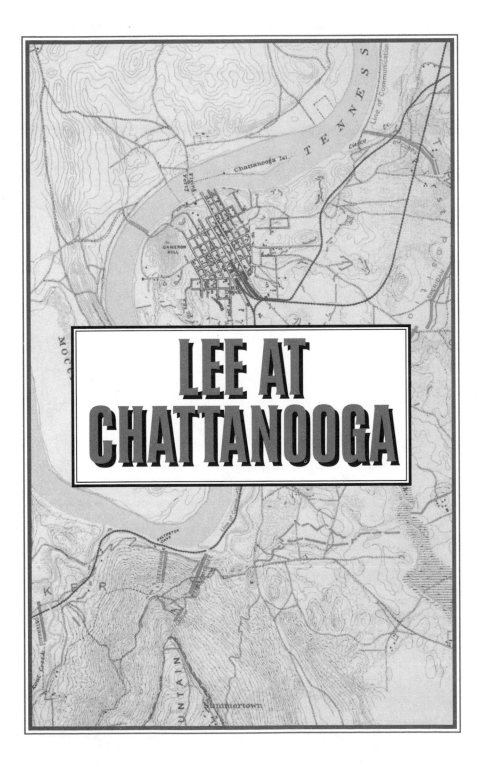

LEE AT CHATTANOOGA

LEE AT CHATTANOOGA

A Novel
OF WHAT MIGHT HAVE BEEN

DENNIS P. McINTIRE

CUMBERLAND HOUSE
NASHVILLE, TENNESSEE

Published by
CUMBERLAND HOUSE PUBLISHING, INC.
431 Harding Industrial Drive
Nashville, Tennessee 37211
www.cumberlandhouse.com

Cover design by Gore Studio, Inc., Nashville, Tennessee.

Library of Congress Cataloging-in-Publication Data

McIntire, Dennis P., 1953–
    Lee at Chattanooga : a novel of what might have been /
Dennis P. McIntire.
        p.   cm.
    ISBN 1-58182-257-X (alk. paper)
    1. Lee, Robert E. (Robert Edward), 1807–1870—Fiction.
2. Tennessee—History—Civil War, 1861–1865—Fiction.
3. Chattanooga (Tenn.), Battle of, 1863—Fiction. 4. Generals—
Fiction. I. Title.
PS3613.C537 L44 2002
813'.6—dc21   2001059865

Printed in the United States of America.

1 2 3 4 5 6 7 8 9 10—05 04 03 02

to my father, Vincent

for all those times in my boyhood, riding in your car,
when I looked out at the hills and fields of Ohio and
imagined the Civil War

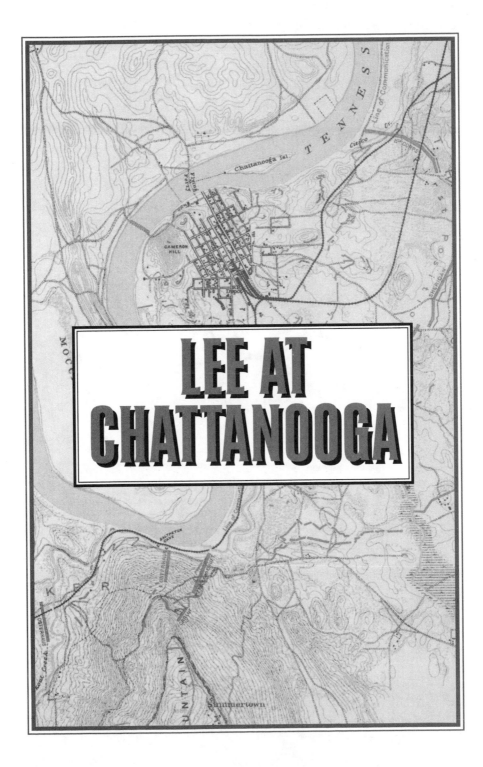

LEE AT CHATTANOOGA

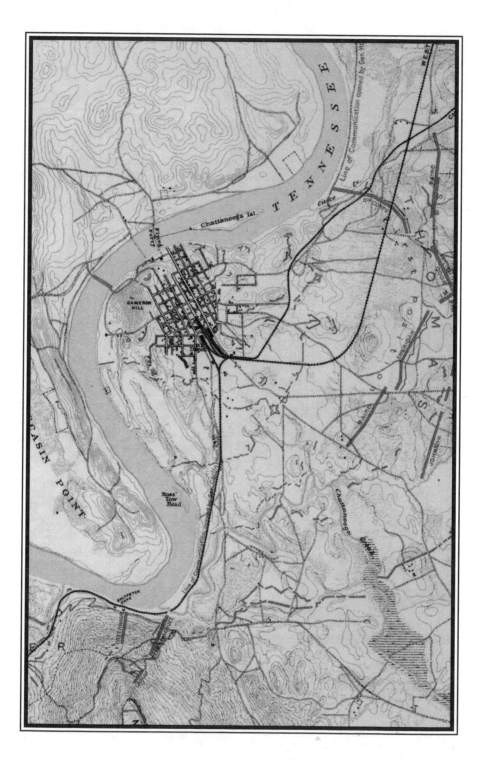

Foreword

WHEN THE SIEGE FINALLY ended, no one could have imagined that it would end the way it did. Not the victorious Federals, nor the defeated Confederates. A thing that ended so incongruously with the way it began.

From start to finish, the siege and struggle for Chattanooga in the latter part of 1863 was dramatic, not only by its rugged setting, but in its unfolding as well; from the near starvation of the Union Army of the Cumberland after being routed at Chickamauga, to its gradual rejuvenation under Ulysses S. Grant. Concomitantly, the jubilant victors of Chickamauga, the Confederate Army of Tennessee, occupying the dominant high ground around Chattanooga, and the holders of the bag into which the beaten Union army was so neatly penned, saw their own readiness and morale erode as the siege progressed. Finally there was the breaking of the siege itself at the battle of Missionary Ridge, as shocking and shameful a defeat for Southern arms as it was a lustrous one for the North, as well as being, to eyewitnesses on both sides who were watching as it happened, unbelievable.

Studies of military history in general and the analysis of military battles in particular very much lend themselves to "what if" theorizing. Had not one action been ordered in a certain engagement, what of another? If not the actual command decision recorded by history, might there have been an alternative? What actually occurred during the Chattanooga campaign of

September through November 1863 is well chronicled by participants and historians alike. But it is the view of the author that if ever there were a compelling subject for a "what if" study of a crucial military action, it is this one. Given the size of the opposing armies, the makeup of their command structures, and the reality of the siege itself, could the battles for Chattanooga have had a different outcome if other circumstances were introduced?

In the sweltering summer of 1863, two calamitous reverses had been inflicted on the aspirations of the newly born Confederate States of America. Up in Pennsylvania, a Southern invasion of the North had been bloodily repulsed at Gettysburg. Down in Mississippi, a Northern invasion of the South succeeded in capturing the strategically vital town of Vicksburg. Both of these Union victories happened in July, on nearly the same days, and the effect on Southern morale was catastrophic.

There was still strength in the Confederacy, to be sure, but with Vicksburg gone, so was the entire Mississippi River, and with the Mississippi gone, the South was literally cut in two. Each side now existed like two halves of a bridge whose span had dropped into the water, each half still standing but the individual components now completely irrelevant to the other. Jefferson Davis had once referred to the Vicksburg stronghold as the nail that held the South together. That summer of 1863 saw the nail forcibly removed.

That same summer, on the fields around Gettysburg, Robert E. Lee's renowned Army of Northern Virginia, believed by many in the North as well as in the South to be unconquerable, was dealt a heartbreaking and crippling defeat. Despite this, Lee managed to bring it safely back to Virginia to fight another day. This in itself was cause for rejoicing in Richmond, as many Southern politicians tried to put the best face on the failed invasion. The bravery of the soldiers was lauded as never before, and there was much talk of fattening up the army with reinforcements. But those in the Southern army who had been there, as well as those civilians perceptive enough to read beyond the glowing accounts, knew the truth. What Lee's army had lost at Gettysburg was muscle tissue.

Lee himself was sickened by the army's losses and deeply depressed over the disastrous campaign. Upon his return to Virginia he immediately submitted an offer of resignation to President Davis. Naturally Davis refused, but it was a new kind of war for the South now. The glorious "old days" were gone.

Yet in that summer of extinguishing hopes, there was still a place and cause for much optimism in the South, and that was in the state of Tennessee. There, a large Rebel army of fifty thousand confronted a slightly larger Union force. Nothing had happened in the Volunteer State for several months, one result of which was that the Rebel Army of Tennessee had become increasingly well trained and supplied. And while catastrophes had occurred with bludgeonlike suddenness east and west, at least it could be truthfully said that here in the center of the Confederacy, nothing bad had happened.

Not yet anyway, said the many cynics and political enemies of the Confederate president, but give it time. Much of their reason for saying this had to do with the general in command of the Army of Tennessee, a man named Braxton Bragg, whom many in the South scorned as a general. Yet he did have positive traits. Bragg was a West Pointer and a Mexican War veteran. As the commanding general of a large army, he had proven himself to be a competent administrator. As a tactician in previous campaigns, he had sometimes performed brilliantly, but here was where the pluses ended and the minuses began, for in these same campaigns he had been inconsistent, and to date he had failed to win a clear-cut victory over his foe. Moreover, his personality was the worst in the Confederate military.

A chronic dyspeptic, which may have had something to do with his caustic manner and seeming dislike of everyone, Bragg was a brutal disciplinarian, heartily disliked by all his soldiers and most of his generals. Yet when all these assets and liabilities were weighed out, he still had one crucial factor in his favor, and that was that the president of the Confederacy, Jefferson Davis, was a devoted and loyal friend.

THAT AUGUST 1863, while the stench of death still hung in the air over Gettysburg and the Union navy was now routinely using Vicksburg to support the further subjugation of the Deep South, things began to happen in Tennessee. The Federal Army of the Cumberland, under the command of Gen. William S. Rosecrans, finally came out of its fortifications around Nashville. In a series of expertly planned quick marches, the bluecoats moved south, catching the Confederates by surprise and forcing their rapid retreat to avoid being encircled. Before the Rebels had time to regroup, the Federals moved out smartly again, once again forcing the gray defenders to fall back. Thus far there had been no fighting, only maneuvering, and the Yankees were clearly driving the team.

Forced from its second defensive position, Bragg's army retreated to the southernmost border of Tennessee, to the important railroad town of Chattanooga, and here Bragg resolved to make his stand. But for a third time the Union commander, like a master fencer, lunged and circled with segments of his army, using the mountainous terrain around Chattanooga to protect and shield his movements. Again the Confederate army, faced with entrapment, was forced to pull back. In the beginning of September 1863, Bragg's Army of Tennessee abandoned Chattanooga and retreated through mountain passes into northern Georgia.

Without a shot having been fired, the Union Army of the Cumberland had forced the Confederates out of Tennessee. Even the cynics and enemies of the Southern president, who were fond of predicting dire events, were stunned. In Richmond calls went out for Bragg's immediate removal. Davis, nonetheless, stood staunchly by his general, but he too was very worried. Also worried was Robert E. Lee, who was following events with his army in Virginia. The president consulted with his Virginia commander, and both men agreed that something needed to be done quickly to turn matters around. Lee and Davis decided to reinforce Bragg's army with a corps from the Army of Northern Virginia. The thing was quickly arranged, and Lee's best general, James Longstreet, the one he later called his "old war horse," along with his entire corps of twelve thousand veterans, was detached from Virginia to begin the long, circuitous journey to Georgia.

This movement was still underway when Rosecrans's army, a portion of which was now occupying Chattanooga, marched out once more. In the latter part of September the Federals pushed south into Georgia. This time they found Bragg's army waiting for them just across the state line. It was here, near and around a quiet wilderness stream called Chickamauga Creek, that the battle was finally joined. For two days the Army of Tennessee and the Army of the Cumberland fought it out in the thick woods and clearings. The battle was one of the fiercest waged in the war, and it was a Union disaster. By the end of the second day, the Federal army, from lowly privates all the way up to the commanding general himself, was fleeing in moblike retreat back to Chattanooga.

It was an astounding and momentous victory for the South. Bragg's army, unleashed at last, had done its work. During the battle, Longstreet's corps arrived from Virginia and immediately joined in, going literally from boxcars to battle in a slashing attack that crumbled the Union line. Chickamauga was exactly the great military triumph that the South needed so badly after Gettysburg and Vicksburg. But as it soon turned out, the attainment was allowed to fall very much short of what it should have been.

The high cost of admission to this great victory in Southern dead and wounded could have been recovered many times over had the triumphant Rebels moved swiftly on the follow-up. The Union army was in chaos. So thoroughly shattered was its organization, that for at least twenty-four hours after the battle it lacked the capability to defend itself from any concerted assault the Rebel army might have chosen to make. Fortunately for the bluecoats, the Rebels made none, and the wrecked Yankee army retreated to Chattanooga.

Although Rosecrans made it back to Chattanooga, his army was far from safety. Now the Confederates had their second chance to destroy the Federals. Cut up and frazzled, its previously adept commanding general now broken and confused, the Army of the Cumberland milled for a time in turmoil, a period in which it was ripe for the harvest. But no reaper came, and by the time the Rebels finally arrived in strength, the opportunity had passed. The Yankees fortified themselves in Chattanooga, and the Army of Tennessee took up positions on the dominating high ground around the town, settling itself in for a siege on a beaten army that, had things been done differently, would not still be in existence. Nor was this lost on the commanders of the victorious Rebel army. Despite the urging of his generals to be turned loose on the escaping Yankees after the battle of Chickamauga had been won, Bragg inexplicably refused to press the assault. What followed then was the beginning of the siege of Chattanooga and Bragg's commanders eventually turning themselves loose against him.

And so it was that immediately after his greatest victory, Bragg came in for his worst attacks, not from his enemies in blue, but from those in gray. For a time, what followed was near mutiny. Nathan Bedford Forrest, Bragg's cavalry chief, after threatening Bragg to his face, stormed out of the camp vowing never to take orders from him again. An anonymously drafted letter was sent to Jefferson Davis signed by several of Bragg's generals. It was a bitter missive, full of recriminations and harsh denunciations of the commanding general's performance during and after the battle.

Davis was greatly alarmed, so much so that he at once set out for Chattanooga in person. He arrived in early October, and there, in an incredible meeting with Bragg's generals, with Bragg himself present and saying nothing, he witnessed these same officers imprecate Bragg's generalship to his face. Even the much respected Longstreet, though not of the Army of Tennessee and not a signatory to the provocative letter, opined aloud to Davis that perhaps it would be better for all if Bragg were relieved of command.

Davis was in a quandary. While wanting very much to stand by Bragg who, like Robert E. Lee, had never criticized him publicly or privately and had always served him loyally, the president was enough of a military man himself to understand that what the generals of the Army of Tennessee had told him was sadly true. A great chance to bag an entire Union army had been missed after Chickamauga. But it did not end there. Confronted with the dilemma of who would replace Bragg if he decided to relieve him, Davis now found the carping generals to be part of the problem.

There was only one among the entire lot of general officers whom Davis felt had the maturity and the ability to command the army, and that was Bragg's senior corps commander, Gen. William J. Hardee. Hardee was older than his colleagues, a West Pointer and a veteran of the Mexican War. Yet when the president asked him about taking the job, Hardee flatly refused. That was that. Bragg would have to stay. But the problem was far from resolved, and Davis knew it. Deeply troubled, he nevertheless returned to Richmond without solving the situation.

WASHINGTON WAS going through its own deep alarm about the Chattanooga situation, and this anxiety was the catalyst for quick action. Immediately after the Chickamauga disaster, twenty thousand soldiers, under the command of Gen. Joseph Hooker, were detached from the eastern theater's Army of the Potomac and sent west by rail. Another Union army of fifteen thousand, commanded by Ambrose E. Burnside, moved into East Tennessee, seizing Knoxville and threatening, albeit from some distance away, the rear of Bragg's besieging army. But this was not all. Gen. William T. Sherman was ordered up from

Vicksburg with twenty thousand battle-tested Westerners. And finally, there was Grant. Idle since capturing Vicksburg, he was now placed in command of all the Union forces in and converging on Chattanooga.

Grant arrived in Chattanooga in October, a short time after Davis had returned to Richmond. His first act was to immediately eliminate the problem of starvation, which had hung heavily over the Army of the Cumberland since its encirclement in Chattanooga. With an innovative scheme and quick action, and using Hooker's troops from the East, Grant seized a critical river crossing known as Brown's Ferry, a steamboat landing on the Tennessee River downstream from Chattanooga and out of range to Confederate artillery harassment. No sooner had the spot been taken than ubiquitous Union transport steamers began unloading supplies, which in turn were carried four miles overland into the back door of Chattanooga. It was derisively called "the cracker line," but it put food in the camps of the beleaguered Federals as well as ammunition in their cartridge boxes. This was Grant at his troublesome best, and what was worse for the Southerners, the Brown's Ferry expedition had been carried out under the very nose of Bragg's army.

Longstreet, who had tried to prevent the Federals from taking the important landing, was beside himself. He and Bragg had never gotten along, and the post-Chickamauga crisis had worsened things even more. Now, with this last Yankee success, the relationship was poisoned beyond any hope of repair. Believing as he did that Brown's Ferry was lost due to Bragg's arrogant refusal to see what was really happening, Longstreet lost all trust in the commanding general of the Army of Tennessee.

This antipathy was fully reciprocated by Bragg. A week after the botched Brown's Ferry episode, he seized on a chance to get rid of Longstreet and his entire corps. Burnside, advancing into East Tennessee, needed to be stopped, and Bragg ordered Longstreet's corps to Knoxville to confront him. Just at the time when the Yankees pinned in Chattanooga were being reinforced in strength, Bragg's besieging force was diminished by twelve thousand battle-seasoned Confederate soldiers.

Yet Bragg was unworried. In one act he had gotten rid of Longstreet and dealt with the problem of Burnside. And as for the growing Federal force to his front, this was of little concern as well. It was all high ground around Chattanooga, and his army had every bit of it. The Yankees had none. So, Bragg reasoned, reinforced or not, if the bluecoats were eager to come on, he would welcome them. He was, he believed, fully prepared with his dug-in army and plentiful artillery to make any upcoming battle into a western version of Lee's great December 1862 victory on the heights overlooking Fredericksburg.

But back in Richmond, Davis continued to watch developments anxiously. He was not nearly as sanguine as his general about the situation there, especially after Longstreet's departure. The Yankees were brewing mischief; there was no doubt about it. Furthermore, he had privately agreed with Longstreet; the capture of Brown's Ferry should never have been allowed to happen, for now it was no longer possible to starve the enemy out of Chattanooga.

Yet there was still hope for a significant victory. As president of the Confederacy, it was Davis's job to always hold out hope, even against long odds. But in Chattanooga it had not yet come to this. The odds there were not yet long, Davis believed, and there were sound reasons to think so. Bragg was right to feel confident about his high ground. It was deadly formidable, ideally suited to the defense. Davis had seen it for himself. And Bragg's army was dug in, and it did indeed have plenty of artillery and abundant room to shift about; the Union Army of the Cumberland was hemmed tightly against the Tennessee River. So given all this, there was more than sufficient reason for hope and firm cause to believe that what had been started and not finished at Chickamauga could be concluded once and for all at Chattanooga.

The Army of the Cumberland could still be destroyed. Davis could see it happening. The Army of Tennessee still had a chance to bag an entire Union army and avenge the dismal summer score of Confederate defeats. Moreover, there was still time to do it, not a lot, but ample. Sherman and his veterans were still a long way off. So too was Burnside. Hooker's troops were on hand, it was true, but they could be dealt with along with the rest if the right plan were devised and acted upon. If the right kind of help could be sent to Braxton Bragg . . .

The right kind of help, Davis pondered. It had to be. Summer had ended, but time remained. The Yankees were still pinned down and would be for a while. The thing in Tennessee was not yet over. Not by a long shot.

HEREIN IS the premise of *Lee at Chattanooga.*

What would have happened had Jefferson Davis decided that the right kind of help to send to Bragg was Robert E. Lee? Could Lee have made the difference there, possibly altering significantly the events of the war? How would he have done against Grant and Sherman, who were fighting on ground more familiar to them than to Lee? And finally, if Davis had sent Lee, what authority would he have given him over Bragg, mindful as he was of Bragg's unswerving loyalty to him?

Serious students of the American Civil War will have no difficulty separating historical fact from what is intended as plausible fiction in this account of the Chattanooga campaign. Within the telling of the story the author has conformed as nearly as possible with the natural terrain of actual events. As much as possible, what really happened in the struggle for Chattanooga in November 1863 is allowed to happen, but only up to a point, and that being where Lee, had he actually had a hand in matters, might have done things differently.

So for the reader then, "kindly to judge," is the story of Lee at Chattanooga.

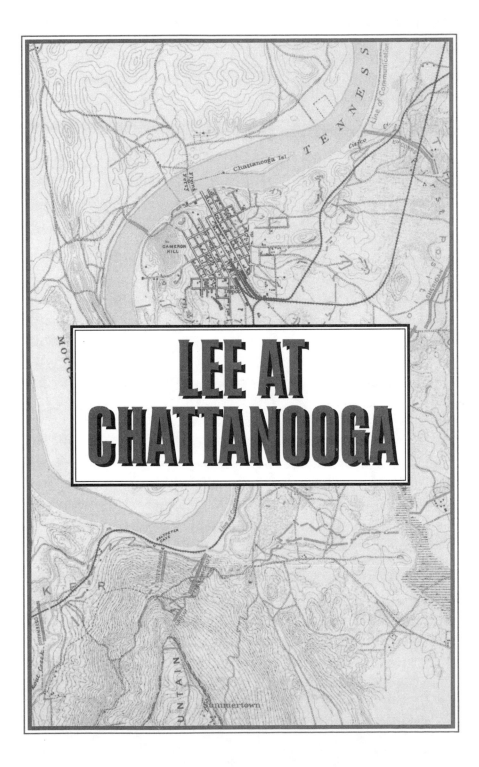

LEE AT
CHATTANOOGA

Prologue

Richmond 1864

I REMEMBER THE DAY THE war ended.

Calling to mind my ride through the fallen capital of the Confederacy that day, it was the ponderous quiet, the deep sullen hush, that was my most vivid recollection. The streets deserted, sidewalks empty, the windows of the buildings curtained or shuttered. I came into the quiet residential district where the Lees lived and it was more of the same, the closed façade of each house like a face of silent pain.

I rode along slowly. There was no need to hurry. No need for any of that anymore. The last three years had been nothing but hurry. Hurry to warn of the enemy's approach. Haste to deliver dispatches. Breakneck gallops to bring up the troops, bring up the guns. Quickly, always quickly.

Now all that was past. There was nothing now to hurry to or hurry from, and the clop, clop, clop of my horse's hooves on the cobblestone street was like the slow winding down of a large clock. Winding down, winding down, finally coming to a stop.

I dismounted in front of the Lee house. The door opened and Major Taylor came out. We looked at each other in silence.

"Is it over then?" he asked hoarsely.

"Yes," I answered.

Taylor's handsome, youthful face held its noble caste as tears welled in his eyes. Then with a soft shudder, he turned away against the door, sobbing quietly into the sleeve of his coat.

My own eyes were as dry as parchment. I waited for a time then I added. "There's been trouble."

Gradually Taylor's shoulders straightened. For a few more moments he held his face against his sleeve, then his arm dropped and he turned slowly to face me again, red eyed but composed.

"Stuart," I said. "He and some of his men broke out of camp this morning and headed off for the hills." I paused before continuing. "There were some civilians killed."

"Civilians," Taylor repeated hollowly.

"Negroes," I told him. "About a half dozen supposedly. A couple were women. The Yankees say that Stuart's men opened fire at random on a group of them. That's the Yankees saying that of course."

Taylor smiled grimly. "Old Jeb always said he'd never live under Yankee rule, didn't he?"

"I don't expect he'll have very long to live under it," I said somberly. "Sheridan's got his whole command after him." Then I asked, "How's the general?"

"He's upstairs," Taylor said.

In the house, just as in the town I had come through, there was quiet, a deep hush emanating from the shadows and the curtained rooms. As Taylor and I went upstairs, our boots sounded loud and unnatural on the wooden steps.

The bedroom door was open. General Lee and his wife were inside. The general was recumbent on the bed, propped up on pillows, the stump of his one leg resting upon a quilt. He was fully dressed in his uniform white shirt and gray trousers, the trouser of his amputated leg folded and neatly pinned below the knee. Mrs. Lee sat in a chair next to the bed and fanned the general's face. Her fan moved slowly and methodically, as though she had been doing it forever. She neither looked up nor ceased her activity as we entered the room. The curtains on the bedroom window were only partially drawn, letting in a wide shaft of the August sunlight, which fell across the room.

Upon the pillow, however, Lee's face was in shadow. Yet he spoke as I approached.

"Good morning, Major Hotchkiss." The voice was firm and strong.

I came to full attention and saluted. "Good morning, General Lee."

There was an expectant pause, and with much chagrin, I realized that I was unable to talk. Lee himself broke the silence.

"Is it concluded then?" he asked.

I managed to nod then willed myself to speak. "It is done, General. The Army of Northern Virginia is surrendered."

There was no movement from the shadowed pillow, only silence. Beside the bed, Mrs. Lee betrayed not the slightest discernible movement or change of feature but continued to fan in steady, ceaseless motion. I stood there, and as I did so I thought, *This is how it must be.* This is how it must be and how it must feel to be in the presence of real royalty. For if there really was such a thing as true aristocracy of the blood, then I was in its presence now, the nobleman lying before me on his sickbed, strong and serene in the face of tragedy, and his noble lady at his side, stoic and enduring.

I went on with my report. "General Johnston has assembled with his army outside of Atlanta, awaiting word on events in Richmond. Upon receiving confirmation of the surrender of the Army of Northern Virginia, he will then issue the order for the Army of Tennessee to stack its arms as well."

Lee received this without comment. But when I related the news of Jeb Stuart's escape, he made an immediate exclamation of regret.

"How I hoped such a thing would not happen," he said, distress evident in his voice. "How I prayed it would not. And now, such a continued and unnecessary waste. Such a senseless further effusion of time, blood, and lives, and all to the avail of nothing."

He lapsed into silence. I waited a few moments then concluded. "General Mahone will come in person as soon as possible to deliver his final report," I said. "And he wishes me to inform you that a detachment of Yankee cavalry will be arriving sometime to provide security for you and Mrs. Lee. Upon the orders of General Grant himself, this house will not be searched, nor are you or Mrs. Lee to be disturbed in any way, nor your movements hindered. Should you desire to move about the city, they will provide your escort."

For the first time Mrs. Lee spoke, in a low icy voice, face and body unmoving as she continued to fan her husband.

"How terribly quaint of Mr. Grant to offer us the protection of his soldiers. And just who would they be protecting us from, I wonder?"

There was nothing to say to this. General Lee had no questions or comments, so Taylor and I went back downstairs.

"If that man lying on the bed up there were a whole man, none of this would be happening right now. You know that, don't you, Jed?" Taylor said bitterly. "Right about now the Yankees would be ruing the day they crossed the Rapidan." His voice trailed off, "Instead of us ruing the day he ever left his own army to go off to Tennessee."

I said nothing. Going outside on the front steps, we lit up cigars and stood silently.

An hour later there came the clopping of many approaching horses, and a column of Union cavalry appeared at the end of the street. They came on and halted short of the house. The officer in charge, a colonel, pressed his animal forward to us and inquired if this was the residence of Gen. Robert E. Lee. Taylor said nothing, so I answered that it was. The Yankee colonel then asked if Lee himself was present in the house and were there any other occupants? I answered his questions, which satisfied him, whereupon he introduced himself as Colonel Somerset, commanding officer of the First Pennsylvania Cavalry.

I recognized the regiment instantly. During the series of midsummer engagements that came to be known collectively as the battle of Richmond, it was this very same First Pennsyl-

vania, along with a brigade of colored troops, that had seized
the vital railroad center at Petersburg and stubbornly held on
until their own help arrived against the frantic but poorly coor-
dinated attacks of A. P. Hill's troops, a disastrous showing that
finished off "Little Powell's" reputation for good, both personally and professionally.

All that seemed like ages ago, but it wasn't. It had only
been a couple of weeks.

The Yankee colonel went on to advise us that he was under
orders not to curtail any movements of the occupants, or hinder
in any way the comings and goings of visitors, but simply to provide security for General Lee and the residents of his house until
such time as a detachment from the provost marshal came along
to take permanent charge. Knowing who these Federals were
obviated the need for any explanation of how they looked, which
was decidedly played out. The troopers were haggard, several
were slightly wounded, and the jaded horses hung their heads
with fatigue. Men, mounts, and equipment were all covered with
mud. Before he took leave of us, the colonel asked if there were
any usable wells close by. Assuming Major Taylor's continued
recalcitrance in the conversation, I was about to answer that I
did not know of any, when Taylor's voice answered from behind
me, informing the Union officer of a well two blocks away and
giving directions.

The colonel thanked Taylor then took charge of his
column. In the kind of brisk efficiency possible only among veteran outfits, the squad divided itself into two parts and posted
each end of the street.

Shortly after this, a solitary gray rider came riding slowly
and somberly toward the house. It was Gen. William Mahone,
commanding general of the now surrendered Army of Northern Virginia, that army's third commander in as many months,
and its shortest tenured, approximately ten days. I had always
respected Mahone and considered him a fine officer, and it was
no fault of his that the rapidity of his elevation through the

command structure of our army during that tragic summer of 1864 was in bleak proportion to the astonishing deterioration of the command structure itself.

Back in May, just before Grant had launched his juggernaut host across the Rapidan, Mahone had been a very competent division commander. A. P. Hill and Richard Ewell were in joint command of the army, with the slightly senior Hill holding the title of commanding general. As formidable as these names looked on paper, those of us who interacted with them on a daily basis knew that each man was a mere fraction of the aggressive officers they had been when winning their laurels and reputations under Lee and Jackson, respectively, in the glorious early days of the war. And as we were all to learn after the war, before the final enemy onslaught, each man was already on the brink of further physical degradation: Hill to the ravages of syphilis and Ewell to brain fever.

To say that James Longstreet was sorely missed then would be a grave understatement, but his loss along with the bulk of his indispensable corps at the last battle for Chattanooga removed him from the war as effectively as a fatal wound. In that same battle, on that same day in Tennessee, fate decreed that some unknown someone in a blue uniform—a single soldier, farmboy or clerk, hero or rogue, unbeknownst to us, the nation, and probably himself—would pull the trigger that would fire the minié ball which would fracture the leg of Gen. Robert E. Lee. Single-handedly, on that cold November afternoon in 1863, that lone unknown soldier inflicted the critical wound that sealed the fate of the Confederacy.

The wound inflicted on Lee did not kill him, although he would never take the field again. With his leg amputated, dangerously straining his already weakened heart, he was to spend the rest of the war on his sickbed in Richmond while the final minutes of the final hour of the existence of the Confederate States of America slipped away. But in that warm May of 1864, as we waited on the south bank of the Rapidan for the enemy to launch his inevitable offensive, the final heartbreak had yet to occur, and we outwardly expressed the view that we could still win. After all, we assured each other, we knew where Grant was coming, and there would be plenty of time before the actual onslaught to form theories on how to stop him.

I say theories because, without the steadfast presence of Lee himself to bristle up the courage of his men like Henry V of old, theory and overly sanguine predictions were all we had to keep up morale, for there was about us then, unspoken and unacknowledged, a dark pall of impending defeat. Still, in the beginning of that May, the defeat had not yet been visited upon us. In preparation to meet the Union assault, General Lee himself, from his sickbed in Richmond, had advised Hill and Ewell exactly how to play it.

Grant would come booming across the Rapidan no later than the first week of May, Lee warned, using three fords, which he then proceeded to name. But once over these fords, Grant would be forced to transit through a very bad place for his army, a region of heavy forest known locally as the Wilderness, where there were only a few roads and no open ground upon which to deploy infantry or artillery in the event of attack. Grant would want to get his army through there quickly, Lee asserted, but he must, under no circumstances, be allowed to do so, for it was there, in the Wilderness, where artillery was useless and the heavy numbers of Yankees could not be used to advantage. It was there that Grant and his army must be hit and hit hard. Nor should the Army of Northern Virginia hold anything back in this assault, for it was absolutely essential to completely embroil the Yankees in the tangled terrain and undergrowth, thereby creating the ultimate mayhem and confusion.

Thus decreed the old warrior, Robert E. Lee, from his sickbed, and we knew he was right. The Gray Fox was missing a leg, and his body had turned frail, but his mind was as alert as ever and the fire still burned. As it turned out, however, tragically for us, in the case of the Gray Fox's two lieutenants who were responsible for carrying all this out, the infirmity was just the opposite.

So in the end, it all happened as we had feared in secret. Grant and the Army of the Potomac came slashing across the Rapidan and into the Wilderness at exactly the places and times expected, but the Yankees were neither stopped nor embroiled. Before the frazzled Ewell and the increasingly incoherent Hill could marshal their forces, Grant had gotten most of his army through the close-packed timber region having scarcely been annoyed. What followed then was a stern chase, with the smaller Army of Northern Virginia frantically trying to catch the Yankees before they made it to Richmond. But the ending was never in doubt, and we all knew it. There was no stopping the bloated Federal corps once they were in open country, and the resurgent Union cavalry, with their well-shod mounts and new repeating rifles, tumbled Jeb Stuart's fiercely swarming troopers from their saddles.

Thus the thing was played out, inexorably and finally, in and around Richmond. And here and now, on the last day in the life of the once mighty Army of Northern Virginia, was its final commander, William Mahone.

He came down gloomily from his horse and spoke to us of a new development brought on by the escape of Stuart and his troopers from Richmond.

"Grant's order allowing officers to keep their sidearms has been rescinded," he said.

"By Grant?" I asked.

Mahone gave a listless shrug. "Him or someone else I reckon." He continued, "The Army of Tennessee's surrendered now as well. I expect that means Sherman and his crowd will be walking into Atlanta at about the same time Grant's troops come in here."

There was a long silence among us.

"I'll take you up to see the general now, sir," Taylor said at length.

His meeting with Lee was a long one, and when Mahone and Taylor came back down there was a distracted finality in the general's manner and speech. As we walked him to his horse, he gazed absently over the rooftops.

"How's the army?" I asked.

"Tolerable well, I reckon," he said, and we smiled at this old repartee, a resilient and deliberately understated statement of morale and pugnacity, harkening back to the old glory days after battles like Fredericksburg and Chancellorsville.

"There was talk of a final review down this street," Mahone went on. "But the Yankees were having none of that." And he added proudly, "Even with the teeth pulled, they still ain't about to turn that dog loose, considerin' how hard they worked to get him on the leash in the first place."

I wanted to say something to comfort him, but there was nothing anyone could say. Fate had cruelly decreed that this courageous officer was to serve, if only for a few short days, as the final commanding officer of what had once been the most dangerous army in the world. And his sole remaining operational duty as head of that army would be to supervise the stacking of its arms.

"Good-bye, General," I said when he was mounted, and what made me say good-bye I did not know, for I was certain to see him again in the later course of the day. As it turned out however, I did not, and it would be ten long years later, when he was a senator in the restored Union State of Virginia, before I would clasp his hand again.

Some time later I was standing on the steps in front of the Lee house when another column of Yankee horsemen came riding down the street. I guessed rightly that this was a cadre from the provost marshal, so I braced myself for trouble. Coming up to the front of the house, a young white officer and four Negro troopers dismounted. I was instantly alarmed, for by their manner they clearly intended to enter the house. I stood in front of the door.

"It is the wish and express order of your General Grant that this house and its occupants be left alone," I said firmly.

The young officer stopped before me and made a show to his men of examining me from head to toe, conspicuously noting that I had no pistol or holster on my belt.

"Where is your sidearm, sir?" he demanded.

"As you can see, I am wearing none," I retorted. "And I will say again, sir, that the orders of your commanding general prohibit any interference with the activities of this house or any of its residents."

"The orders of the secretary of war in Washington dictate otherwise," the Union officer said blandly and with a slight smirk. Then he returned to his first concern. "As you are not wearing your weapon, sir, I assume you have placed it somewhere. Where is it?"

"Since when does any provost guard not take its orders from the commanding general of its army?" I asked heatedly, refusing to be put off.

"I will not bandy words with you, sir!" the young Federal all but shouted sharply. "You are surrendered, sir, and rate no explanation from me! It is enough for you to know that in view of the flight of certain units of your calvary, in direct defiance of the original terms of the armistice, as well as the atrocity committed upon unarmed and defenseless members of Richmond's Negro population by these same renegades, all officers of the former Army of Northern Virginia are to immediately surrender their firearms." And he added significantly, "Including every one of its former commanders."

Suddenly Taylor was at my side and bristling with rage. "How dare you appear in the doorway of this house, with that uniform and your Negroes, and complain of atrocities, sir!" he fumed furiously.

"Place him under arrest," the Union officer ordered, to which Taylor immediately responded by throwing his riding gauntlets heavily into the man's face. "At your service, you Yankee swine!" he hissed.

"Bind his hands!" the Federal commanded in a shaky voice, unnecessarily as it was, for the members of his detachment swarmed forward to subdue and disarm the struggling Taylor and did just that. The young officer was flushed and angered but also intimidated, for he stayed well out of the way as the murderously silent Taylor was hustled down the steps.

"I will see General Lee now," the man said to me coldly. "You can either lead me to him, or I will go in and find him myself, and you can follow your friend in arrest."

I led the way inside, not out of any fear of this Yankee or his stockade, but in total preemption of him and his Negro sergeant having unfettered access to Mrs. Lee's house.

We went up the stairs. The door to General Lee's room was open. He was recumbent on the bed as before, his face still in shadow. Mrs. Lee had drawn her frail, arthritic form up to its full stature and stood next to the bed like a sentinel. The Negro sergeant stayed in the hallway. As I entered the room, followed close behind by the young Union officer, she frowned.

"Mrs. Lee, I cannot prevent this," I began.

"It is all right, Major," she replied. "For I perceive nothing of a stature that should trouble us overmuch."

The young Federal appeared not to hear this. His eyes went intently from Mrs. Lee to the grayclad figure on the bed, and it was evident that he was very much aware of the company he was in and fully cognizant of the unique opportunity that this access presented for his own self-enhancement.

He removed his cap and bowed gallantly to Mrs. Lee. "Madame, I am most regretful of this intrusion, which, unfortunately, is unavoidable."

Mrs. Lee did not stir. Turning to the bed, the young man bowed again. "General Lee, good day to you sir. I am Captain C. Charles Pennington III." He quickly and suavely added, "If

I may, General, perhaps you will recall meeting my father in Washington just before the war. He was—."

"Major Hotchkiss, what is all this?" Lee broke in sharply.

"He wants your revolver, General," I answered.

His speech interrupted, the Union officer glared at me. I looked back at him coolly. "It is the thing General Mahone told us to expect, sir," I added.

"Yes," said Lee, and his voice was strong. "Major Hotchkiss, kindly reach up on the top shelf of the armoire, and there you will find the object sought. Give it to this officer, if you please, and let that be a termination to this tiresome interlude."

Relinquishing the general's sidearm to this Yankee pup bothered me much more than it did the general. I was aware of a deep flush on my face as I thrust the weapon into his hands. Mrs. Lee had turned about, showing the unwelcome visitor the furious back of her head. The young captain, twice rebuffed and clearly resenting it, let his eyes flicker one last time over Lee's prostrate form, then bowing stiffly, he strode out of the room. I followed him and the sergeant down the stairs and out to the stoop.

Outside the house the blue-uniformed officer removed the revolver slowly from the holster, examining it long and attentively before restoring it to its sheath, and there was a look of naked triumph on his face that I could not endure to see. But he had not forgotten about me.

"That leaves you, Major," he said. "Will you tell me where you have hidden your sidearm, or perhaps we'll need to search the house."

I pointed mutely toward my horse, whereupon, at the orders of the officer, two troopers dismounted and rummaged through my saddlebags, one of them pulling out my holster and cartridge box. Next they went to Taylor's horse and commenced a search through his belongings, but I was not concerned with this, for my mind was fixed on something else.

At that moment I did not want the war to be over. I stared at the Federal officer and saw a soft, comfortable face, well fed and healthy and totally unformed by any experience or life event outside of his own choosing and pleasure. How one such as him had come by his uniform and authority to carry out what he had just done, I did not know, but he was undoubtedly somebody's pet, the bright and darling sycophant of some Northern power lord. And so when I asked him, "What engagements were you in, sir?"—not to hear the answer, which I already knew, but to hear how he would make it—he gave me a disdainful look then glanced away, saying nothing. That was answer enough. Of course there were no engagements for him to speak of. He would have been much too smart to have gone to war before now. At this moment, however, with the dangerous world rendered safe and secure and the once fearsome Army of Northern Virginia no longer a threat to someone riding about the streets of Richmond in a tailored new blue uniform, here came this stripling in his leisured arrogance to do the bidding of his masters.

But the world was not to be entirely safe, I then decided. For after all the rivers of blood and the thousands upon thousands of maimings over the past four years, there was more than enough room on the butcher's list for a mere broken nose and hopefully a tooth or two and the despoiling of a clean white cotton shirt by a few bloodstains.

I stepped forward but instantly felt both my arms caught in a strong grip. Silently, and with all my strength, wholly intent on my target, I tried to break free, straining against my bonds to close the distance and deliver the blow to this hated enemy. But I was held fast. The Negro sergeant and another trooper worked my arms behind me and forced me slowly back against the door of the house.

I let out a gasp. Hearing this, the Federal officer turned and realized immediately what had almost happened. His initial look of consternation turned to anger, and I thought for sure that I was about to follow Taylor in being placed under arrest. But he said nothing, holding Lee's holstered pistol tightly

under his arm, a distracted gleam in his eye. His men having finished with their search through Taylor's saddlebags, he walked
quickly down the steps and mounted his horse. The two Negro
troopers kept hold of me until the column was well started
down the street.

"How well you protect your new master," I said to the
sergeant after he released me.

The black man gave me a long reproachful look.

"The Lord Jesus is my master, Major, an' no one else. An'
there ain't nothin' walkin' this earth that *He* needs protection
from. But that ain't the case with you, sir, especially if you still
got a mind to sass folks wearin' blue. Ain't no good gonna come
from that, and seeing's how you appear to be the only one left
to watch over that old man upstairs, I reckon I'd be mindin' my
manners."

After they had gone I went back upstairs. The door to the
general's room was closed. I knocked softly. The door opened
and Mrs. Lee came quietly out.

"Mrs. Lee, I am deeply sorry for what has happened," I said
earnestly. "Is there anything I can do to make things better? Is
the general badly upset?"

Mrs. Lee smiled and placed her hand on my arm. "He is
fine, Major Hotchkiss. He is trying to sleep. And do not be troubled, for no real harm nor embarrassment can come to those who
put themselves in the hands of the Lord." Then she said anxiously, "Poor dear Major Taylor. What is likely to come of him do
you suppose?"

"Very little I think," I said. "At any rate, as soon as your
son gets here, I'll find him. Don't worry."

"Thank you, Major. Now in the meantime, you must come
downstairs with me. It is time you had something to eat."

Mrs. Lee presided over my lunch, a meager broth and
some bread, and we spoke no more of the incident. Afterward
she returned to her husband's bedside and I resumed my post
outside the house. The afternoon was sultry and oppressive, and

a deep soul weariness was upon me. I leaned against the railing and my mind wandered far away, so far that I quite lost track of time and where I was. I had no idea how much time had elapsed before Custis Lee came riding up to the house.

"Well, Jed."

"Well, Custis."

He dismounted and for a moment we looked at each other wordlessly.

"The Yankees put Taylor under arrest," I said.

Custis nodded. "I heard. How's the general?"

I told him then told him about the confiscation of the general's service revolver from his sickroom. Custis had not heard this, and he listened in bitter silence. When I was finished, he said quietly but with deep feeling, "I suppose it does no good to wish the Yankees damned and in hell, does it?"

"No," I said flatly. "No good at all." Then I asked what news there was of Stuart and his renegade troopers.

"Nothing that could be called good news," Custis replied. "He's got the whole of the Yankee cavalry off chasing him." Then he brightened. "Of course it's not like that's never happened before, is it? And maybe Jeb wants to take one last ride around the Yankee army for old time's sake before he gives up," Custis suggested with a grim smile, but the humor was wide of the mark.

Now that Custis was there I could go back and rejoin the army, but before I did I told him I would make sure that Taylor was all right. "And I'll try to come by tonight if I learn any other news that might be of interest to the general," I promised.

Custis waved and went into the house. I rode off, not knowing that I would never again return to this street or this house or that I would never see General Lee alive again.

The war was over.

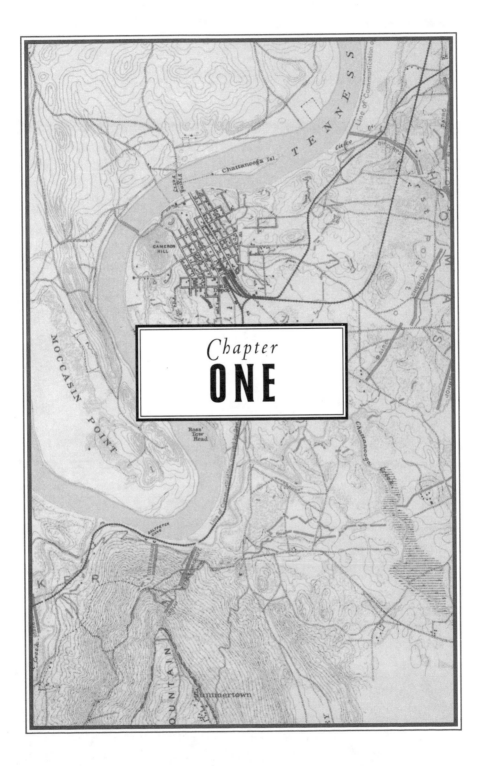

Chapter
ONE

$\mathcal{M}$Y NAME IS Jedediah Hotchkiss.

During the war I fought on the side of the rebellion, in the Army of Northern Virginia. I was that army's chief topographical officer, and Robert E. Lee was my general.

I was a Northerner by birth, from Upstate New York, and a schoolteacher before the war. I lived in several places during my life, but when I got to Virginia I stayed out of love. Not love for a woman just then, but for the beauty and serene magnificence of the Shenandoah Valley and the Blue Ridge Mountains. My wanderlust was permanently cured.

There I married and started a family. And when the war broke out there was not the slightest question in my mind of which side to take. There were two fundamental reasons for this, the first having to do with where I had come from, and the second embracing where I ended up. Growing up in the North had never endeared me to New England abolitionists, whose highly selective altruism toward their lesser man I always suspected. I was against slavery myself, but what of it? Having this belief, which was only a matter of Scripture, not to mention common sense, certainly did not entitle me to rate myself as some enlightened entity in the eyes of God, to be exalted above my fellow citizens. Yet I could never rid myself of the suspicion that for quite a number of well-heeled abolitionists, abolitionism was a holier-than-thou nosegay, to be worn ostentatiously on the lapel whenever possible, and that feeling sorry for the poor Negro was an end to itself, justifying their highly developed sense of moral superiority over others, which was, I believed, apart from everything else, what they were really all about.

So as the doctrine and the vanities of the abolitionists had never come close to touching me, even when I was a Northerner, there was nothing for me to break free from once the war between North and South broke out. But the same could not be said for my real home, late discovered in my life though it was. For this was Virginia, and the beautiful Shenandoah Valley, which, apart from the face of my wife, Sara, was the most beautiful and spiritual thing I had ever looked upon. There was never a matter of choosing sides.

And so it was altogether fitting and natural that the first Confederate general I worked for, and the first army in which I served, were those whose names were, and still are today, indelibly linked to the defense of the Valley I loved. The little army took its name after it, the Army of Shenandoah, and the general in command of it was, of course, Thomas Jackson. Stonewall.

I was his mapmaker. He was a demanding officer, not at all likable, but I learned my trade under him. One of the first tasks he assigned to me, as the war began to pick up and the Yankees were making their first incursions into the Shenandoah, was to make a map of the entire valley. This was no small thing, but I did it and took immense pride in how he then proceeded to use it, drubbing the wits out of the separate Union columns and forcing them all to scurry off for safety like granary rats from an old woman's broom.

When Jackson's army became a part of the Army of Northern Virginia under Robert E. Lee, my direct superior was the chief engineer of the Army of Northern Virginia, the kindly Maj. James K. Boswell. He became one of my best and dearest friends in the army, but he was killed in the battle of Chancellorsville in the same panicked volley from our own troops that mortally wounded and eventually killed Stonewall. It was at this time that I was made the chief of engineers of James Longstreet's First Corps, and it was in this capacity that I served directly under Robert E. Lee during his time in the Chattanooga theater, serving the old man, not only as his topographical officer, but for a time as his personal aide and orderly. These were seemingly trivial collateral duties, but it caused me my most anxious times in the entire war.

I survived the war. The North won, we lost, and after the surrender of the Army of Northern Virginia outside of Richmond that August 1864, we were all allowed to return to our homes, whereupon, as the victorious Ulysses S. Grant decreed, we were "not to be disturbed by United States authority" so long as we all did what the decree said, which was to "observe paroles and the laws in force where they reside." Speaking for myself, this was exactly what I did. I was sick of the war and counted myself lucky to have gotten out in one piece, or without any missing pieces. I returned to my wife and family in what was left of the Shenandoah Valley, taking scrupulous care to "observe my parole" as well as "the laws in force where I resided," and got on with my life.

But those blood-drenched years were not easily forgotten, nor was the enmity gone. A couple of weeks after his escape from Richmond, Stuart and several of his troopers were finally captured after a running battle with pursuing Federal cavalry. When, after a drumhead military trial, presided over by the Yankee government's infamous Committee on the Conduct of the War, he was hanged for war crimes committed upon civilians, to many Southerners the hour seemed darker even than when the Army of Northern Virginia had surrendered.

"The last cavalier and defender of the Southern civilization!" a radical newspaper in Charleston cried defiantly.

"He was indeed," a radical newspaper in Boston agreed. "And so he had to hang."

Bile and wormwood this was to Southerners, but though our resentment was still capable of being kindled, for all but the wild and reckless, our fighting spirit was quenched. About the war somebody, a Northerner of course, wrote, "In our youths our hearts were touched by fire." He was right, although that fire was a long way from what touched us then, defeated Rebels, much older than our years, trying to make a living in the midst of the ruined South. It seemed odd to me at first that the great eloquent summations of the war mostly came from Northern

pens. Where were all the Southern writers and poets, I wondered and then decided they were all dead. Dead or broken.
Killed off in the wood lots and forests of northern Virginia or
the sun-drenched fields of Maryland and Pennsylvania. Or
frozen to death on the windswept plain in front of Chattanooga, away off in Tennessee, or in one of the many ravines
and thickets of Missionary Ridge.

And all the passion and zeal that might drive a man to write
was extinguished in a deadly volley or shell burst or stifled forever with the amputation of an arm or a leg. In the end we came
away with one more dependency on the North, a dependency
on their poets to remember for future generations the valor of
our soldiers as well as theirs. And it was just as well, because, for
Southerners, poetry was a bad way to make a living.

Those former soldiers of the Southland who had somehow
escaped death in the war were now challenged by life. During
the war they had seldom eaten well, and for many the peace that
followed brought little change. All scrounged for their daily
bread. Gray veterans who had once stood in stalwart battle lines,
survived the killing grounds of Antietam and Gettysburg, or the
final battles around Richmond, were now hardscrabble farmers
or hired laborers, or worst of the lot, public nuisances hanging
about town squares: quarrelsome, loquacious alcoholics who, for
a drink, told their stories of valor and heroism to anyone who
would listen. And generals and colonels who had once led fierce,
shrieking charges that sent their blue enemies reeling were glad
to find work selling insurance. Or, as was the case with the general who had ordered most of them, making a living as an
administrator at a rural Virginia campus. Shortly after the surrender of his old army, General Lee moved his family from Richmond to the small town of Lexington, deep in the Virginia hills,
the home of the famed Virginia Military Institute, where his
eldest son, Custis, had taken a job as a professor. Close by there
was a small college, Washington College it was called, which had
been bankrupted by the war. My general became its president.

In those postwar years, while we were all being "reconstructed," there were times when I would have given nearly anything to see the old general again. But he never traveled, and Lexington was far out of the way of most populated areas. Only years later did I get my chance to pay him a visit.

In the autumn of 1867, I was invited to visit Knoxville by a close friend of mine from the war, Patrick Cleburne, whom I had met during my tour of duty in the ill-fated Chattanooga campaign. He had become active in Tennessee politics and greatly desired me to visit him while he was staying in Knoxville. Here was my propitious opportunity to call on General Lee as well, for Lexington was only a short side trip off my route to Tennessee. Immediately, I sent a letter to General Lee in care of Washington College, paying him my renewed respects, informing him of my upcoming travel, and asking for permission, provided it was convenient, for me to pay a call. The reply came not from Lee but from Mrs. Lee. The general had been ill recently, she said, but was recovering well and looked forward to my visit.

And that was how I met my traveling companion, Edward Deslauries, with whom I shared my visit to Lexington. I met him by chance the morning I was checking out of the hotel in Charlottesville. I was making inquiries at the desk about transportation down to Lexington. Deslauries, overhearing my questions and my destination, introduced himself. As soon as I told him my name, which to my surprise he said that he knew well from the war years, he proposed that we have breakfast. He told me that by what he had overheard me saying, we not only shared the same destination of travel, but that our reason for going to Lexington was identical as well, to make a call on General Lee.

It was then that his name clarified itself in my mind, and I realized that I was having breakfast with none other than that very same Deslauries who had served during the war as personal secretary to Jefferson Davis. This in turn made me recall times during the war when I had heard officers returning from visits to the Richmond White House making humorous references about "Jeff's grave old 'butler.'"

That was Deslauries.

Yet meeting him in person for the first time, I found him to be not very grave at all, but very pleasant both for his sincere cordiality and his conversational proficiency. He was indeed naturally sober and elderly, although not as old as I imagined based on what I had heard about him. I guessed him to be in his early fifties, a short man, trim, with short graying hair and a close-cropped gray beard. He was fastidious in movement, and that morning was impeccably dressed in a gray flannel suit, which made him appear in my eyes as a stately scholar with the weight of some yet-to-be-written thesis hanging on his thoughts. This impression, as it turned out, was entirely accurate.

Like myself, Deslauries had written to ask to visit the general, and as had been my circumstance, was responded to by Mrs. Lee, informing him of the general's recent illness but also of his anticipation of the visit. Deslauries was to have arrived a couple of days before me, but the weather, the worst I recalled since living in Virginia, had changed everything. He was traveling by rail to Covington, which was only a dozen miles from Lexington, and he had arranged for a horse and buggy to take him the rest of the way. The rains, however, had been severe, flooding a portion of the track between Charlottesville and Covington, thereby forcing him to lay up in Charlottesville. Now with the line clear, Deslauries suggested that we travel together and offered to share with me his transportation to Lexington, which I gratefully accepted.

His purpose in visiting the general, he told me, was to solicit the general's input with regard to a book he was writing, "long overdue," he asserted, "to correct many misapprehensions about the Confederacy," on what would have been the Confederate States of America's foreign policy toward Europe and the Caribbean if the South had won the war. "A story that needs telling to the world!" Deslauries added with some animation. "For the civilized nations need to be aware that our country, had it been allowed to live, would have been a vibrant, contributing member of the world community. President Davis was an internationalist, sir, with marvelous theories for the efficacy of international trade, theories that would have become reality once our independence was won. It was a side of him that few people knew!"

Aside from such tangents as this, although the matter was clearly close to his heart, I found Deslauries to be a likable companion and one with fascinating stories to tell, for in his role as the president's secretary and confidant, he knew much and shared with me anecdotes and facts that soldiers such as I, serving in the field, never knew or suspected. One such account was that after the battle of Gettysburg, Lee had sent Davis a letter of resignation.

I was aghast. "Why, the war might just as well have ended right there in the summer of '63 if Lee had resigned," I exclaimed. "Obviously the president did not even consider it."

"Not for a moment," said Deslauries. "But he was terribly worried for the general, for on its merits the letter did have strong persuasive qualities. The general touched upon certain infirmities of mind and body that prevented him from moving among his army as a general should, in order to see his instructions carried out. He suggested that a younger man would do better. 'And how,' he asked in his letter, almost pleadingly I thought, and so did Mr. Davis, 'when I have not the power to carry out my own wishes, can I be expected to carry out the higher wishes of others?' It was a good point, but the president was having none of it."

Deslauries had other stories as well, on lesser officials and other gossip of the late Confederacy, which he was glad to share and I was more than willing to hear, so that the train ride to Covington was quite agreeable. As was to be expected, however, the talk always returned to the man we were traveling to visit, an officer who had started so inauspiciously as a mere adviser to Jefferson Davis and soon became the field general of legend throughout the world. It was our discussion of General Lee's heartbreaking defeat at Gettysburg that brought Deslauries to the subject of Braxton Bragg's resounding win at Chickamauga only two months later, and the follow-up siege of Chattanooga, as well as the growing idea of the president to send Lee there in the hope of reinforcing this success and salvaging the war.

When I expressed interest in knowing more about the events leading up to General Lee's assignment to the Chattanooga theater, I found Deslauries to be surprisingly forthcoming. I thought this was probably due to the fact that in the aftermath of what eventually happened to the general there, and concomitantly to the hopes of the entire Confederacy, he, as I, was still trying to make some sense of it all. Therefore he was glad for the opportunity to discuss it with someone such as I, who had viewed the events firsthand.

"President Davis was very alarmed to receive the general's offer of resignation after Gettysburg," Deslauries began. "For that battle had done nothing to diminish Lee's stature in the eyes of the president. All he wanted for Lee just then was rest, for with the Army of Northern Virginia safely back on Southern soil, as it was then, Mr. Davis was immeasurably relieved, and greatly heartened in the renewal of our struggle for independence." And here Deslauries frowned. "That was why the military situation in Tennessee took on all importance. After the wonderful news of Chickamauga, it was in the West that Mr. Davis believed that the Confederacy could and should recover its old resurgence, beginning, first and foremost, with the total destruction of the Union Army of the Cumberland in Chattanooga. This would bring Tennessee solidly back into our fold and compel the Yankees to look apprehensively at reinforcing their gains in Mississippi. Another unopposed advance into

Kentucky by Bragg's army would be a real possibility. Oh yes, toward the end of the summer of 1863, Mr. Davis grew positively obsessed about bringing on a victory in Tennessee."

"Was this when the president came up with the idea of sending the general there?" I asked.

Deslauries thought for moment. "If not about that time, then very soon after," he said.

"He knew General Lee would not be happy about being asked to go," Deslauries continued. "But I believe the president had made up his mind to ask him for some time. He confided to me, however, that he would not order Lee to go, as he could never order him to leave his own army. But he did feel, and I agreed with him, that by merely formulating the request, as president of the Confederacy, Lee would bend himself to the will of his country. It turned out we were right.

"The day General Lee arrived in Richmond to discuss the Chattanooga affair, Mr. Davis seemed very depressed," Deslauries recalled. "He was looking out the window, and when I came in, he pointed out and said, 'Look at that.' There was a chilly, steady rain falling, one of those rains that signaled the onset of winter. There were slick puddles on the marble steps of the square and dark stains on the Grecian columns of the capital building. Beyond the heights, the rooftops of the city glistened silver and shiny under the low dark clouds.

"'Quite a rainstorm,' I agreed, then realized that the president was talking about the curling, wisping smoke coming from the countless chimneys."

"THIN SMOKE from meager fires," Jefferson Davis said morbidly. "Everyone trying to keep warm."

Yet as soon as General Lee arrived, the president's mood changed. Davis smiled broadly when he shook the general's hand and asked after Mrs. Lee. Each man assured the other that he was in good health. I wasn't sure that cither was exactly telling the truth, except perhaps Mr. Davis who, in the short period of time since his number-one general had entered the room, was very much improved in disposition.

Lee refused the offer of refreshments. He was regal as always in his trim gray uniform, and at this meeting he was very somber. He and Davis came to the main topic gradually. At the president's request, Lee gave him an overview of the condition of the Army of Northern Virginia and the current tactical situation. It was another of those "all quiet on the Potomac" interludes that the Yankees so favored, so there was really little to discuss in terms of belligerent action. Davis asked a few more questions, which the general answered, then after a long, deliberative silence, he asked Lee if he had read and studied a certain letter that he had sent him. Lee replied that he had and, withdrawing a small packet from the pocket of his tunic, placed it on the table in front of the president.

This letter was a word-for-word copy of the letter that had been sent to Davis by General Bragg's outraged commanders, written after Chickamauga, Deslauries explained. And the subject of the letter was the Army of Tennessee's commander, the much-maligned Bragg.

AT THIS point in his narrative, Deslauries shook his head. "I read the letter when Mr. Davis first received it. In large part it was, or should have been, an embarrassment to the authors, for it contained much spiteful innuendo against General Bragg that did nothing to address the main issue. Yet when the authors finally did essay the main issue, which was Bragg's competency as a commander after Chickamauga, they did it very well, and not with diatribe but specifics. It was these specifics that carried weight with Mr. Davis, particulars of a complete breakdown of tactical leadership in the field. General Bragg's disgusted subordinates alleged that the chance to destroy the Army of the Cumberland in its entirety after Chickamauga had been botched not once but twice. And if these allegations were correct, and it seemed very much like they were, as much as Mr. Davis wanted to give the benefit of the doubt to General Bragg, that commanding general had ignored the advice of his field commanders, and by stubbornly setting his sights on avoiding a defeat, he had succeeded only in averting total victory. This letter was the reason for Mr. Davis's visit to Chattanooga that October, and when he returned to Richmond I saw that he was still very apprehensive about the situation there. None of the generals he sounded out about replacing General Bragg desired his job. So there it was, Braxton Bragg still in charge, his commanders still seething and resentful, and the situation still up in the air. That was when he thought about Lee.

Deslauries resumed his narrative of the meeting between General Lee and President Davis.

As THEY sat there, Davis pointed to the letter that Lee had placed on the table before him. "I think you will agree, General, that this makes for lamentable reading."

"Yes," Lee replied. "Quite so. A very troubling affair at a most inopportune time. A most unfortunate time."

"Indeed," said the president. "We must do something to assist General Bragg's army. We must do something to alter this situation there. Do you not agree?"

Lee returned the president's gaze unfalteringly. He was an intuitive man and knew, if only by way of the letter that President Davis had forwarded him in preparation for this meeting, that the affair in Tennessee was to be the salient topic of this interview. Replying calmly he said, "I agree that some sort of intervention in the affairs there would be most prudent, especially in light of this correspondence." He nodded toward the envelope. "Yet I assume that when you speak of assistance now, you are speaking of assistance to be granted in addition to that which has already been provided from this theater."

He was reminding the president of the reallocation of Longstreet's corps, which he had detached to Bragg's theater of operations just before Chickamauga. Davis acknowledged this, which gave him an opportunity to raise a troubling side issue regarding Bragg's use of that corps.

"The latest word I have is that General Bragg has ordered General Longstreet and the First Corps up to Knoxville to keep an eye on General Burnside," he said. "Does this coincide with what you know, General?"

Lee nodded in assent, and Davis continued. "Apparently General Bragg feels that General Burnside's advance from that direction, slow as it has been, constitutes an immediate threat to his right flank, even from that distance. Would you think this constitutes such a threat?"

Lee thought a moment before answering. "No, Mr. President," he announced. "Certainly not to warrant reducing the besieging force on Missionary Ridge by twelve thousand men just at the time when the Federal army in Chattanooga is beginning to expand their own numbers. Yet," he added equivocally and diplomatically, "it is not my right flank; it is General Bragg's. And I can only assume from this great distance that as the commanding general of his army, he made the determination as he saw fit."

The president gave a judicious nod. "That part is true, General. I don't fault General Bragg for his decision to send a force to block Burnside, and naturally it was his decision to make. But the idea of having the premier corps of the Army of Northern Virginia sitting idly in the far reaches of the Tennessee wilderness, keeping at bay only an equal number of Union troops whose commander is clearly not disposed to descend on Chattanooga with any speed to help lift the siege—this, General, does not sit well with me. Nor with you, I would assume."

Lee's silence was his assent.

Davis continued. "At any rate, the further General Burnside is from Chattanooga the better. And to my way of thinking, Knoxville is at least far enough away from Chattanooga to allow better use to be made of General Longstreet's corps, and to keep the focus squarely on the main front, which is Chattanooga and General Rosecrans's trapped Yankee army. Once again, General Lee, I assume I am speaking to your like mind on the matter."

The general agreed, and the president grew reflective at this point, brooding upon the letter on the table before him. Then he made his pitch.

"General Lee," he began, "I feel that this matter at Chattanooga is imperative enough to warrant the personal attention of someone such as yourself. The attention, I mean to say, of yourself."

Having said this, he looked straight into the general's face and waited for a reaction. There was none. Not at first. Lee only asked, "Are you proposing then, Mr. President, to relieve General Bragg?"

"That I am not, General," the president answered. "I say to you in confidence that there might be a time when I will have to do that, but as yet I think it would not do. For now I think we must use what we have and who we have. Although," he added pointedly, "this is not to preclude sending what assistance we may."

Davis believed he had answered Lee's question. He waited to see if there was more, but the general said nothing.

"General Lee," the president continued, "what I am asking you to do is to go there yourself, to see General Bragg for yourself. I know we still have the means of destroying an enemy army there if we act with dispatch. A victory at Chattanooga by either capturing or destroying an entire Yankee army would be of inestimable value to the morale of our struggling country, and such an achievement would go far in countering the reverses of this summer."

In response to this, Deslauries noticed Lee's face flush, knowing this was an indirect reference of sorts to the events of June and July in Pennsylvania as well as Mississippi.

The general stared at the table, betraying no trace of his own feeling in the matter. At length he asked, "Mr. President, what would be my specific orders?"

Davis had considered this carefully. "General Lee, if you were to go there, my first and immediate message to General Bragg would be that General Longstreet's corps is to be removed from his operational authority and returned to you. Therefore, your first order would be to take charge, in person, of that component of your army that is in Tennessee at this time, and second, to work out a plan for its sound tactical disengagement from all military affairs in that state for return to duty with the Army of Northern Virginia." Then, significantly, he used the phrase, "at the proper time."

The president had hoped to see a pleased reaction from his guest, but Lee made no audible answer for several moments. Finally, he asked, "And what would be my further orders?"

Here Davis took a long deliberation. With a slight frown he picked up the letter on the table and placed it in his waistcoat pocket.

"I must confess, General Lee, that in expressing my concerns openly to you, the use of the word 'orders' makes me uncomfortable." He paused for some moments then said gravely, "General, I would like you to go to Chattanooga and pay a visit to General Bragg. See him. See his army. Acquaint yourself with the situation there. Things have been stalled on that front for far too long. I would like you to examine things with a fresh eye." Then he added, "With a predator's eye, sir."

Lee responded crisply, "Sir, you are telling me that you wish me to serve as Bragg's adviser."

Davis returned his gaze head-on. "More than that, General."

"What then?" Lee pressed his inquiry.

"I want you to be a catalyst, General. An enabler. I wish for you to devise a plan by which the Army of Tennessee, with the help of General Longstreet's First Corps, can inflict a profound defeat upon the enemy. Complete and total. Not on the scale of merely causing their evacuation or retreat, for we both know what a meaningless cocked hat a win like that would be at this stage. No sir. I speak of destroying the Federal Army of the Cumberland sequestered in Chattanooga. I have been there myself, General Lee, and I tell you, sir, it can still be done. The gates of opportunity are far from closed there. They must not be allowed to close before we act!'

The president had allowed himself to get more worked up than he wanted. Now he leaned back in his chair and pulled at his cuffs.

"And this plan that you would have me devise, Mr. President," Lee noted with an unnatural flatness in his voice. "What then would I do with it?"

"I want you to bring it to the attention of General Bragg and myself right away," Davis replied eagerly. "Especially General Bragg, for his immediate cooperation. And I can assure you that you will have his cooperation, General."

Davis said this as a reassurance, but the stoic look on Lee's face spoke much to the contrary. He was not looking at the president but gazing downward, slowly shaking his head, as though listening to the report of a courier who had brought severe news from the battlefield.

The president studied his general for several moments then quietly urged him to speak his mind.

Lee did not answer right away. At last he raised his head and calmly stated, "Mr. President, you must know that this relationship you propose can serve only to manufacture trouble between generals."

Davis smiled. "Trouble among some, General Lee, but not with such an officer as yourself."

The general was not mollified by the president's compliment. He only repeated, "This troubles me deeply. This truly troubles me deeply." His countenance was no longer a blank expression. His doubts were clearly reflected in his features, and there was also a trace of alarm in his protest, which in turn caused Davis to defend his point even more strenuously.

"General Lee," he said, "I concede to you that these arrangements are highly irregular, but what we are about here is a much-needed victory for our country. I am convinced there is one to be had at Chattanooga."

Davis placed his hand on his coat pocket where he had placed the letter from General Bragg's generals. Solemnly he added, "This correspondence calls for action before it is too late, General. I am aware of your reservations and concerns in this matter, but have you considered that what you fear most might not happen? The 'trouble between generals,' as you say, might not come about? I know you are acquainted with General Bragg and his . . . eccentricities. But he too is acquainted with you and your prowess. You hold the admiration of all the South, of all our nation, General Lee. I know that includes General Bragg. An officer of your stature and ability can be a sound and strengthening influence on others. I believe this will be of immeasurable value to our cause if you would go to Chattanooga."

Lee's face was dark with skepticism. Then Davis climaxed his appeal in his most personal terms. "General Lee," he implored, "I am asking you to go to Tennessee. Will you undertake this great task?"

The general did not answer quickly. His face was a portrait of foreboding as Davis watched him anxiously.

"YOU KNOW," Deslauries interrupted his narrative again, "afterward, the president told me that he wanted so much for General Lee to see the situation with the hope and optimism that he did. Mr. Davis, being a former military man himself, was fully appreciative of and sympathetic to General Lee's misgivings. But as he expressed so earnestly to me after the meeting, this was a different situation, and General Lee was a special kind of general, the kind of officer who commanded such vast respect that he could get anything he wanted from anyone simply by asking. 'I see it as clear as day, Mr. Deslauries,' the president told me. 'Cannot General Lee see it as well? His mere presence on Missionary Ridge would be enough to alter the situation, start things moving, blow the clouds away.'"

Then he resumed the story of the meeting between Davis and Lee in the Richmond White House.

THE LAST question Lee asked was how long he would be expected to serve in Tennessee.

Davis's answer was immediate and forthright. "General, after the crucial matter is brought to a head there, for better or for worse, I am inclined to leave that decision to you. You may stay or return whenever you like. And when you decide that it is time to depart from that theater, you will return to Virginia with General Longstreet's corps."

Lee was solemn, reticent, but he replied firmly, "Mr. President, it is impossible for me to deny your request. I would only ask you to allow me sufficient time to make the necessary arrangements within my army to deal with my absence. Thereupon I will be ready to remove myself to Tennessee at the soonest moment."

The smile that Davis bestowed on his premier general at that moment was almost jubilant. "General Lee," he said, "I consider your concurrence in this matter to be a personal favor to me. And I assure you, sir, I will be forever grateful."

Lee replied formally, "You honor me, sir."

HERE DESLAURIES added his own observation.

"At the time I thought his reply a trifle too formal. For Mr. Davis was quite happy and relieved and wanted the general to feel the same way. This of course was beyond his power, but he desired very much to mollify and reassure the officer who had given everything in support of the Confederacy and Jefferson Davis.

THE PRESIDENT noted Lee's concerns. "You are troubled, General, and I understood your reasons. The circumstances in Tennessee are unique and demand unprecedented solutions. But we *can* win there, General. You will see it as well. And if it turns out that our endeavors there result in the destruction of a Yankee army, then all our misgivings now will appear as so many trifles. This by no means implies that I take your hesitations lightly, for I do not. I am quite conscious of the fact that sending the commander of one army to look over the shoulder of another is a thing to be avoided. But in this instance, I am not as uneasy in my mind as you are, for I know the merit of both generals."

Here he smiled and hoped Lee would as well, but the Virginian did not.

"THE REST of the meeting fell upon me," Deslauries continued. "I proceeded to brief and make available to General Lee copies of General Bragg's correspondences on the condition of his army to date, as well as his appraisals of the Federal host. Also, prior to his departure, he would be given every bit of intelligence the War Department had regarding the movement of the other Union forces converging on that theater. General Lee and Mr. Davis agreed to meet again within the week to finalize any details. It was during this interim that I drafted the telegram that would go out to Generals Bragg and Longstreet to inform them of General Lee's imminent arrival."

I took note of this and asked with regard to Deslauries's composing of telegrams, "As well as the one that had my name on it?"

Deslauries chuckled. "The very one. How did you receive it? Were you delighted to serve a tour as the great general's chief aide, or did you feel otherwise?"

"Quite the otherwise, I assure you," I said ruefully. In response to Deslauries's curiosity in the matter, I related how his wires had been received at General Longstreet's headquarters in Tennessee.

"The day of your telegram, I was summoned to the general's tent. 'I've got a couple of telegrams for you to read,' he said.

"The general handed me a dispatch of several pages, but as I read the first paragraph I felt as though a hand had reached out and seized me.

The scene came back to me most vividly as I described it to Deslauries.

"No!" I exclaimed. "I don't believe it! General Lee is coming to Tennessee! Why, General, this is wonderful news!"

Seeing the serious look on his face I demurred somewhat. "Well, is it not wonderful news, sir?"

"Read on," he said.

After I did so, I was a good deal more pensive myself, but far from being as saturnine as my chief.

"What do you think?" General Longstreet asked.

"Well, we're not working for Bragg anymore, and that can't be bad," I said. "And as for the rest of what Richmond is trying to say . . . I'm not quite sure I get the gist of it, but it sounds like we'll all be back in our own country pretty soon. After all, it says very clearly that General Lee will take First Corps back to Virginia as soon as he sees fit. That's good news."

"Yes," General Longstreet agreed. "But the part about his looking in on the situation at Chattanooga is what has me concerned. I'm not sure what kind of news that is."

Then he handed me another telegram, this one only a single page long. As soon as I read it, I gasped and sat down. "Oh no, sir," I protested. "I'm to be General Lee's aide. Forgive me, sir, but this is a big mistake!"

Longstreet watched my anguish with grim amusement.

"But why me?" I asked unhappily.

"Who the hell else?" he growled at me.

DESLAURIES LAUGHED. "General Lee's aide, Walter Taylor, was as mortified as you were, poor fellow. We heard he was very despondent over being left behind. But in the view of the War Department, and the view of the president as well, it was essential that the general's departure from the Army of Northern Virginia be kept a matter of the utmost secrecy for as long as possible. Therefore it was deemed mandatory that Major Taylor, as well as Traveller, should stay conspicuously with the army and allow themselves to be seen by everyone, including recently paroled Federal prisoners. General Lee could take whoever else he needed or wanted from his staff until he reached Atlanta; thereupon it was the responsibility of the Army of Tennessee to attend to his needs." And here Deslauries gave me a significant look. "Which, by your own account to the War Department, did not happen."

"It most assuredly did not!" I said emphatically, mildly surprised that after all the years the memory of the oversight could still elicit such a recoil.

"At any rate, that was how General Lee came to travel to Chattanooga," Deslauries said. Then he gave a sigh. "And the rest is history. Nothing was the same for us after he came back."

Deslauries fell silent, and neither of us felt like going any further on the subject just then.

"You were a military man, Major," Deslauries said at length. "Do you suppose we could have won the war had the general not been disabled at Chattanooga? What if he would have come back to Virginia as the same general? Do you suppose it would have made a difference?"

I shook my head. "I used to wonder about that, but I don't bother with it anymore. To tell you the truth, I don't think it would have made much of a difference in the end. Even if he were a whole man, I don't think his generalship in 1864 would have accrued the same results that his generalship got us in '62 or '63. There is no way."

Deslauries seemed troubled by this. "I'm not sure I take your meaning," he said.

"Let's not forget, General Lee was not getting the help he was accustomed to receiving from his lieutenants earlier in the war," I said. "And when General Grant launched his campaign in 1864, there were far fewer of them. General Jackson was long dead. Generals Hill and Ewell were already well started in their mental declines. And just as important, many of the old fire-eating commanders at the division and brigade levels were gone. Pelham was dead. Pender was dead. Pettigrew and Barksdale. Trimble captured. These men could never be replaced."

"But the army, Major," Deslauries insisted. "There was always a vast difference between General Lee's army and the Army of the Potomac."

"And in the last twelve months of the war the difference was vast and getting vaster," I laughed. "They were constantly getting bigger and we were getting smaller. On the way up to Gettysburg, one of the soldiers asked me, 'Major, why is it that no matter how many of those damn Yankees we shoot down, there always seems to be more and more of them?' 'What does it matter?' I retorted and reminded him of what our newspapers used to say back when the war started, how one good South-erner could whip seven paper-collar Yankees, and we both had a good laugh.'"

Deslauries frowned. I had the sense that my forthright views and anecdote had offended some long and deeply held premise of his own.

"You appear to have harbored little hope that the war could have been won after 1863," he remarked in a more criti-cal tone.

I shrugged. "I don't know," I lied. My real answer would have been a resounding yes had I chosen to answer truthfully. Perhaps more accurate would have been to say, "Absolutely yes" that the war was all up by the end of 1863, and "probably yes" that it had been all up from the very start, now that the years had put so many of our misconceptions, self-deceptions, and false hopes in clear perspective. I chose to be disingenuous, not out of any disrespect for Deslauries, but from a conviction that it had long since ceased to matter. Anytime I chanced upon a "could we have won?" conversation I tried to go the other way. In my mind, getting involved in such speculations was tantamount to talking to a drunk, a thing to be avoided unless one had a great deal of time on one's hands. To me it had always been a tiresome debate, nothing more than an opening for profitless interchanges on the "if onlys" and the "might have beens" of battles like the Seven Days, Gettysburg, or the Wilderness.

Deslauries was looking at me attentively. "But what about before the end of 1863?" he asked. "Indeed, what if we had won a great victory at Chattanooga? Would you then have thought the war winable?"

"If we had won a great victory at Chattanooga," I repeated. "No, I would not have thought the war winable. All it would have meant would be a reprieve."

As I expected, Deslauries reacted strongly. "Oh, no sir!" he declared, shaking his head emphatically. "Not at all, Major Hotchkiss, not at all! If I may say, sir, I believe you were far too much of a pessimist then! Things were going on in our government to bring about a victory of which you and your comrades in arms could have had no inkling."

I was tempted to make a sharp rejoinder, accusing Deslauries and his frock-coated colleagues in Richmond of the same myopia with regard to their view of what could be accomplished on the battlefield against legions of well-equipped Yankees. Instead I answered quietly, "I was not a pessimist at the start of the Chattanooga campaign, sir, but I learned to become one."

"I would be most interested to hear your account of those days," Deslauries said. "Other than his written report after he returned to Virginia, General Lee addressed no other correspondence to the president about it. Nor did I ever hear Mr. Davis speak at any length on the matter when it was all finished."

"Yes, Major," he urged. "Not now, for we are both tired, but later I would hear all about it, all about the details of General Lee's tour of duty there. And," he added good-naturedly, "I would learn as well the circumstances that caused such an intelligent and sagacious man as you so obviously are to topple from the lofty heights of the old Rebel optimism into the dark ravines of demoralization."

I agreed to tell him all about it just as soon as time and comfort would permit.

We arrived at Covington, and it was only on this final leg of the journey, by carriage, that our trip turned into a hardship. We were blown and buffeted by a nonstop rain, which checked our progress to a soaking crawl along interminably muddy roads, and it was here, at a rain-soaked farm, where we first heard the news that Robert E. Lee of Lexington, Virginia, had taken a sudden relapse in health and died.

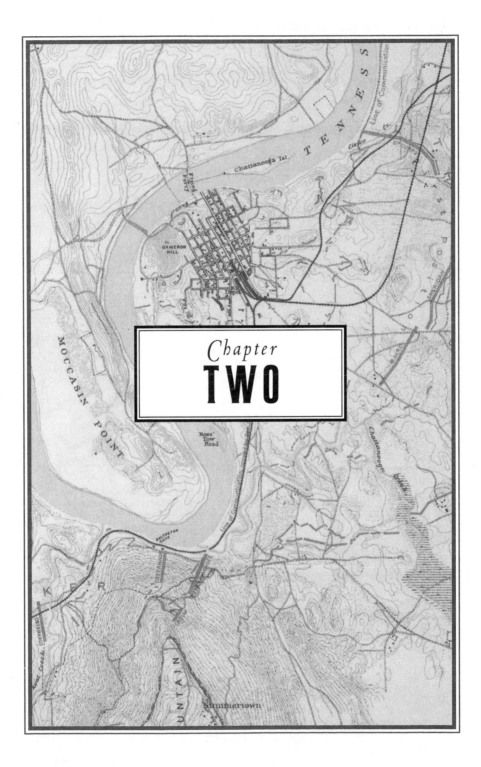

Chapter
TWO

$\mathcal{R}$OBERT E. LEE WAS dead.

He had spent the last three years of his life in the obscurity of a remote town in the Shenandoah Valley, living out these final years as a college president the same way he had lived as a general. The man in charge. The man who others looked to when a final decision was needed. Respected. Awed. Worshiped from a distance. Always the distance.

The day of his funeral was a pouring rain. Both Deslauries and I had, each for our own reasons, come a long distance with the purpose of visiting a living General Lee. Yet as it turned out, we arrived in the small town of Lexington just in time to witness the famous man's funeral. He had died suddenly, after a short illness, and his passing caught everyone by surprise. But for this, there would have been on hand for the funeral many more people from across the South, where he was still revered as a saint. This and the unprecedented heavy rains, which flooded and mired the county on a scale heretofore rarely experienced by the local residents, thus kept outsiders away. But the news of the general's death struck former Confederates and secessionists wherever they were. And wherever they were, they mourned.

Robert E. Lee was dead, and the lost cause was lost for good.

Deslauries and I walked side by side in the funeral procession, which made its way in a pelting rain toward the chapel of the college. I had no way of knowing what a lifelong civilian like the dignified Deslauries was making of the deluge, but to me it seemed fitting to the somber occasion. As a senior staff officer in Lee's Army of Northern Virginia during the war of secession, I had endured countless marches in the rain in the wake of this man, and today might have been one more of those, except for the preponderance of fancy umbrellas that blossomed over the slogging column, never part of the equipage carried by Lee's veterans. Nor was the general mounted for this march.

Behind the hearse came Traveler, bridled and saddled and chafing at the slow pace of the procession, pawing the ground in irritation and splashing his handler with mud. A band and contingent of cadets from the nearby Virginia Military Institute served as the uniformed honor guard. The citizens of Lexington lined the street, the men removing their hats when the casket passed, both men and women openly weeping.

Reaching the chapel of Washington College, the coffin was taken inside and the mourners crowded in after. The pews quickly filled, and most of us stood against the walls. The service for the dead was performed by the local Episcopalian minister, whom I recognized immediately as William Pendleton, white haired and pious, just as I had last seen him at the surrender in Richmond three years hence, but now looking much more at peace with himself in the frock of a small-town clergyman than he had in the gray uniform as Lee's chief of artillery.

As the former artilleryman gave his intonation, I looked around the assembly for other familiar faces. Deslauries and I had only just arrived in time to join the procession, so there had been no opportunity to mingle or introduce ourselves. The majority of the dark-suited, somber-faced congregation were clearly faculty members and affiliates of Washington College, Lee's last command. Mrs. Lee, permanently confined to a wheelchair and swaddled with blankets, was near the coffin. In the pew next to her were two of her sons, Custis and Rooney.

The service was concluded, and Mrs. Lee was wheeled out. Custis and Rooney remained in the chapel for a time, acknowledging the mourners who filed by the coffin.

I was welcomed warmly by Custis. So too was Deslauries, since Custis, who spent most of the war in Richmond as one of the War Department's military liaison officers, naturally remembered President Davis's secretary.

"You must come down to the house," he told us. "My mother would be pleased to speak to you both. Rooney and I shall be along shortly."

It was a short walk to the residence where General Lee had lived his last years and final hours. The house was an exceedingly comfortable dwelling, built, as I was informed, by the college for its presidents. It was already crowded when Deslauries and I arrived. My umbrella had done little to prevent the blowing rain from soaking my overcoat, and once inside I was glad to remove it, hoping for a fire in front of which I could place myself and my damp clothes. I had to settle for a cup of lukewarm tea instead, as the main room downstairs had only one blazing hearth, and this was where Mrs. Lee sat in her wheelchair and received her guests. Custis and Rooney took up station on either side of her.

The widow of Robert E. Lee and the great-granddaughter of Martha Washington received us with stately mien. Much of her late husband's aura surrounded her as well. Her quick eyes had the depth of ages past. Meeting her again after the passage of several years, I was struck anew at how she seemed like a living bridge back to the great Washington himself and his fractious colleagues of schoolboy legend, who founded an extraordinary, albeit turbulent, nation. A blanket lay across her lap, and even though she was seated in a wheelchair, I felt no sense of diminution in anything about her. There was certainly none in her bearing.

"Mr. Deslauries, Major Hotchkiss, dear gentlemen. Thank you for coming."

Bowing, each of us in turn clasped her extended hand.

"How regretful I am of the circumstances that prevented you from seeing the general before his unfortunate lapse," she said. "I fear your trip to these parts was wasted."

Immediately we made voluble protestations to the contrary. Speaking to Deslauries, she said, "I know, kind sir, that you were most desirous to have the general examine the fruits of some political research you were doing. Perhaps one of my sons could provide you with some service in that regard, so as not to have rendered your trip here bereft of substance?"

"Absolutely no, I beseech you, Madame," Deslauries protested fervently. "I would not think of imposing at this time on the grief of you or your family."

"Not at all, Mr. Deslauries," Custis spoke up. "I would be happy to review your material if it would please you and do my utmost to offer any such observations as might have occurred to my father."

"You are very kind," Deslauries responded.

Mrs. Lee's eyes rested on me. "I am happy for the opportunity to see you again, Major Hotchkiss. I only wish it could have been under suitable circumstances. In our last conversations, the general reminisced much on those dreadful battlefields and spoke often to me of the indispensable service you rendered him during the time he was put upon by our authorities to travel in person to Chattanooga."

This last was clearly pejorative, if not of the "authorities," which in truth was Jefferson Davis, singular, then at least of the decision.

"I am pleased also to be able to express my own gratitude for your scrupulous attendance on my husband," she added.

Flushing, I bowed deeply. "It was an exalted privilege Madame," I said sincerely.

"Where are you gentlemen staying?" asked Rooney.

"A place called the New Aberdeen Inn," I said, and to my alarm both Lee sons rolled their eyes.

"Oh, dear," said Mrs. Lee. "I suppose you could find no other accommodations on such short notice?"

"As you say, Madame, on such short notice we could not," Deslauries answered, looking at the three of them nonplused. "But it appeared to us as a most warmly agreeable and accommodating lodging upon our arrival here in Lexington. Is this not the case?"

"I daresay you will find the accommodations quite agreeable," Custis said disparagingly. "Of that I have heard as much. But be assured you will recompense the innkeeper, a Mr. Campbell, fully for every measure of comfort that his premises bestow. I am not aware of many hardworking people hereabout who can afford his price, and those who can are loath to pay the cost for an overnight lodging that is not one penny less than that of the better hotels in Richmond."

"The sad thing is that the man is supposedly a native-born Virginian," said Rooney. "But his usurious effrontery is that of a Boston Yankee. This is made all the more atrocious by the fact that he did no service in the war. Perhaps you gentlemen will be able to find someone here who may have spare accommodations in their homes."

I was about to say something but saw that Mrs. Lee's eyes had already left us and her attention was on the next person in line behind us.

"Come back later, gentlemen, when the house clears out a bit, and I am sure we will have more time to talk," said Custis.

Saying that we would do so, we took our leave of Mrs. Lee. We stayed for a while, visiting with some of the other guests. The military side of the Lee family was vastly underrepresented, although many of the officers and soldiers who had served him faithfully during the war years would arrive in later days to pay their respects, when the weather cleared.

I spoke to those veterans who were present and found out what gossip I could about old colleagues, most of whom were managing to scratch out a living. It was a somber reunion, although not unhappy. I was glad for such news as I learned of my former brothers in arms, for especially in the final year of the war, the Army of Northern Virginia was indeed a family, beleaguered and doomed, but always proud and defiant.

The rain was still coming down heavily when Deslauries and I left the house. We hurried along under our umbrellas in troubled frames of mind over what Custis and Rooney had said about our lodging and our innkeeper. As we approached the inn Deslauries shouted above the downpour, "It will be well nigh impossible to find other accommodations now. And to think we considered ourselves so lucky to have found such a place when we first arrived."

We had indeed considered ourselves lucky. Upon our arrival in Lexington, about which we knew nothing, we had discovered the inn by way of a large pitch bonfire burning in the front yard, sputtering and hissing defiance at the rain. This was an entirely uplifting sight, as we had spent all of the previous night at a ferry landing, waiting for daylight so as to carefully gauge the depth and current of a stream we were hoping to cross without drowning. Spending the night inside a small carriage in a pounding rain was an extremely cold and damp experience, and so, coming into Lexington on the morning of the funeral and seeing that the large bonfire signified an inn, we made immediately for it.

As our carriage had come in the drive, a heavy-booted figure covered with a large oilskin coat came out of somewhere and immediately headed up the team, leading the horses quickly up the drive and checking them the instant the door to the carriage was before the covered porch. When we had alighted, I saw to my great surprise that this adept livery person was an elderly Negro woman.

A sign over the door read, THE NEW ABERDEEN INN AND TAVERN, A. CAMPBELL, HOST. A quick look around once inside was all we needed to conclude that we had been led there by an auspicious star. The downstairs room was the tavern, a tidy, homey space with an immaculately swept floor and, at one end, a blazing fire burning in a large stone hearth. Travelers such as we, who had been subjected to the worst excesses of weather, could not have imagined a more welcome sight. But were there vacancies, we worriedly asked the innkeeper, who had introduced himself as Mr. Campbell, and to our vast relief he assured us that there were. He was a middle-aged man, serious and alert, with an exceedingly fit, robust appearance. So healthy did he look in fact that I wanted to ask him what theater he had been in during the war. But Deslauries was telling him that we were in a hurry to get to the funeral, whereupon the innkeeper gave directions on how we could walk directly to the general's house. He assured us that in the meantime he would attend to the carriage team and see to our bags.

That had been several hours ago, and we had gone to join the funeral feeling most pleased and fortunate about the state of our lodgings, especially having arrived in town so recently. Now, upon our return and forewarned as we were of what we might expect, the cozy inside of the tavern was not nearly so inviting.

"Good afternoon, gentlemen," the innkeeper greeted us. "Your bags have been taken upstairs. Shall I show you the way?"

"Thank you, not just yet," said Deslauries studiously. "If you would be so kind, I would like to examine your prices, for as you recall, in our haste to get to the funeral, we did not have a chance to discuss that issue."

"By all means, sir," replied the innkeeper with full equanimity. "You'll find the current rates there," and pointed to a chalkboard hanging on the wall. Then he added, "Hopefully you have had the opportunity to make your own inquiries about our reputation with some of the inhabitants."

We have indeed, I remarked to myself dryly, at the same time noticing that the innkeeper showed no reticence in making such a comment. Rather a cool customer, I thought.

Deslauries made a show of frowning at the chalkboard, a trifle too theatrically to my way of thinking. Then, repeating the criticism voiced by Custis, he said, "Forgive me, sir, but I cannot help but note that these rates are nearly identical to the rates one can expect at one of the finer hotels in Richmond."

Deslauries's expectation of some contrite word or explanation on the part of the innkeeper was immediately dashed.

The man looked amused. "Familiar as I am with the various hostelries of Richmond, I must say I find myself somewhat baffled at your employment of the word 'finer,' kind traveler," he said with a raised eyebrow. "The last time I stayed in what was supposed to be one of the 'finest' hotels there, the wall-paper was hangin' down, the window looked out on a lot of charred buildings and litter-strewn lots, and I fancied I could still smell the smoke from the fire. But maybe things have spruced up since then."

Deslauries listened in shocked silence. Recovering now, he struck an attitude of offended dignity. "I will have you know, sir, that I am a citizen of Richmond!"

The innkeeper looked back at him unapologetically but said in a friendly tone nevertheless, "Then please permit me to bid you welcome to Lexington, kind sir, of which I am a citizen, and hope your stay is a pleasant one. And insofar as you will permit me to be your host, your comfort will be a matter of my strictest duty, for I am an honest man of business, sir, honestly proud of my hospice and happy to put its accommodations at your service."

Unsure of how to respond to this effusion of benign intentions, Deslauries regarded the man gravely.

I studied the chalkboard as well. "Let us hope we find that to be the case then," I said nonchalantly, not looking at the innkeeper but aware of his sharp glance in my direction. "Your board indicates that a hot bath is included in the price of the lodging. May I inquire as to whether that is a full bath, such as one might expect in a city accommodation?"

"Most assuredly, kind traveler," the innkeeper replied, able to suppress all but the slightest vestige of irritation. I noted his pique with amused satisfaction. He had turned to look at me full on, his body turned squarely in my direction, and I suspected that this was probably how he met all such insurrections to his authority. "Which is to say full immersion in a large body tub," he continued, holding me in his gaze. "Water boiled to proper temperature, with attendant close by for replenishment on call. Fifteen-minute time limit, and if the bath is not desired during your stay," he gave a sidelong glance at Deslauries, "twenty-five cents will be deducted from the final bill. Shall I show you to your rooms, gentlemen, or would you like more time to think the matter over?"

As if in collusion with the innkeeper, the roar of the rain on the roof redoubled, and gusts of wind shook the windows. I looked at Deslauries. I could see he was still not mollified, but he nevertheless nodded his acquiescence.

The rooms were small, each just large enough to hold a bed, armoire, and washstand. But like the tavern downstairs, everything was scrubbed and dusted, and the bed linens were washed and ironed. Deslauries expressed his desire for a nap, while I opted for a bath. We agreed to meet in the tavern in approximately one hour, whereupon we would discuss paying another call on the Lee family.

My bath was nothing less than splendid, the chill and wetness of the last two days dissipating from my body in the blissfully hot water, brought continually from the kitchen by a hardworking young Negro boy. So wonderful was my soaking that when my allotted period was up—scrupulously timed by the innkeeper, for I had set my own watch on a nearby chair, and precisely at the end of fifteen minutes he appeared with my towels—I informed him that I would like another fifteen.

To this he readily assented, informing me cordially not to worry, but that he would take care to add an extra twenty-five cents to my bill. In the meantime, he would immediately send the boy with more hot water and please enjoy the bath.

After he had gone I could not help but smile. Custis was right; the hospitality of our earnest innkeeper was neither free nor cheap. With my trip to Knoxville still ahead, I would be spending a good deal more money in Lexington than I had intended. Nevertheless I could see no alternative. Despite Rooney's suggestion, I was quite averse to soliciting total strangers for lodging. Furthermore I now had to admit that the amenities of Mr. Campbell's New Aberdeen Inn, however priced, were not lacking in any detail.

After my bath I went downstairs to wait for Deslauries. Quiescent now, sitting in dry clothes before a warm hearth, I did not want to move. Dormancy was a luxury, and I indulged it fully. Comfortable as I was in my body, my mind was depressed, and my thoughts glum and cheerless. It was the funeral that had done it.

For the past few years I had lived my life quietly, devoted myself to my family, and deliberately not thought about the war. But with this visit to General Lee's home, which was now his final resting place, memories from that time the Yankee poet had alluded to were inevitably stirred to life. It was beginning to settle in on me that the general from that passionate time, who my uniformed comrades and I had attended, the clairvoyant upon whom we had all pinned our faith and our lives, was departed. A morose spell was upon me, and the fervor and heartbreak of four blood-drenched years of war that I had put out of my mind after the surrender, years following in the wake of a white-haired commander who was now gone from the earth, refused any longer to keep their place in the obscure closet of my memory where they had been banished.

Deslauries joined me wordlessly, sitting down at the table, and for a long time we both stared into the fire. At last he broke the long silence.

"Well," he sighed and said nothing else. Yet there was no need, for the single word and the tone in which it was uttered were sufficient. It summed up the war, all the brilliant campaigns, and all the bravely fought battles, all of which had proved to no avail.

Well.

All the sacrifices, unmatched. The singleness of purpose, the love and faith in a commander, unwavering, which had all gone for naught.

Well.

And that commander was now dead. Dead and buried, never to mount his horse again. Marse Robert. Uncle Bobby. Gone forever and the war over. The war lost.

Well, well, well.

We had all, Deslauries included, although he had not been a soldier, in our own place and our own way given the fullest measure of our talents, given our entire selves, to the defense of a cause, the protection of an idea. It had been a consuming thing then, drawing us above ourselves and our own self-interests. The Northern poet was right. There had indeed been a fire in our hearts. A fire that drew us toward it when the flames were high and strong, and continued to draw us closer, seeking the warmth, even when the flames were fading in the embers.

We had taken sides in a great tragic struggle and, despite all that we and thousands upon thousands of others had given, our side was vanquished. And for reasons known only to God, in a bloody contest where so many had died, when it was all over I found myself among the spared. Being a practical man, I did not dwell overlong on why this had happened but accepted my blessing and tried to be deserving, returning to my family and with my wife striving to raise our children as righteous Christians.

I could not speak for Deslauries about any privations he might have undergone during the war. But as for me, a serving Confederate officer, I had undergone many. And as a soldier I endured them as the war brought them and forgot them promptly when they were past. But now and again there were moments when the memories returned, like now, in front of an innkeeper's fire in Lexington, Virginia, only a few hours after the funeral of Gen. Robert E. Lee, commander, Army of Northern Virginia.

"Let's have a drink," I said to Deslauries and motioned for the innkeeper. We each ordered a bourbon, and when our host returned with the tray, Deslauries inquired innocently, "And were you yourself acquainted with General Lee, Mr. Campbell? He or some members of his family having been your guests at one time, perhaps?"

"No sir," replied the innkeeper. "Although I often used to see him riding his magnificent horse about the town and country, as he was fond of doing."

Deslauries continued in a light, conversational tone. "And if I may inquire, sir, were you a participant in the late war of Southern Rebellion?"

"I was not, sir," the innkeeper said emphatically. And he added with equal firmness, "I saw not the slightest reason for it."

"Ah. A wise choice given how things turned out. Clearly a man of practicality over sentiment," Deslauries declared. His reproof was veiled, but I saw that the innkeeper, no man of deficient alertness, noted this immediately. For his unsophisticated ways, our host was no yokel, and I was beginning to suspect that he might indeed be a good deal more. Cloaking his recognition of the censure every bit as deftly as Deslauries had issued it, the innkeeper gave a self-deprecating smile.

"Thank you, sir, I try to be practical," he said. "Seems to me if everyone in the world was as practical as the Savior intended them to be, there wouldn't need to be no wars."

We made no response to this, waiting for him to set down the tray. Instead, he shifted it from one arm to the other.

"Mind if I tell you a little story?" he asked then went on without waiting for an answer. "No, gents, I weren't in the army," he said, the smile still on his face but his eyes looking defiantly at Deslauries. "But four and more years of tryin' to scrape out a livin' in these parts seemed a right loyal thing for a citizen of the Old Dominion to be about back then. That was to my way of thinkin' leastways, but then I ain't near as smart as some. Still, I learned a lot about soldierin' too. It was an expensive education, gentlemen, paid in full by yours truly. And there weren't no government standing by to protect. Certainly not from Washington nor from Richmond either. I used to have a farm over near Covington, and for the first couple of years after the insanity started, I managed to tend my crops and get by with pretty good luck. The dogs barkin' down at the bend would always let me know if I was about to be visited by some band of patriots on either side, which gave me about five minutes to get the cow and the horses shooed off into the swamp.

But one particular day the dogs was off somewhere, and my luck with them.

"The cow was tied to the post, and I was leading my two ponies out of the barn when all of a sudden here comes a column of Yankee horse soldiers, clompin' into the yard like they owned the place. There was a young whelp of an officer at their head, and I yelled to him that this was private property, and where in the hell did they think they was goin' and also for him to tell his lame-brained troopers to stay on the road instead of cantering all through my vegetable patch.

"Well, he reins up and glares at me, trying to look all stern and hickory, then he sings out, 'You have an impudent way of greeting visitors, Mr. Farmer.'

"'Well, I don't recall invitin' any visitors here to be greeted in the first place!' I sings back at him.

"He didn't say nothin' to that but gives me another sissy glare, then he and the others looked around, and that's when they started takin' special note of the cow and the ponies.

"'Seen any Reb cavalry?' the officer asks.

"'No,' I said. 'And why would I want to tell you if I did?'

"Now if it was me, I'd have given up on asking any more questions, but not this one. He kept right at it.

"'So you ain't seen no Reb cavalry at all?'

"'Can't say that I have.'

"'How 'bout Reb infantry?'

"'Can't say that I have.'

"'Artillery?'

"Same answer.

"Then he says, "You ain't too far from a damn fool, are you?'

"'Nope,' I answers. 'I reckon there's only about twenty feet separatin' us.'

"That was when the sergeant comes up, and I braced myself, since sergeants was usually the ones that started trouble.

"'I reckon this gentleman didn't get the word up here that there's a war on,' he remarks real saucylike, speakin' to his officer but lookin' at me. 'I'd figure that an able-bodied man like your-self would be off with the Reb army,' he says to me.

"'Well, you figured wrong,' I said. 'I don't own no slaves, and I don't give a hang for any Richmond politicians nor any of their problems.'

"'Well then, that bein' the case, maybe you want to join up with us, since we all feel the same way about it,' the sergeant says with a smirk, and his troopers laughed.

"'Search the buildings!' the officer orders, and right about then I might've done somethin' stupid but extremely satisfying except that the sergeant drew his revolver and laid it across his saddle.

"'No need to take offense, Mr. Farmer,' he says all serene-like and still with the smirk. 'These here are dangerous parts for us, since not all your neighbors are as peaceable and law-abiding as you are.'

"'I reckon so,' I shot back. 'But maybe if you'd git on back north where you belong instead of pokin' your noses around where you ain't wanted, it'd be a lot less dangerous!'

"I'll tell you straight, gentlemen, bein' forced to stand still and watch while a bunch of muddy saddle-humpers go into your house brazen as they please, and hearin' their clod boots walkin' around inside, goin' through rooms and openin' doors and cupboards, why it's enough to make a sane man feel like he wants to bust right open.

"The ones that went in the barn came out carrying my brand-new harness and all the rest of my livery, cool as you please. If I'd had a gun on me I think I would have pulled it out and used it right then, hang the consequences. The Yankee sergeant knew it too, as I caught him playin' with the hammer on his revolver all smuglike.

"'We'll need to confiscate your livestock,' the officer tells me. 'To keep them from falling into enemy hands.'

"I didn't say nothin'. Couldn't say or do a blasted thing, except build up steam like an old boiler fit to bust.

"'We'll bring 'em back as soon as the war's over,' cracks the sergeant, and the others laughed.

"So there they went," the innkeeper continued. "Horse thieves in uniform, ridin' off with my stock, and me wishin' a gut shot for each one of them.

"Well, the next day I'm sittin' in the yard, tryin' to figure out what to do next when lo and behold, 'look away Dixieland,' here comes a troop of *grayback* cavalry into the yard, lookin' all martial and warlike.

"'Well, don't hope spring eternal,' I says to myself, 'and only a whole day late! And ain't it peculiar, but what do you think the first thing this bunch of heroes want to know is? 'Seen any Yanks?' the fellow in charge asks, and I'm thinkin' somebody in Richmond or Washington ought to have the job of herdin' these fools together so they can get down to fightin' like they say they want. Well, I was still hot about bein' robbed on my own land and on my own doorstep by a pack of pasty-faced New England paper collars, and I didn't waste any time lettin' this new set of Napoleons know about it. 'A passel of 'em came through here just yesterday and took my livestock,' I said. 'Where were you fellas then? They left here headin' north. If you hurry you might just be able to catch them and get my animals back!'

"Well, they didn't say nothin' to this but kind of looks me over, and then one fellow asks, smart-alecky like, 'How come you ain't in the army?' Well, right then I thinks, 'Hello, Andrew, these boys are startin' to sound an awful lot like the bully Yankees, just different accents. So to the smart-alecky one I says, 'I reckon I ain't in the army since somebody needs to stay at home and raise livestock for soldier boys to steal!'

"They didn't take kindly to that, but I didn't care since I was beginnin' not to take too kindly to them, hang the flag they were totin'. Then another one drawls out, 'Kinda suspicious ain't it?'

"'What's suspicious?' I says. And he says, 'That the Yankees didn't burn your place like they's been doin' up the valley. What do you make of that, Mr. Gentleman Farmer?'

"Now I considered this a right ill-mannered thing to say to a man on his own property and in his own yard, especially a yokel with a Georgia accent tryin' to act all high and mighty up here in Virginia. If it had been just the two of us, I'd've dragged his big dumb carcass off his big dumb crow-bait horse and taught him a lesson in manners to take back home to his red-clay peanut farmers.

"'I'll tell you what I makes of it,' I fires back at him. 'It tells me that even low-born, thievin' Yankees might have some manners, which is more than I can say about some of the folks on the other side. So put that in your sack with your goober peas, Mr. Brave Cavalier!'

"Well, as you might imagine, that was getting' on to fightin' words, but I was past carin', as the situation had long since 'deteriorated,' as the generals say. The Georgia goober made a show like he was thinkin' to come off his horse and lay into me, but he didn't, just like I knew he wouldn't all along. Brotherly love was by the boards now, so I wasn't real surprised when the whole thing played out again, the house and the out-buildings searched same as the Yankees did the day before, but worst was that, before they rode off, I had to stand there and watch while they gathered up all my chickens, every single one! Chased 'em down they did, too! All through the barnyard, out in the field, even under the shed! Not even the Yankees bothered doing that! 'Send the bill to Richmond!' the officer in charge of these bandits tells me as they rode away, while the goober calls out, 'We'll keep a sharp eye out for your livestock, Mr. Thomas Jefferson!' and the rest of them laughed, same way as the Yankees!"

Pausing now, the innkeeper looked at us with self-righteous scorn. "I'll have you know, sirs, that right then I did the only thing I could do, what every citizen in every country that calls itself civilized is supposed to have a right to do. I wrote two letters raising holy hell on having my income taken away, and demanding compensation. I sent one to Abe Lincoln and the other to Jeff Davis himself, demanding that whichever one was my rightful president do the right thing and pay me back in full. Well you won't be surprised when I tell you I never heard nothin' from neither one. So since then, gentlemen, I ain't had no use for wars, politicians, noble causes, nor least of all, soldiers."

Throughout his long diatribe we had been waiting for him to pour our drinks, but we were being shown that the innkeeper was altogether a man on his own schedule when put on the defensive. His rebuttal to both of us concluded, he once again resumed his role as host. Putting down the tray at last, he set the glasses in front of us. Then with a deft, experienced hand, he poured three fingers of bourbon into each of our glasses. "If I leave the bottle you'll need to put down a deposit," he declared.

I shook my head. "How much do I owe you?"

"Four bits for the both of them," he answered.

I looked up in surprise. "Two bits a glass," I remarked as I fumbled in my change purse. "That's rather a surprising price to be charged out here, when it's less than half that in Richmond. Nevertheless," I smiled, as I laid out the coins. "No doubt you would say, 'This isn't Richmond.'"

The innkeeper said nothing to this, but looking at me the same way a blacksmith might look at a loose shoe on a horse, he called over his shoulder, "Nathan, fetch that whiskey barrel over here."

The Negro boy who had tended my bath arrived cradling a wooden cask. The innkeeper took it from him and twirled it up to rest on his shoulders. "Lookee here," he said to me, and pointed to the stark black letters stenciled on the wood, which read, BOURBON COUNTY, KENTUCKY.

"'Bourbon County, Kentucky' is what that says, kind traveler," the innkeeper announced. " I know you can read, but I'm just addin' to the point. Bourbon County, from the state of Kentucky. Educated folks as you both certainly are, I'm sure I don't need to remind you that there ain't no direct line between here and there. And that if you think on it, you'll recollect that there's many a river, mountain range, and forest that divides these two spots. So that this very barrel, along with its companions, the nectar of which reposes in the glasses before you, had to come by rail across two states and part of a third just to reach Covington, and that the railroads don't move neither boxes nor bodies for free, I know I don't need to remind you neither. Now from Covington, this barrel and its companions had to come over here by freight wagon, but what with all the rain we've been havin', makin' a mess of roads and fords, haulin' fees have spiked considerable. But never mind that, gentlemen. Never mind any of that. The fact is that it's here, good bourbon whiskey, in spite of long distance, flooded roads, and bad weather. Right here in Lexington, Virginia, waitin' to be set down in front of a thirsty customer on command. The genuine article, sirs. Not some cheap rye. Not some watered-down local swill, but the real thing. And as much of it as you want for as long as you want, so long as you pay up." He thumped the barrel proudly. "Bourbon whiskey was what you ordered, kind travelers, and Bourbon County, Kentucky, whiskey is what you got. You'll know it for yourselves just as soon as you taste it, if you know anything about it at all." He swung the cask back into the arms of the Negro boy. "And the going price," he affirmed, looking straight at me as he scooped up my coins, "is two bits a glass."

As he departed he called to the boy, "Nathan, mind you stoke up that fire so's our guests will be comfortable."

After the innkeeper had gone, I smiled at Deslauries, who shook his head and grimaced. "What a garrulous fellow," he exclaimed irritably. "I'm sure I've never met the like. And certainly *not* a Richmonder, I'm happy to proclaim. In fact, I would be quite surprised to learn that his ill-shod, cow-manured boots had ever set foot on a single cobblestone in any respectable district of that fair, longsuffering city. I rather suppose he thinks he told us off."

"I rather suppose he does," I laughed.

Still looking disdainful, Deslauries raised his glass to his lips. He sipped once then again. His face lightened. "It would appear, however, that our loquacious host is no liar insofar as his certification of his house spirits is concerned," he declared with satisfaction. "For I believe this is indeed the genuine whiskey of our poor sister, Kentucky."

Then he looked at me seriously. "As I promised you on the way down here, Major, there would be a time when I would want to hear, in your own words, your perceptions and views on what transpired in the much-lamented Chattanooga campaign in the late fall of 1863, while our dear General Lee was out there. Would you feel up to telling me about it?"

I shrugged. "What do you want to know?"

"Everything, naturally. And right from the time General Lee arrived."

I considered for a while whether I wanted to go into the whole thing then. It was over and done, and the lead player recently buried. But Deslauries's eyes were eager for me to relate a critical part of the history of the Confederacy that I had witnessed, most of the time at the side of the great general himself. And now it was appropriate, I decided. An appropriate story and an appropriate time to tell it. So with a drink of my whiskey and shifting in my chair, I began to relate to Deslauries the story of Lee at Chattanooga.

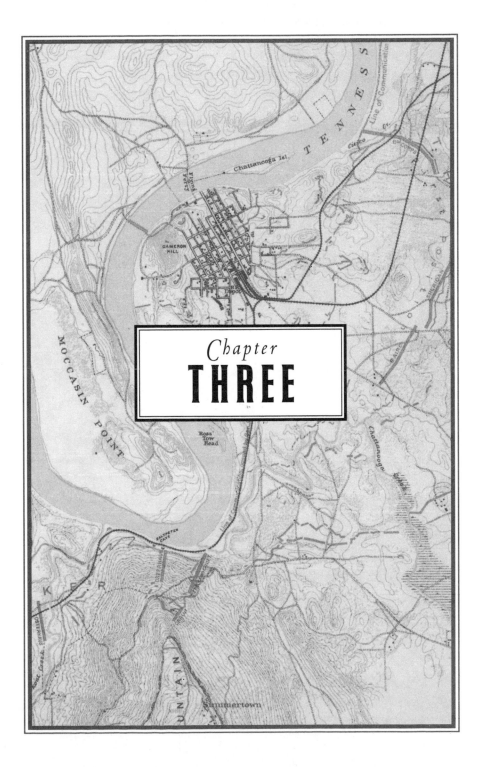

Chapter
THREE

*I*N THE SOFT LIGHT of a three-quarter moon I could see all the way up the road that ran parallel to the railroad tracks. That was where the cavalry escort would be coming from if they were coming, but I already knew they weren't coming.

The rail yard was deserted. Moon glow bathed the vacant storage platforms, darkened sheds, and empty tracks. There were no human beings around at all, except for the occasional invalid sentry nodding off in some quiet corner, trying to keep warm. They used the wounded and convalescents for picket duty here, and I thought bitterly, these were the only ones from the Army of Tennessee on hand to greet the train that was only minutes away, bringing the man in whose hands alone were carried the fragile eggs of the Confederacy.

I had been around the entire rail yard twice. I had stopped at the telegrapher's and at the stationmaster's; no one had heard anything about any escort from General Bragg's headquarters to meet the train. "An escort for who?" the stationmaster inquired. I briefly gave credence to the idea that they might be on the way even as I sat there, but quickly gave up that notion. Not a chance. This was business as usual in General Bragg's Army of Tennessee, as all of us who had come over from Virginia had come to find out. Botched business as usual, from the disagreeable commanding general himself, to his malevolent chief of staff, down to every one of his twitchy, prune-faced staff officers.

No sir, Jed old boy, I told myself, you've got this one on your own.

So I sat there on my horse in the still moonlight in an empty rail yard. I had brought along an extra mount for the general, and both the animals had their heads down, probably dozing. I had my head down too, so that I didn't see the crippled old butternut until he was up beside me.

"Major?" he called out.

This soldier was a tall lean man, his face obscured by a large slouch hat. He had only one leg and used his rifle as a crutch. Immediately my hopes rose.

"Yes," I said. "Did you come from the telegraph office? Is the escort on its way?"

He leaned heavily on his rifle. "Why no suh, reckon I don't know nothin' 'bout no escort or such." He gestured over his shoulder. "I was settin' on them barls' yonder when I seen you pull up in the moonlight. Came out here to take a gander 'cause you look mighty familiar. I reckon you might be Major Hotchkiss, what's with Old Pete and the First Corps."

"That's right," I said. "And who might you be?"

The man touched his hat in salute. "Sergeant Goner Wickett, Hood's division, Longstreet's corps. My first name's Lucius, but folks took to callin' me Goner after Sharpsburg. Took a shell fragment square in the chest and laid in a corn field all day. Figured my time had come, but it warn't to be. At nightfall I managed to crawl back to my camp, and all the boys told me they'd given me up as a goner. Since then the name stuck. And its powerful nice to see someone from the old corps tonight, Major. It gets a tad lonesome sometimes since the boys all left."

I smiled and extended my hand down to him. "Nice to meet you as well, Sergeant Goner. I feel the same way sometimes." I pointed to the emptiness between his left knee and the ground. "Looks like you ran into another spell of bad luck."

He nodded. "Ain't no two ways 'bout that. A Yankee solid at Chickmawga took it off clean as a whistle. Had to lay up a bit to heal. Then when all my boys piled onto the boxcars for Knoxville, the doc made me stay put. Said I warn't no travelin' case even though I knew better. Now I go roun' kickin' myself with the one leg I got left for not climbin' on one of them cars with my Texas pards."

I couldn't suppress a laugh. I had long been awed by the toughness and risibility of the typical Rebel soldier and marveled where it came from.

"How're the boys doin' over there, Major? Been any fightin'?"

"The boys are fine," I said. "No fighting. Just sitting."

There came just then the long wail of a train whistle from off in the darkness.

"Sergeant, I've got to meet someone on that train," I told him. Could I trouble you to hold the horses?"

"No trouble a'tall," he replied.

I dismounted and handed him the reins. I was still distracted about the missing escort, which should have been lined up behind me along the track, but now I was nervous as well. The whistle sounded again, much nearer, and I could hear the chuffing of the engine. The sergeant was looking at me curiously.

"Don't usually get no trains pullin' in here this time of night," he commented. When I made no reply, his face brightened with an idea. "Hey, Major, this ain't Old Pete yer waitin' on is it? Old Pete and some of the boys?"

"No, Sergeant, it's not Old Pete I'm afraid," I said, forcing a smile, in spite of my increasing agitation.

There was another wail, piercingly close, and suddenly a headlight came into sight. The locomotive huffed slowly into the yard, blowing noise and steam and smoke. As it came on, I noted that it wasn't much of a train at all. There were several flatcars loaded with supplies, and one boxlike car behind the tender, the type used to carry wounded. That was all, and there was not a soldier in sight anywhere, none in the cab, none on the boxcar, none on the flatcars. It was then, to my absolute horror, that I realized that there could be something worse than not having an escort from Bragg's headquarters on hand to meet the train, and that was not having one on the train itself.

It was scarcely believable, but there it was. The thing was to have been arranged by Bragg's chief of staff, a heavily armed guard detail to ride along from Dalton, down the line. But this had gone the same route as the cavalry escort. To my over-wrought mind just then, this was nothing short of criminal. If Robert E. Lee was aboard this train, and he had better be, then any scratch band of Union cavalry that might have been on the prowl that night could have killed or captured the first soldier of the Confederacy without even so much as a sharp fight. I resolved to report all this in detail to General Longstreet at the soonest opportunity along with my heartfelt petition to serve on the firing squad for General Bragg's chief of staff.

In a cloud of rolling steam, the locomotive came to a loud, hissing stop. The horses pawed back out of the wet cloud. Two of the train crew jumped down from the cab and ran back to the medical car, placing a step stool by the stairs. The other two members of the crew craned their necks out of the cab, looking back expectantly.

The two men waited at the bottom of the steps, and then a figure emerged on the platform of the car. Amid the wafting steam he was visually indistinguishable just then, wearing a wide-brimmed hat and long, heavy coat. This lone passenger took hold of the railing and stepped slowly down the iron stairs then onto the platform, where he was helped to the ground by the two members of the train crew. General Lee was on Tennessee soil.

Behind me, I heard the sergeant make an astonished exclamation. My own heart was thumping, and I was conscious of how, seeing the old man again, I felt like a child.

I stepped forward and snapped my arm up in crisp salute.

"Good evening, General! Major Jedediah Hotchkiss at your service, sir!"

The general said nothing at first but peered at me through the steam. "I believe this is not Dalton?" he said.

"No sir," I answered. "This is Chickamauga Station."

"The final stop then," he said. "We are near the Army of Tennessee, I assume. Near Chattanooga."

"Yes, General. General Bragg's headquarters is only a few miles away. We can ride from here." Somewhat flustered in my own mind just then, I was tempted to make some sort of apology for the missing escort, but General Lee's own apparent disorientation held me back. He was peering at me again, and then he broke into a cordial smile. "Why Major Hotchkiss, of course! And how are you tonight, sir?"

"Very good, General Lee, thank you. And it's very good to see you, sir."

The train men brought out the general's baggage, two bags. While these were being secured to my horse, I saw the general noticing the one-legged sergeant who was standing at ramrod-stiff attention, hat removed, holding the reins of the horses.

"At ease, Sergeant," I said. "General Lee, this is one of Hood's men, wounded at Chickamauga."

"Good evening, Sergeant," said Lee.

"Evenin', General," the sergeant replied, staring at him with bright, shining eyes and then blurting out excitedly, "And God bless you, sir! God bless! Why I says to myself, 'Goner old boy, that ain't no one but Mars' Robert come glidin' out of that car, hanged if it ain't! Mars' Robert hisself or you're a blind old hound!'" Then, mastering himself, he snapped back to attention and sounded off. "Sergeant Goner Wickett, General! Hood's division of Longstreet's corps, Army of Northern Virginia!"

General Lee's tired smile was genuine. He saluted, and nodded toward the man's missing leg. "Did that happen at Chickamauga, Sergeant?"

"Yes sir," the man answered immediately. "Ain't nothin General. General Hood hisself got worse!"

Lee nodded gravely. "Yes. I saw General Hood in Richmond before I came here. He is recovering nicely from the wound he sustained in that great victory. I hope you will take every care to mend yourself as well."

"T'ain't nothin' at all, General," the sergeant replied, his voice becoming excited again. "You shoulda seen the boys that day, General. I wisht you'd been there to see 'em run when we hit 'em! Why we swept them bluebellies outta bush, gully, and gopher hole! But then your boys always knew how to lick Yankees, General, and that's a fact!"

Lee's smile broadened.

"We've got to be going now, Sergeant," I said, putting my hand on his shoulder. "General Lee needs to get up to Missionary Ridge tonight."

The sergeant nodded. He held the bridle as Lee mounted his horse. There was silence now except for the panting of the locomotive. As we rode into the moonlight I looked back to see the sergeant standing at attention, hat over his heart, and behind him were the two train crewmen standing by the car, and two more looking out of the cab, not a one moving or speaking.

"Are you feeling all right, General?" I asked anxiously, as we left the rail yard.

"Quite so, Major, thank you," Lee replied. Then he asked, "And how was our friend General Longstreet when you saw him last?"

I noted the lightness in his tone as he posed this query, and it made me feel better.

"Quite well and in good health, General," I answered. "And right now he's keeping a weather eye on Burnside over in East Tennessee."

"Has General Burnside shown any recent advance toward Chattanooga?" Lee asked.

"No sir, he's just sitting behind his works in Knoxville."

Lee gave me an inquisitive look. "How do you know that?" he asked. "From General Bragg's people?"

"No, General. I get a wire every couple of days from General Longstreet's headquarters, informing me of the situation over there, to be passed on to you when you got here."

Lee fell silent for a time, and I was grateful, being occupied with keeping us on the road as well as fretting over other details of General Lee's safety, which would not be absolved until we were safely within the confines of the Army of Tennessee on Missionary Ridge. I had selected a good mount for the general, or so I hoped. Not at all like Traveler, of course, but a sturdy, well-behaved pony that thus far was bearing his rider well.

There was not a time in the war when I felt so much of the world on my shoulders, not even under Stonewall, when he was in one of his impatient fits for "a terrain map, Mr. Hotchkiss. A terrain map at the soonest! Ride out at once, sir!" Those had been stressful times, but here was a wholly new challenge. Delivered into my hands for safekeeping, in a strange land with unfamiliar people, was an obviously tired first general of the Confederacy. With no escort and no protection, save my own revolver, it was all on me to get this indispensable asset to his destination.

We rode along in silence; the general seemingly inclined to be alone with his thoughts or his weariness. I took the lead and was grateful for the moonlight on the trail. It all seemed like a dream to me just then, a troubling, uneasy dream, taking place in an alien landscape of unkempt wilderness, rocks, and steep precipices, all in moonlight. And in the midst of all this was the fantastic, unnerving reality of General Lee's presence. A gray man riding along in moon glow, and his guide, to lead him safely through this luminous nocturnal setting, was me. And it was not a dream.

Suddenly General Lee came up alongside.

"What have you heard of General Sherman, Major? Are his whereabouts known? It was reported to me in Richmond that he is on his way from Memphis, coming here."

"That is my knowledge as well, General," I answered.

"There are twenty thousand men in his force, I have heard."

"At least that many, sir."

"I assume General Bragg has cavalry out trying to pinpoint General Sherman's location?"

I paused before answering. Everyone in the Army of Tennessee and Longstreet's corps as well had heard about the ugly incident between cavalry commander Bedford Forrest and Braxton Bragg that had taken place after Chickamauga.

"General Lee," I began. "You should be aware, sir, if you are not already, that Generals Forrest and Bragg had a severe falling out after Chickamauga. As a result, General Forrest refuses to take orders from General Bragg or allow any part of his command to do so. What cavalry is left in the Army of Tennessee that does not belong to Forrest is under the command of General Wheeler."

"Very well," said Lee. "So then, has General Wheeler received reconnaissance taskings?"

"I'm afraid I don't know the answer to that, General," I replied.

"Has any portion of the Army of Tennessee been assigned to search out General Sherman?"

"I myself am not aware of any such taskings, sir," I answered uneasily. I was painfully cognizant that my "I don't know's" were beginning to sound repetitive.

"I'm sorry I can't be of more help on that, General," I explained. "The fact is, since I've been back here, I've never been present at any of General Bragg's councils. I'm not even invited to staff officers call. Whatever I manage to learn comes to me largely secondhand."

Lee gave me a reassuring smile. "I see, Major. I believe I understand." He was silent for a time then asked seriously. "What I would like to know, Major, is your own assessment of the Army of Tennessee's intelligence gathering. You have had much to compare it with. You were a part of General Jackson's apparatus. You know how we do things in Virginia. How do they obtain sound information here? What kind of reports does General Bragg receive about the enemy forces converging here, and in your mind, what is their accuracy?"

These were crucial questions that the general expected me to answer. I took time before I made my reply. As an engineer I preferred to deal with known facts, incontrovertible evidence gathered from personal survey. But there was no such luxury here. Nor time. My assessment would not be scientific diagnosis, but opinion and nothing more. But it had to be right. This was Robert E. Lee asking.

"General," I began. "I cannot say with certainty what General Bragg and his staff know or do not know about the Yankee forces converging on Chattanooga. I do know what I have observed and heard since my attachment here, and frankly, General, it makes me uneasy. From what I have seen, or in this case, from what I have failed to see, it is my impression that there is no aggressive reconnaissance whatsoever taking place outside of this immediate theater, which means no one is out looking for General Sherman. As for the presence of General Burnside's army in Knoxville, I firmly believe that General Bragg has left entirely with General Longstreet the responsibility for dealing with him."

I took another pause to collect my thoughts, for what I was going to say next was controversial to say the least, and poisonous if I were wrong, although I did not then, or now, ever believe I was.

"But most disquieting, General Lee," I continued, "is the light regard that I note General Bragg and his staff seem to exhibit about the enemy forces gathering here. That and the complacency which has suborned all aggressive mindsets. All talk of an attack on the Army of the Cumberland is long past. Instead the boasting is of how the Yankees will be destroyed when they finally come out to attack the impregnable positions of the Army of Tennessee. 'Another Fredericksburg waiting to happen,' I heard one officer call it. 'Only a matter of time.' But that's not the truth, General Lee. That's not how it is at all. Time is with the Yankees. The fact is they don't have to come out and do anything. A few weeks ago they were eating mules and stray dogs, but not anymore. They've got a supply line better than ours right now. And with all the loud talk of impregnable positions and fatal fields of fire and the like, well, General, all I can say is that's something General Bragg's engineers will have to answer for in blood."

Lee looked at me. "What do you mean by that, Major?"

I had not intended this last to come out so forcefully, but as an engineer myself, what I was referring to was a gross, and to my mind inexcusable, oversight that was frequently allowed to happen by supervisory infantry officers when not properly watched over by someone trained in the science of military fortifications.

"General Lee," I said, "this army that we're going to, this Army of Tennessee, is in one of the most exceptional defensive positions I have ever seen. Better than Mayre's Heights even, sir, and you know I wouldn't say that lightly. Missionary Ridge is a natural wall to keep an enemy bottled up in Chattanooga. And when you're on top of the ridge from any location, there's a great appearance of domination, you look right down on the Yankees and the town. But that's the problem, General; looks count for too much with this army. Way too much, because looking down on the enemy makes this army think they don't have to fortify properly!"

I was warming anew to my topic, and so made a point of lowering my voice. "It's the usual thing that all soldiers do if they're not told otherwise, sir. They fortify where it's easiest to dig instead of in the place that's best for overlapping fire. And I'm beginning to think that a lot of these so-called engineers out here aren't much better than the infantry privates when it comes to having a trained eye. They believe the strongest part of any hill is right at the top, so what they've got along the line of Missionary Ridge are a lot of batteries and rifle pits with blind spots. You'll see for yourself, General, the number of trenches that aren't sited properly. They look formidable enough until you take a close look, then you can see that the enemy would have to be charging right up on the muzzles themselves before they'd be of any use!"

General Lee looked concerned. "Did you speak of this to any of their people?" he asked.

"Yes sir," I replied. "Back when we first got here I pointed out one of the worst-case batteries to one of the staff engineers. Thought I was doing him a favor. He agreed with me then he said, 'Well, Major, if the Yankee infantry gets this far up the Ridge, we've had it anyway.' I saw that battery yesterday, General. Nothing's changed."

General Lee said nothing to this, but I knew he had listened closely. He became absorbed in thought once more, and we rode along in silence. He dropped behind me, and looking back once, I noted how he appeared in the moon glow, a gray man riding along in a pale gray light.

It was very strange to actually have the general here, and once again, most unsettling. By ordering the general to come here in person, the Richmond government was saying unequivocally that this theater was now the most important in the Confederacy. After Gettysburg and Vicksburg, I could somewhat understand this view. Chattanooga was certainly crucial to hold, and the chance to destroy an entire Yankee army should not be permitted to pass. On this Richmond had a point. High-ranking attention was certainly warranted. But did it warrant sending the man himself?

"IT DID," Deslauries broke in. "It was. The president was adamant on that point."

"To be sure," I said in deference to the man who was the chief aide to the former president of the Confederacy.

"Yet," I went on. "It all seemed so misplaced, so very unnatural, to have Robert E. Lee present out in that untamed country, among all those Westerners. It was unsettling to imagine *him* anywhere else but with the Army of Northern Virginia, defending the heart of the Confederacy before Richmond."

I stopped and waited for Deslauries to respond. This was unquestionably my bias, my right to have it and express it rooted in the "center of the universe" vanity of every soldier, which declares that whatever theater his own army serves in is the most critical. And my theater, my army, and my loyalty was, then as now, northern Virginia.

Yet Deslauries said nothing to this, and I resumed my narrative.

WHEN LEE spoke again he asked, "Major, what is your view of this army's offensive capability? Would the officers and men be eager to attack?"

I stopped my horse to let the general come up. "In my view they would not, General," I said. "In my view they are content to sit in their works on the high ground and wait, which is to say hope, for the enemy to attack."

Lee looked at me thoughtfully. "Yet surely this was not always the case," he opined.

I knew what he was referring to. "It was certainly not the case right after Chickamauga, General. But it is now." I answered.

"Very troubling," Lee remarked sagely. "To hear this about the very same army that fought so bravely and gallantly at Perryville and Murfreesboro."

"And Chickamauga," I added. But to myself I thought, *Perhaps it is no longer the same army.* No longer the same set of warriors who fought a larger army to a standstill at Perryville and rocked the Army of the Cumberland back on its startled heels at Murfreesboro, not to mention nearly finishing off this same force at Chickamauga. But something had broken after that battle, something that must have been festering long before then, something that had caused this formerly belligerent, hard-hitting army to atrophy to its present state of sullen inactivity and outright cynicism. They looked and acted like garrison troops now, and they would have to be remade. It was indeed the stark truth that if the present Army of Tennessee was to be remade into anything resembling the cut-and-slash legion it had once been, capable of destroying the Yankee army in Chattanooga, the glowing embers from these past successes would have to be patiently fanned into new flames. In short, it was a job for a real general.

And Lee would see it for himself, I thought. Hopefully see everything, just as he always did, the strengths as well as the weaknesses of what he had to work with, then come up with a plan to win. Classic Lee, the classic engineer officer. As we rode along, Lee fell into a silence so prolonged that I was startled to hear his voice when he asked his next question, an all-important one.

"And what about this General Grant, Major?"

"He's a pretty big name out here, sir," I said. "The Yankees make quite a fuss over him. I suppose some of our people do too. The first thing he did when he got here was to open a supply line at Brown's Ferry, downriver from Chattanooga and out of range of the batteries on Lookout Mountain. He hasn't done much since then except have his army dig a lot of trenches."

"Well," Lee noted, "if all he has done so far is to open up a supply line for his army then properly entrench it, I daresay he is doing quite well. But we will see about this man in the days to come. Perhaps we will find a way to take his true measure." And he added, "before all his help arrives."

The general fell silent once more, and my mind went back to a few days before when I had gotten my own first glimpse of the man Grant. I had been reconnoitering beyond Missionary Ridge, at a small rise in front of Missionary Ridge called Orchard Knob, the Army of Tennessee's forward position, and closest to the main Union line around Chattanooga. A signal sergeant handed me a telescope and invited me to have a look at the conqueror of Vicksburg. I held the device to my eye and there, riding out on the flat plain in front of the Federal lines, I saw a group of mounted men. Clearly they were officers; I could easily make out their wide-brimmed slouch hats and the gold markings on their long coats. They ambled along, talking among themselves, and occasionally scanning Missionary Ridge with their field glasses. In the lead of this group was a small-framed man on a very large

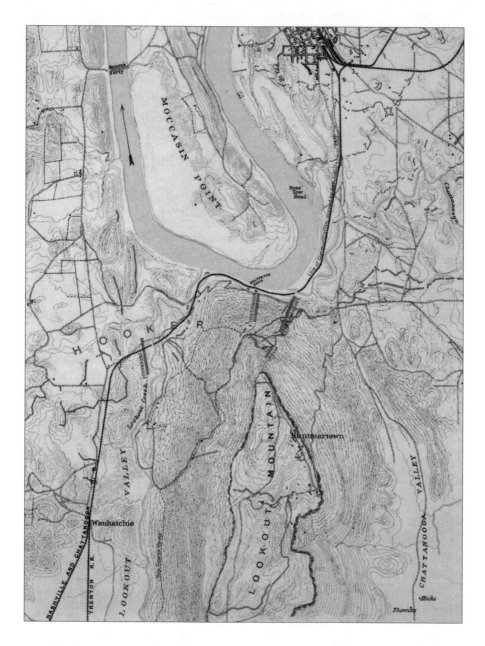

*Lookout Mountain dominates the terrain to the south of Chattanooga.
Brown's Ferry is shown connecting the one side of the river to
the jut of land known as Moccasin Point.*

black horse. He rode along easily, puffs of smoke from a pipe or cigar blowing away from his face. Then he turned and said something to the group, pointing to the very position where I was, and the rest of the officers all raised their glasses and took a long survey. Concluding this, the calm man on the black horse led the group in a slow meander back toward the Union lines.

I handed the glasses back to the signal sergeant and spoke to the lieutenant in command of the two-piece battery posted there.

"A couple of shots from your guns might take some of the complacency out of their manner," I suggested with a smile.

The lieutenant shook his head. "Aw there ain't no cause to start such a fuss, Major. Yanks is spiteful folks. If we opened fire, they'd shell this little camp with every gun they had, hang the waste of ammunition, just to prove what bully boys they was."

Recalling this incident afresh, and with new dissatisfaction, I considered relating it to Lee.

Ahead was a rise in the road, and suddenly forms appeared in the moonlight. It was a picket outpost that I had passed through earlier, but now a spasm of panic went through me. I was not in Tennessee anymore but back in Virginia, in a tangle of wilderness on a wild and lurid night full of death and smoke, seconds before a fatal volley, trying to keep up with a battle-crazed Stonewall Jackson who was galloping toward a group of shadowy figures just such as these.

I whirled my horse squarely in front of a startled General Lee.

"Don't shoot!" I commanded. "We are friends!"

The forms in the road were still, and I cursed to myself, realizing that my violent actions had undoubtedly unnerved them.

"And just what friend goes thar?" a voice from up the road drawled warily.

"Major Jedediah Hotchkiss of Longstreet's corps," I replied. "I passed through here an hour ago."

"That so now," said the voice. "Well maybe y'did, maybe y'dint. Who's that yer with?"

"General Robert E. Lee of the Army of Northern Virginia. En route to see General Bragg."

There was an astonished silence from the darkness ahead, where I could imagine pipes being removed from startled mouths. A long stillness followed then the same voice drawled out, "That so now. Well maybe 'tis, maybe t'aint."

There was a stirring among the moonlit forms, and a disgusted voice bellowed, "By thunder, Posey, you could make Jesus cuss!" Then this voice called down sternly, "Come ahead on and get recognized!"

As we passed wordlessly through the picket post, the soldiers lined the road and stared at General Lee. Then one of them asked me, "This h'yar be the same General Lee what's been lickin' the Yanks over in Virginny?"

"Yes," I answered with a bit of pride.

We rode on, and from behind I heard the same soldier exclaim, "Well, Lord have mercy!"

We passed through the sleeping camp of the Army of Tennessee, arriving at General Bragg's headquarters, which was a small farmhouse. As we came into the yard, I noted the darkened windows and absence of anyone, save for the duty orderly who approached us with a lantern, holding it high and peering intently toward General Lee. Upon my sharp query he informed me that General Bragg had been obliged to turn in early for the night, due to a slight illness. None of the other staff were present either, he went on apologetically, still looking at General Lee, but said that accommodations had been prepared for the general, which he would lead us to.

Alarmed and angered, I was unable to do anything about either. Here was another typical Army of Tennessee reception given to the foremost general of the Confederacy: no one around, headquarters lights out, the commanding general in bed, and one gawky orderly to lead the way to heaven knew what kind of quarters for Robert E. Lee. For the second time that night I tasted deep bile.

The orderly led us off through the camp, about a quarter of a mile, to a wind-sheltered hollow where a large tent was pitched and two soldiers tended to a bonfire in front. Upon quick inspection of the tent and its furnishing, I was relieved to find it suitable, at least to my expectations of what General Lee would need for his comfort. Happily Lee agreed. After turning down an offer of food from the orderly, he announced his wish to retire for the night.

He had said little since our arrival on Missionary Ridge, and he had expressed no displeasure upon hearing that General Bragg was unavailable to see him that evening. It occurred to me that the old Virginian might actually have been glad to do nothing but retire after his long and arduous trip without the need to engage in any further protocol. I hoped so, at any rate, for just then my sense of helplessness and incapacity to get anything done through the Army of Tennessee chain of command was weighing upon me heavily.

I took my gear and saddle and made a bed for myself near Lee's tent. It was cold, just like every night had been since I arrived in Tennessee, and I still hadn't gotten used to it. Flare-ups of hot anger over the day's debacles kept me somewhat warm as I settled down to sleep.

Finally, I tried to let it all go and get some rest. He's here now, I thought, and whatever was supposed to come of it would begin with tomorrow's dawn.

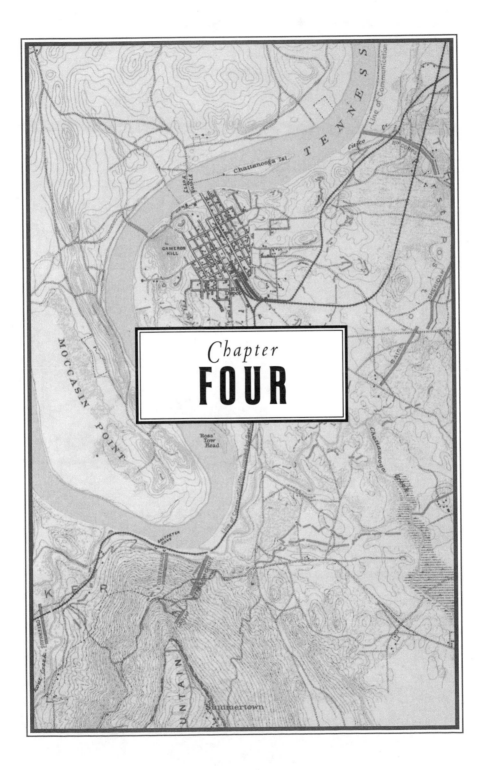

Chapter
FOUR

*A*WAKENING AT DAYBREAK I went to the general's tent and found him up and dressed. He greeted me genially, and in response to my question told me that he had slept well. Looking at him, I wasn't so sure. Prior to his arrival the night before, I had not seen General Lee for months. Viewing him now in the daylight, I tried to recall if his hair and face had always been so white.

An orderly had been assigned from General Bragg's headquarters to cook his breakfast, and as he did so, General Lee and I stood outside the tent. The general surveyed the encampment keenly and was himself being looked over as well. Soldiers passing nearby pointed and stared; the news of his arrival had obviously spread quickly through the regimental camps. An officer, the chief of staff, approached from the direction of General Bragg's headquarters. He was a stern-visaged, nervous colonel whom I thoroughly detested.

Stopping in front of General Lee he saluted and in a formal tone conveyed the respects of General Bragg, welcoming Lee to the Army of Tennessee. After Lee's equally formal thanks, the colonel went on to say that General Bragg was very much looking forward to meeting the general later that morning.

In other words, "Not now," I thought.

Lee replied that he would be pleased to meet General Bragg whenever it was convenient. The colonel nodded stiffly and was about to depart when Lee said casually that while waiting for his visit with Bragg, he was most anxious to take a ride along Missionary Ridge and to have a look at the enemy positions. If there were no objections, Lee continued placidly, he and his aide, Major Hotchkiss, would start right away.

Obviously taken aback by Lee's request, the colonel stammered that he could think of no objections, which I knew was not the same as outright permission. For my part I enjoyed his discomfiture. Having been around General Bragg's staff, I knew the kind of things that made them fret, and I was totally unsympathetic. In the many disagreeable associations I had had with them, I had come to notice that they almost constantly wore the same expressions on their faces, which was that of having been taken aback or discomfited by something.

So it was with the colonel right now. General Lee's request had been unexpected, which meant he would now be risking the ire of the moody, unpredictable Bragg with the news that Lee was riding about Bragg's army on his own.

Frowning, the colonel took his leave of General Lee and started quickly back for headquarters. Immediately I followed after him. When we were a sufficient distance from Lee's tent, I called out to him. He turned to confront me with a glare.

Taking care to keep a cordial tone in my voice, I voiced to him my distress over the matter of the missing cavalry escort of the night before. The colonel regarded me coldly.

"I gave the necessary orders, Major, and in a timely fashion. If there is any blame, it must rest with the obviously unreliable elements of our cavalry. Do you have any other business with me, sir?"

I had none. Abruptly he was off again without a word. I watched him go, biting my lip.

Back at Lee's tent the general was waiting for me, ready to get started. The orderlies brought up the horses, and we started off at a leisurely pace along the ridge. Soldiers and officers alike stared out from their campfires.

"Hey, Major," a man called out. "That be Robert E. Lee?"

I nodded.

"Well, I'll be!" the man exclaimed. "Hey Gen'ral, are you takin' over from General Bragg?"

Continuing in my role as spokesman, I said, "Not at all. General Bragg commands this army."

"Well, dog it all, Major," the soldier shouted. "Come back when you have some good news."

This brought laughter all around.

At another spot a soldier called out that he and his friends had heard that Lee and Bragg were going to switch armies, Lee taking the one in Tennessee and Bragg going back to Virginia. Was it true? he wanted to know.

"Absolutely not," I answered.

"Well I reckon that's a good thing then," said the soldier. "If Bragg went to Virginia, he'd give the Yankees Richmond in a week!"

I suppressed a smile and we rode on. Lee remained oblivious and unperturbed by this irreverent Western raillery.

"How well do the men eat out here, Major?"

"Poorly, sir."

"Because of the enemy?"

"No sir. The supply system falls very short of the mark up here. Practically nonexistent actually. Everybody scrounges."

Lee fell silent again.

I was taking him to a site on the ridge that afforded one of the better views of besieged Chattanooga and the winding Tennessee River. Reaching the spot, we dismounted, and I led the general to the top of a parapet from which could be seen nearly the whole slope of Missionary Ridge as well as the flat, scrubbily wooded ground out to the furthest Rebel position, the knoll known as Orchard Knob. Beyond was the treeless, open plain in front of Chattanooga.

"Rather a magnificent country, Major," Lee commented quietly.

"It is indeed, General."

Lee looked out over the landscape intently. He had brought binoculars, and as he scanned I filled him in on the details of the terrain and the visible dispositions of both Union and Confederate armies.

The Army of the Cumberland, occupying the town of Chattanooga, was held in place and besieged by way of a north-to-south crescent of dominant high ground east of the town,

held in strength by the Rebels. The strongest part of this fortified crescent, and its vital center, was Missionary Ridge. The
northernmost tip of the Confederate arc touched the river north
of Chattanooga. The bottom of the arc was solidly fixed south of
the town by the steep, rugged slopes of Lookout Mountain.

The Federal lines were a much smaller arc surrounding the
town itself. Yet with the time they had been given, their works had
become quite formidable, with two strong earthen forts anchoring each extremity. North of Chattanooga, the Union left, a series
of redoubts had been expertly laid out for enfilade fire and close-
in defense, and the Yankees had named the works Fort Grose.
South of Chattanooga, on the extreme Union right, was another
defensive construction called Fort Negley. This fort was by far the
more formidable of the two, laid out every bit as skillfully as its
counterpart but with more redoubts covering greater space. From
the elevation of Missionary Ridge, it resembled a five-pointed star.

"If there's anything the Yankees know how to do well it's
build defensive works," I remarked with acerbity as I saw the
general studying both forts.

He smiled. "Yes, Major. They have undeniably made good
use of their time."

He pointed to the long pontoon bridge that connected
Chattanooga to the other side of the river and upon which now
was visible a steady movement of wagons.

"So the Army of the Cumberland is being supplied now?"

"Yes sir," I answered. "Ever since Grant arrived."

"And Brown's Ferry is the spot?"

"Yes sir," I said.

"Yes," he said thoughtfully. Then pointing toward Lookout Mountain he said, "I have been told that the best vantage
point for this whole theater is up there."

"That's right, General. I can take you there anytime you
like."

"Good," said Lee. "Today if there's time. If not, tomorrow
first thing."

He gazed out over the landscape. He was thinking, and as I watched him, it seemed to me that he was also troubled. At one point he waved his arm to the far side of the Tennessee River, far beyond Chattanooga. "And somewhere out there is General Sherman, I understand."

"That's right, General."

"Not counting his force, I've been told that there are upwards of forty thousand of the enemy in and around Chattanooga now, including General Hooker's reinforcements from the Army of the Potomac."

"Yes sir, I'd guess that's correct," I answered.

Lee looked at me keenly. "Has this been confirmed by General Bragg's people?"

"I'm afraid I don't know that, sir."

"What is the strength at Brown's Ferry?"

"I'm aware that some part of Hooker's Easterners are there, General. The rest are encamped at the base of Lookout Mountain on the valley side."

This was no answer at all. Lee gave me a questioning glance. "In what strength, Major? A regiment? A brigade perhaps?"

"I'm sorry, General, but I don't know the answer to that."

Just like last night, I was beginning to squirm under this specific line of questioning. But it was also my belief that nobody on Bragg's staff could have answered General Lee's questions either. Information about the enemy that the general was seeking was the stuff of cavalry, probing and identifying numbers and units. Yet ever since Forrest had stormed out of Bragg's tent several weeks back, there had been very little cavalry to speak of, which was bad for Bragg's army. Reflecting on the circumstances that had brought on this bad state of affairs, it seemed to me that the Army of Tennessee was not so much a single Confederate force as it was a conglomerate of feudal, warring chieftains.

Lee appeared to be reading my thoughts. "It's all right, Major. I recall what you told me last night about Bragg and his cavalry commander.

"Yes sir, General Forrest."

"I have heard much of this gallant officer, Forrest. Are you well acquainted with him?"

"No sir. Since I arrived here with Longstreet's corps, back in September, I've only seen him twice, and that was at a distance."

Lee nodded, then said, "Major, when we get back, there are two things I would like you to do. First is to telegraph General Longstreet that I have arrived here in Tennessee and that I desire to meet with him as soon as possible. This would mean that he must necessarily come here, causing him to leave his army. But if General Burnside is quiescent on his front right now, I do very much desire it. And I would like him to get my request as soon as possible."

"Yes sir," I said. "I'll see that it goes out from Chickamauga Station right away."

Lee continued. "The other thing I wish, Major, is a meeting with General Forrest. I would like you to communicate to this officer my respects and that I would be deeply honored to receive a call from him at the soonest opportunity."

Lee saw the troubled look on my face. "What is it, Major?"

"General, that might not be so easy to arrange," I said. "It is my understanding that Forrest's feud with General Bragg was a particularly rancorous one. Forrest stated unequivocally that he would no longer take orders from the man, and that he even now considers his cavalry severed from this army and refuses to even come within its camp."

Lee gave a soft smile. "Almost like the quarrel between Jackson and Hill back in Virginia, eh, Major?"

"Much worse I think, General."

"Well, send a message to General Forrest regardless, Major Hotchkiss. Perhaps he will speak to me."

We were walking back to the horses, and I said, "General Lee, I wonder if I might ask you a question?"

"Certainly, Major."

"Sir, what exactly were you sent here to do?"

Lee looked at me. "Why naturally to offer my assistance to General Bragg in bringing this matter to a satisfactory conclusion."

"And how long will you stay, General?"

Lee looked amused. "Meaning perhaps how long will the rest of you be staying?"

I smiled self-consciously at Lee's perception.

"You do not think we can be of service here, Major?" Lee asked in a jesting tone.

"It's not a matter of that, General," I answered. "We've already been of excellent service here. But now it's whether or not we're wanted."

Lee appeared to reflect on this. "We must all serve where we are needed, sir," he said, adding soberly, "or where we are ordered. At any rate, Major, we must stay here until this matter is settled. One way or the other. To the good of the cause above all else."

BRAGG'S STAFF was waiting outside the house as we rode up. After we had dismounted, the chief of staff came forward and introduced General Lee to the other officers. All of them scrutinized the Virginian closely. I had always found them to be a twitchy, unpleasant lot, just like their colonel and just like their commanding general. As the round of introductions was made, I noticed an uneasy protocol that I had never seen with this group. Some of the officers saluted, heels tightly together. Others bowed.

General Longstreet should see this, I thought.

When this was completed, the chief of staff briefed Lee on the administrative arrangements being made for his convenience. Orderlies would be assigned full time to see to his comfort and billeting needs. Couriers would be made available to him upon request at any time. At this time Lee interrupted, graciously thanking the colonel and adding that he could make use of one courier immediately, to deliver a letter that he had written to General Forrest.

As had happened earlier that morning, the colonel was totally ambushed by Lee's request, giving the general a rattled look even while acquiescing to it. The invoked name of Nathan Bedford Forrest had done it. Behind the colonel, his staff exchanged apprehensive glances.

The administrative details concluded, the colonel led General Lee inside the house, the rest of us following.

In the main room General Bragg was waiting, splendidly uniformed. He arose busily from his desk as we entered, my cynical interpretation being that this was to suggest that he was hard at work on other absorbing matters. Now he came around the desk to greet the Virginian. "General Lee, welcome to the Army of Tennessee. We are honored to have you."

General Bragg did not smile but said this somewhat severely, shaking Lee's hand in rigid formality, complete with a stiff bow. While far from being a warm greeting, it was not a hostile one either. It was just Braxton Bragg being himself, as anyone who had even had the slightest contact with the man would have expected.

"I myself am delighted to see you, General Bragg, and to be with this splendid army that has done so much," Lee said warmly. "And now that I am here, please allow me to express, first and foremost, my personal congratulations to you on your inspiring victory at Chickamauga."

And thanks to an entire corps from the Army of Northern Virginia, I could not help thinking unkindly.

Bragg thanked Lee for the compliment then returned to the other side of his desk, motioning Lee to a chair. When they were both seated, he boomed out suddenly, "So General Lee, has President Davis sent you to take command here?"

If Bragg had intended the question as a jest, it was without mirth. Whatever the intent, the bluntness and unsuitability of the comment was in appalling bad taste. Characteristically, Lee appeared to take no notice.

"I am under no such orders, General, as I hope you are aware," Lee smiled. "Quite the contrary, as a matter of fact, for your great victory at Chickamauga gives sufficient cause to argue that this army has done quite well with its present commanding general."

Probably against his own wishes, Bragg could not help looking pleased by this deft compliment. Straightaway, he then asked Lee if he had seen the Federal positions around Chattanooga. Lee replied that he had and followed up by saying he was anxious to hear General Bragg's appraisal of the military situation. Bragg's response was immediate.

"They must abandon Chattanooga soon or starve," he declared. "Right now they are clinging to their trenches in the hope of luring us to a destructive attack. It is their only expectation of success. But very soon, necessity will overtake them and they will have to pull out. Once they are out of their defensive works and back across the Tennessee, I intend to pursue and defeat them in large segments."

Hearing this, I was dumbfounded and incredulous that I had heard the commanding general of the Army of Tennessee say such a thing out loud. I looked at him and thought that the man was out of his mind. *The Yankees must leave or starve?* It was General Bragg's own army that was in danger of starvation as winter approached. *Defeat the enemy in large segments after they had recrossed the Tennessee?* How? Where? What on earth was he talking about? I looked at his staff for similar reactions and saw only blank expressions. *A council of fools,* I thought, and looked at Lee.

Lee had listened courteously to Bragg's summation. He nodded and for several seconds appeared to be mulling over what he had been told. But when he spoke again it was to change the subject completely.

"And what do you know of General Sherman's whereabouts, General?"

At this question Bragg blinked. I had seen him do it before. Nobody could blink like Bragg. His deep dark eyes, set under thick eyebrows and never once lit by a gleam of humor that I had ever seen or could even imagine, gave his visage a look of constant severity. He blinked again at Lee's question, and his face became, once more for his staff to emulate, a living model of a man taken aback.

At last Bragg gave his answer. "General Sherman is coming east from Memphis," he said. "The roads are bad and he is proceeding slowly." This was old news that everyone already knew. *Quit stalling, General Bragg,* I growled to myself. Bragg continued, "I expect his army to swing well north of Chattanooga, then east, in order to reach his true objective, which is Knoxville and the reinforcement of General Burnside."

Once again, I could scarcely believe my ears. Sherman heading for Knoxville? Avoiding Chattanooga and his friend Grant? It was preposterous. *Ask him how he knows that, General Lee,* I fumed. *Ask the fool if he knows where General Sherman is right now.*

Lee of course did neither. Motioning me over to the table, he had me spread out a large map of southern Tennessee that he had brought from Richmond.

"This map of your theater has many points of interest to me that I am most eager to inquire about, with your forbearance, General Bragg," Lee said. "But by your leave, I think now would be a fortuitous time to relay to you intelligence made available to me in Richmond with which you might not be acquainted. Intelligence particularly related to General Sherman's objective. I would set these forth to you if we might be left in privacy right now."

Bragg and his staff looked warily at one another. Then upon his hesitant nod, everyone began leaving the room. I was the last one out, and as I looked over my shoulder, I saw General Lee standing over the map. Still seated, Bragg was looking up at Lee and blinking.

THE CONFERENCE was a long one. Gradually Bragg's officers drifted away. Well over an hour had passed before the door to the house opened and Lee came out by himself. He was not inclined to talk, and during the short ride back to his tent he said nothing. I had no way of knowing what kind of absurdity Bragg might have dished out to the general in private, or what kind of lame excuses he might have made to explain away the ever-worsening military situation of his army. To me it was a frightening possibility that Braxton Bragg believed his own nonsense. Be this as it may, as I looked at the pensive General Lee just then, I felt certain that he had taken his own proper sounding of Braxton Bragg.

He knows the situation now, I thought, *and it can't make him feel too good. This is not Virginia, Marse Robert, bless your heart, this is Tennessee. Ulysses S. Grant himself is down there, working himself up for a fight. General Sherman's on his way to help. And up here is Braxton Bragg.*

Once more I was struck at how much General Lee had aged. Not in the face, which was still handsome and finely sculpted, and certainly not in the eyes, where alert intelligence lived and fire still burned, but again in his peculiar whiteness of hair, skin, and pallor. And in his stride too, which was shorter. But that had come about after Gettysburg.

Back then I was no different from anyone else in the Army of Northern Virginia, from the highest-educated officer down to the lowliest private. We all revered the man. And not just as the unquestioned supreme soldier of both the North and the South, but as a cherished uncle—lofty, dignified, and distant, to be feared as well as loved, and never understood by any of us not of his generation. Where he led we would follow, and ultimately we would win, even when things looked darkest. It was every bit the way we felt back in those years. Our optimism was like the optimism of children, to be sure, and looking back on that beginning of the end, it was hopelessly naive. But whatever else might be said of it, it made us cheerful in the dreary times and kept us strong when there was hardly anything to eat. And, I thought, if this Western army of Bragg's, this Army of Tennessee, got to know General Lee even a part of the way we know him, they too would be regenerated. It could not help but be so. And just then, riding back to Lee's tent, despite the fact that Lee was obviously troubled over what he had seen and heard thus far on Missionary Ridge, I began to believe again.

BACK AT his tent, General Lee informed me, "Major, we will go to Lookout Mountain first thing tomorrow morning. I am quite keen to see the view from up there."

"There's plenty of time to go today, if you like, sir," I told him.

He shook his head. "I have been informed that this afternoon I should expect calls from some of this army's commanders, whom I am anxious to meet. In the meantime, Major, I think I will rest a bit."

"As you wish, General," I said. "I'll see to it that you're not disturbed until your visitors arrive."

The general went into his tent, closing the flap after him. I sat down by the fire, had a smoke, and wrote a long letter to Sara, my wife. My fireside was quiet, and I ended up dozing off. I had no idea how long I slept, but when I awoke I saw that the flap of the general's tent was open.

I wandered over and peered inside, where I saw General Lee sitting at a camp table and studying the map that he had tried to review with General Bragg.

"How are you doing, General?" I inquired. "May I get you anything, sir?"

He glanced up. "No, Major. I need nothing at present, thank you," he replied and went back to his map.

A short time later two senior officers rode up and dismounted. The general's first visitors were the two corps commanders of the Army of Tennessee, one a professional politician, the other a professional soldier.

John Breckinridge was a former vice president of the United States and, just prior to the war, the Southern Democrats' nominee for president. William J. Hardee was a former West Point commandant and the author of the U.S. Army's official textbook on close-order infantry drill, a junior officers bible used as much by both sides during the war as it was before. They made a balanced contrast. Handsome and genial, General Breckinridge appeared boyish and ruddy with his large, flaring brigand's moustache. Handsome as well as stern visaged, Hardee was several years older and bore himself like the consummate lifelong army officer he was. While my attachment to the Army of Tennessee had not brought me in close proximity to either officer, they had always received me cordially when the occasion presented itself.

I saluted then announced their presence to General Lee, who came out personally to escort them into his tent. Their visit lasted an hour. The two Western generals bore grave looks when they first shook hands with Lee. I had the sense that they had braced themselves in expectation of some message from Richmond that the general might pass on to them, and the message could be either good or bad: "You're to be commended . . . ," "You're to be censored . . . ," "You're being promoted . . . ," "You're being relieved . . ." But by the time they left all that had changed. Both men were in high spirits. General Lee walked them to their horses, reminiscing with General Hardee about their time during the war in Mexico.

THAT WAS the way he had, I asserted proudly to Deslauries. "Such was the infectious spirit of General Lee. He was never reluctant to use the tools at hand and never lacking in the skill to improve them."

"President Davis considered both Hardee and Breckinridge to be able officers and quite up to their duties as corps commanders," Deslauries observed. "As he saw during his visit to this army, unfortunately, they were not beyond that."

He was referring to Davis's visit to Chattanooga and his stormy meeting with General Bragg's rebellious commanders, when for a time he was searching for an officer to replace Bragg as head of the army.

"Of course, General Breckinridge was never really under consideration," the former presidential secretary added casually, sipping his bourbon. "He was clearly too fledgling, too new to his then-present level of command. 'A novitiate,' Mr. Davis called him, 'to the precious art, attainable by only the highest tier of commanders, to seek and bring about the destruction of an entire enemy army.' That left only Hardee as the logical choice, and of course Hardee wanted nothing to do with the job."

I gave a start. "Hardee?" I asked. This was the first I had heard that the president had even considered that general to replace Bragg, let alone actually asked him to do so.

Deslauries gave me a sober, inquisitive look. "You did not consider General Hardee an excellent officer?" he asked.

"I did indeed consider him so," I replied. "Just not so . . . excellent as a candidate for commander in chief of such a large and important army." I added, "It seemed to me that General Hardee had certain . . . shortcomings, discernible to the attentive observer, that would obviously preclude him from being considered for such a high responsibility."

"'Obviously'?" Deslauries repeated my word. "Such as?"

"Still too much the commandant of cadets," was my immediate rejoinder.

That observation seemed to sit well with my companion, and he added, "The president was surprised when General Hardee turned him down. He quite expected a career soldier such as the man was to step forward at once. Although . . ." Here Deslauries resorted to disingenuous tact, "He later expressed admiration of the general's humility and his wisdom in knowing his own limitations as a commander." He added archly, "And by that, allowing Mr. Davis to know them also.

"All this is not to say that the president was not pleased overall by the caliber of the leading officers in the Army of Tennessee," Deslauries continued, as though compelled to make the argument. "He was. Generals Breckinridge and Hardee had his utmost confidence in their assigned roles. And he was quite enamored of the talent of that army's divisional commanders as well. One in particular he considered as one of the best in the Confederate service. He later called this man another Stonewall Jackson waiting to bloom."

"That would be Cleburne," I volunteered flatly.

"Yes," confirmed the presidential secretary. "I was given to understand that General Lee was quite taken when he discovered him."

"It's true," I noted. "He was the key officer upon whom General Lee decided to base his offensive plan against the Yankees in Chattanooga. General Cleburne's initial success was to be crucial to everything else. That he pulled it off as expected did not surprise anyone who knew him. Furthermore, I am convinced that General Lee had decided on General Cleburne's key role quite early, probably only a few minutes after they met.

"As for comparing him to General Jackson," I added, "I would say that he had already bloomed by the time General Lee came to Chattanooga. I worked under General Jackson in the Valley and knew him well. But I also became quite close to General Cleburne. I used to joke with him, telling him I was wracking my brains trying to figure out how we might steal him from the western theater and get him over with the Army of Northern Virginia. Actually, I don't suppose it was all that much of a joke. General Jackson was brilliant and fiercely aggressive, but very rigid. Everything had to be done according to his way, and he did not like any of his officers knowing more than he did about anything. General Cleburne was never like that; he lived in a wider world. He had served in the British army before emigrating here from Ireland, and that was demonstrated in the way his men were trained. He was every bit the soldier General Jackson was but not the least bit provincial."

And I continued my story.

THROUGHOUT THE rest of that afternoon General Lee was called upon by various divisional and brigade commanders. Cleburne was the last to arrive. He rode into the campsite alone and waved a cheery greeting to me after he dismounted.

"Well, Jed, it looks as though your commanding general has arrived."

"He has indeed, sir. He's looking forward to meeting you."

"Almost didn't believe it when I heard that General Lee was here in person. But now there's hope, I daresay. I also hope you put in a good word for me."

"Why, naturally, I didn't think that necessary given your wide notoriety," I quipped.

The Irishman laughed. "Haven't been seeing much of you around division these past days. I'll be looking forward to a game of chess next time you drop by for supper." He nodded toward the general's tent. "This is a real honor. You know how you feel when you finally meet someone you've read so much about? All my boys are glad he's come, although none of us ever would have figured him leaving Virginia to come here, what with the Army of the Potomac on the loose."

"Oh, they're not really on the loose," I said disparagingly. "They won't come out of hibernation until next spring."

I announced Cleburne's arrival to the general then straightaway mounted up to undertake an errand of my own. As per the general's orders, immediately after touring Missionary Ridge that morning, I had ridden to Chickamauga Station and submitted General Lee's summons to General Longstreet on the telegraph. Following up on this now, I returned to the telegraph office and was pleased to learn that an acknowledgment had been received from General Longstreet outside of Knoxville.

Upon my return to Missionary Ridge, I was surprised to see General Cleburne's horse still tethered near General Lee's tent. Obviously Lee was finding much to discuss with the young general. Much more time passed before General Cleburne finally emerged from the tent. He walked toward his horse slowly, his face frowning in thought, yet he gave me a friendly smile when I joined him.

"Everything all right, General?" I asked.

"Oh yes," he replied. Then he added, nodding back in the direction of General Lee's tent, "That's quite a man in there, Jed. Classic Caesar type, I think. Knows just what he's playing at and cool as a Natchez gambler. With a general like that I can see how you boys in the East managed to win so often against long odds. You're lucky to have him. Now I guess we are too."

On the particulars of what General Lee had said to him General Cleburne was not forthcoming to me. When he reached his horse he gave me a pat on the shoulder. "Drop by soon, Major. And if you bring some of your excellent Virginia tobacco, I might be induced to parole a quantity of bourbon as fair exchange."

"Consider it an agreement," I laughed. "I'll see you soon."

With a jaunty wave of his hand, General Cleburne rode off. Going back to General Lee's tent I found him once more poring over a map.

I told him of General Longstreet's acknowledgment, which pleased him. Then he said. "I've just had a very interesting meeting with General Cleburne, Major. Pray tell, what is your impression of the man?"

"He's the absolute best they've got," I answered without hesitation.

Lee nodded. "Yes. He is certainly one of the most intelligent division commanders I have ever met. I have been asking him questions, laying out certain scenarios. He seems to be quite a forward-thinking officer. One not daunted by risks as long as they are calculated ones."

"That sounds like General Cleburne," I said.

"He was not born in this country I understand?"

"No sir. He emigrated here from Ireland and was practicing law in Helena, Arkansas, when the war broke out. He's had a military background, though, with service in the British army."

"He is well regarded by the other generals of this army I think?" Lee queried.

"Absolutely sir," I assured him. "I've been told that General Bragg has more than once spoken highly of him. In this army, that's something."

"That is good, then," Lee said musingly. "That is very good." He looked at his map for a moment then said, "Tomorrow morning, Major, first thing, I would like for you to take me up Lookout Mountain."

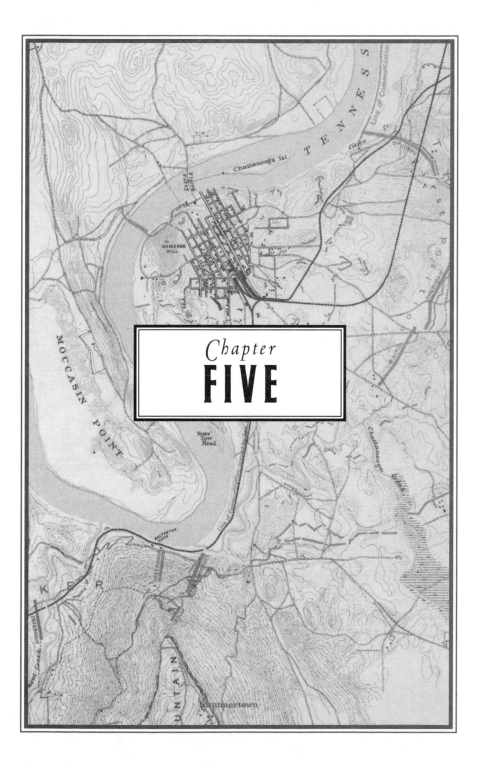

Chapter
FIVE

Right after breakfast we left camp for the summit of Lookout Mountain. We wound our way upward on the wide trail, but the last part of the road was steep and rutted. I navigated my horse carefully while at the same time casting anxious glances over my shoulder at the general. He was coming on slowly, head down, and it was difficult to tell whether he was watching the road or lost in thought. Anxiety stoked my imagination to morbid extremes, and I reflected fearfully on a tragic circumstance of fate that would result in a lost war and a lost cause should a pony make a misstep on an obscure Tennessee mountain road and throw an elderly rider onto hard stones.

I reached the crest of the rise and was greatly relieved when General Lee was up beside me.

Upon the general's request, our first inspection was of the lone battery that General Bragg had placed here. Four guns were situated atop a cliff that commanded a spectacular view of Chattanooga and Missionary Ridge beyond. As we approached this artillery camp through a grove of trees, I became aware of strange goings on. I had visited this site several times before, and now the sentry, who I recognized and who I knew recognized me, upon seeing that I was being followed by another officer, turned and hurried off for the camp. Puzzled by this action, I rode on and saw several soldiers ducking quickly into their shelters while others wandered in a deliberate fashion in the opposite direction from our approach, trying to affect an air of nonchalance but failing miserably. The captain in charge of the four-gun battery, an Alabamian, came forward nervously. His greeting was to me, but his eyes were riveted on the general, who was just coming out of the woods beyond the camp.

"Howdy, Jedediah. Nice to see you again," he said in a casual tone, but like his men he was a bad actor. Then, his eyes still on the approaching general, he snapped at the sentry standing nearby, "Why, that ain't General Bragg!"

The general came up beside me, and I said, "General Lee, may I present to you Captain Garrity, the battery commander."

At the mention of the general's name the captain's jaw dropped open. Rumor being capricious, as always, it was obvious that the news of the general's arrival, which had spread rapidly among the camps of Missionary Ridge, had not reached this altitude.

"Good morning, Captain," Lee said, but for a moment the captain continued only to gape. In a moment, he saluted and shot a savage look at the still-nonplused sentry as he motioned him forward to hold the horses.

"I believe I would like to take stock of your view from up here, sir," Lee said when we dismounted. He walked toward the precipice, and I held back the captain who made a move to walk beside him.

"He'll want to have a look on his own," I whispered to him. "He'll call if he wants you."

Aided by field glasses, Lee began a close scrutiny of the Federal works around Chattanooga. As he did so, I noticed the gunners emerging from their shelters to gawk while others drifted back from the edge of the camp.

"What on earth is going in?" I asked the captain, who had not taken his eyes off Lee. "What's everyone so skittish about? They look like a bunch of frightened squirrels."

"They thought it was General Bragg," the captain said absently, then he exclaimed, "Lawdy, Jedediah, is that old man General Lee himself? What on earth is he doing out here? To relieve General Bragg?"

I told him about Lee's arrival then went on to pursue my own point. "Why would General Bragg's coming up here get everyone so upset?" I asked.

"Word is that General Bragg ain't too happy with the work we've been doin' up here," the captain said. "He thinks we got a lot of extra people could be put to better use down on Missionary Ridge. As you might imagine, nobody up here wants to get pegged to go down there. These are right hospitable surroundings compared to what's below. Plus we run our own show up here, and the boys have gotten used to not being crowded." He added tersely, "And it ain't like General Bragg gave us the right tools to do the job, is it? I mean if he wants us to shoot at Yankee wagon trains all the way across the river, maybe we ought to have the proper guns to do a proper job, I mean these ain't 32-pounders, are they, so what's he expect?"

At this point Lee beckoned and we went forward, the captain nervously.

The general waved his arm along the sweeping view of Chattanooga and the myriad of tent cities in and around its confines. On the plain beyond the town, dark masses of infantry could be seen exercising at drill, the sunlight catching the accumulated bayonets.

"And what have we here, Captain?" he asked.

"Well, General," the artillerist answered, "that there's the Yankee Army of the Cumberland, all bottled up in Chattanooga."

"And what have you observed this army doing since you've been up here?"

The captain nodded at the distant formations. "Just a whole lot of that, General, and not much else."

"Do they ever sortie beyond their own works?"

"Oh, my goodness, no sir!" exclaimed the Alabamian. "Why them Yanks ain't stupid."

Lee gave him an inquisitive look. "What do you mean by that, Captain?"

The man took off his hat and pointed to Missionary Ridge. "Why that's just what our boys there are waitin' on, General. And hopin' for. A chance to pull off a massacre."

"Massacre," Lee repeated.

"Yes sir," the captain asserted. "Whenever they decide to go against Missionary Ridge, that's what'll happen." And he added brightly, "Just like your own boys pulled off last year at Fredericksburg."

Lee nodded. "Thank you, Captain. Let us all hope for such an opportunity." He turned to me. "This will do for here, I think, Major. Let us continue on, if you please."

We traveled along on level ground for about half a mile, sometimes hemmed in by trees, other times out in the open with more of the grand spectacle before us. Our goal was the unsurpassed vantage point on the western side of Lookout Mountain, which commanded a sensational view to the north and west. We dismounted in a grove of trees, and I led the way forward onto a large slab of rock and the breathtaking panorama.

To the north was the winding, bending Tennessee River, across which rose the wooded slopes of what was known locally as Moccasin Point, an area held within a loop of the river so as to resemble a giant moccasin. Stretching away to the west was the wide expanse of Lookout Valley, which ran along a north-south line for many miles, parallel to the spine of Lookout Mountain. To the west, far beyond, were the foothills of the Great Mountains.

"The locals call this Sunset Rock, General," I said. "For obvious reasons."

"Quite grand," Lee said, taking in the view. "Really quite grand." Then he added, "Up until now I would have ventured to say that perhaps the most magnificent vista in all the states might have been from the mountain peaks in Maryland. But this certainly rivals that."

"Not the same kind of country, though, General," I said.

"No," he agreed. "It is not the same. This is wild and unkempt in a way that the other is not, but there is a natural beauty to it nonetheless."

It was a cool, clear sunny day, and the view was unlimited. From this elevated point the encampments of Hooker's division from the Army of the Potomac, camped along the western base of Lookout Mountain, could be seen in detail. Halfway up the peninsula of Moccasin Point, across the river on its western side, columns of smoke rose above the trees.

Lee pointed to the smoke and observed, "I assume that is Brown's Ferry."

"Yes sir," I replied.

"And the smoke is from their supply transports."

"Yes sir."

He swung his glasses to the west and scanned the clear expanse of Lookout Valley. His surveillance was meticulous, and for a long time neither of us spoke.

"So it was by way of this valley that our old adversary, General Hooker, arrived on the scene," Lee said at last.

"That's right, sir," I replied and described to Lee the attempt Longstreet had made to intercept them in a wild night battle nearly a month ago, a Wagnerian scene, with the wind blowing and bonfires blazing on the heights of this very mountain, with Longstreet thundering about, and signal torches going up and down the slopes of the mountain as he tried in vain to drive the bluecoats back.

"More men might have made the issue certain," Lee remarked sagely.

I said nothing. Longstreet had expressed the same view to Bragg after the fight. This was another of Bragg's great follies and the final straw between the two generals. Now, this Federal force to whom the valley had not been denied was camped comfortably astride it, protecting Brown's Ferry and the supply-laden transports.

Lee scanned the Union camp. Just like their counterparts in the Army of the Cumberland were doing in Chattanooga, dark masses of infantry could be seen drilling and countermarching, bayonets glinting, serene in their position, heedless and apparently fearless of who or what might be watching from the heights of Lookout Mountain.

"Five thousand was the number I was given in Richmond as to the size of General Hooker's division," Lee commented, glasses still to his eyes. "That's probably correct. Not much more than that anyway."

I said nothing. I was very much savoring the irony of the moment. Down below was the very same Yankee general and undoubtedly some of the very same regiments that had been soundly whipped by Lee and Jackson at Chancellorsville, nearly six months before. What would they think if they knew that the same general who had broken them in a panic then was looking down upon them now?

Suddenly Lee turned to me. "You have an alert, logical mind, Major. What do you think General Grant is doing?"

"Waiting for General Sherman, sir."

"Yes. I believe that as well. And all the while he is inactive, his army is being resupplied. While our own Army of Tennessee—," he gestured in the direction of Missionary Ridge, "—which also chooses to be inactive, is not."

I could see Lee was vexed, and I knew the cause. It was the view that had done it, an unobscured display that told only the truth. From here the untroubled, unworried Union forces could be seen in their untroubled, unharassed camps. And steamboats unloaded supplies in perfect serenity at an unthreatened landing to be taken at will across an unthreatened pontoon bridge into a town and to an army that was supposed to be besieged. It was a scene to boil the blood of any good Confederate soldier, I thought, and Bragg and his gaggle of staff should come up here every day and get a good dose of outrage.

The general's glasses were trained on the Union camp once more. He studied the vista for a long time then swung his binoculars in a slow arc northward, up Lookout Valley, until he came to the smoke-smudged region that marked Brown's Ferry. Again his glasses lingered, and I noticed his mouth drawn tight, an unmistakable sign of anger, and marveled at his concentration. At length he lowered the glasses, mouth set, jaw still tense.

Glancing over the region with his own eyes, he put up his hand. "And somewhere out there comes General Sherman. Somewhere, somewhere."

"General Bragg could give you no solid views on his whereabouts yesterday?" I asked.

"He expressed his views on the matter," Lee replied. "But with all due respect to the general, I am not sure I share them. They are based, I fear, on wishful surmises and old reconnaissances. I certainly do not agree with his prognostication that General Sherman's army is directed toward Knoxville. It is here they are coming. Right here." His brow furrowed in thought, then he added, "Yet, I believe we will have some time before he arrives. Several days at least, possibly a week. I was informed in Richmond that his departure from Memphis was delayed and the roads are indeed very bad. That will be to our advantage."

He made one last survey, this a quick one: valley, Union camp, Brown's Ferry. Then he was finished, returning his field glasses to their case and snapping the lid decisively. *This is the start of it,* I thought. *Whatever he ultimately decides to dish out to the Yankees, he's preparing the broth right now.*

Taking notice of a nearby boulder, he made for it with the obvious intention of using it as a seat. Just before he reached it, however, he stumbled heavily, only barely regaining his balance. In an instant I was beside him.

"General, are you all right?"

Lee smiled. "Yes . . . yes."

I seated him on the rock.

"I fear this thin mountain air takes some getting used to," he observed. "It was so for many of us in Mexico, years ago."

I was genuinely alarmed. "Would you like a swallow of water, sir?"

Lee shook his head. He was looking out over the countryside again, apparently all right, his thoughts back on the matter at hand. I stood back but kept my eyes on him anxiously. Once again I marked how pale and white he was. Too pale and too white, and much too valuable to be climbing around on rocks in some remote theater of the war, I fumed. Suddenly I was angry. What was Richmond doing, what were they thinking about? What was Jefferson Davis thinking about in sending the last hope of the new Confederacy, who this day was looking, very disturbingly, like a tired old man, to this place, alone and unaccompanied? To arrive by himself in the middle of the night at a shabby railhead, to step out of a boxcar to a reception of one officer and a one-legged soldier? Had everything in this war come down to one man now? It was absurd. More than absurd, it was depressing.

Lee broke into my resentful soliloquy just then with a calm reflection. "I have no personal recollection of this General Grant, Major. Other than the attendant publicity on his recent exploits, I can recall nothing else of the man. However, I believe we can expect him to use these people of his to their fullest capacity. That is certain. Nor do I doubt for a moment that he has not formulated a plan of his own, even as we speak. But he will do nothing just yet. He will wait for General Sherman."

I listened, saying nothing. The general stood up. He no longer appeared wobbly. "Major, when we get back to Missionary Ridge, there are two tasks of extreme importance I would like you to undertake."

"Certainly, General."

Lee waved his hand in the direction of Chattanooga. "Over the next few days I would like a new map of this theater, with certain clarifications and reexaminations of the enemy's positions. There are certain aspects of terrain between our two lines that I would like to see plotted. I will give you the specifics when we return and tell you exactly where I desire the utmost detail. Yet I fear this will be rather time consuming for you, Major, and may require you to make a nuisance of yourself with some of General Bragg's people in the furthermost units, for such surveys as I will require must necessarily be based on first-hand observations."

"Of course, General," I said. "That will not be a problem."

Lee smiled. "Thank you, Major." Then he added. "The second thing I would like you to do is a matter of some immediacy, and I would like you to act on this before anything else. I want you to arrange, through General Bragg's staff, the movement of my quarters from its current site on Missionary Ridge to another spot. Close to the army, of course, but not among it. In fact, Chickamauga Station would be just such a spot. I would find its proximity to the telegraph convenient. And outside of couriers who could check in at certain times, I am not desirous to trouble General Bragg for any orderlies from his army to attend me."

Seeing the bewilderment and consternation on my face, Lee made his explanation gently. "I am rather tired at the moment, Major, and I would like a couple of days to rest in private. I do not expect anything to happen that soon, and so I would use the time to rest up from my journey. Also there is much to study in this problem, and whenever General Longstreet arrives, I would have our conference a private one."

"I'll be happy to arrange that as you wish, sir," I told him, lying through my teeth. I didn't like it one bit. If Lee wasn't actually ill, he certainly wasn't in full health either. At least on Missionary Ridge there would be people constantly in the area of his camp—and doctors available. But if I went along with his request, knowing of his fatigue, and he were to die alone in his tent in this godforsaken country, what could I say by way of explanation? How could I face anyone in the Army of Northern Virginia after that? How could I face myself after that?

When we returned to Missionary Ridge I went about seeing to General Lee's wishes. I fully expected to face a troubling barrage of questions from Bragg's chief of staff when I brought up the matter of General Lee's relocation to Chickamauga Station. I had answers prepared in my head as best I could for what I believed would be a hostile cross-examination. As it turned out, I could have spared myself the worry. Hearing my request on behalf of General Lee, the colonel immediately gave the necessary orders to his subordinates and asked not a single question. Apparently life under Braxton Bragg had doused any curiosity he might have had, or else made it a liability. The thing was to be carried out first thing the next morning.

For the rest of the day, Lee stayed in his tent, studying maps and reading over a sheaf of documents he had brought with him from Richmond. I noticed the title on two of these. One was the most recent report from the War Department in Richmond regarding the Vicksburg campaign. The other was the formal report submitted by General Bragg concerning the battle of Murfreesboro.

Based on what the general had confided to me on Lookout Mountain that afternoon, that he was tired and wanted rest, I expected him to make an early night of it. Yet, close to midnight, when I returned from a trip to the telegraph at Chickamauga Station, I was surprised to find the lantern still burning in the general's tent and the general himself sitting at his camp desk. This being the case, I was able to report to him some good news. Longstreet had telegraphed from outside Knoxville, informing the general that he would proceed to Lee's location as soon as rail transportation could be arranged. As expected, Lee was pleased.

He still showed no disposition to go to bed, so I went outside and settled myself down by the fire. *He needs less sleep than I do,* I thought, and pulled out my pipe and tobacco, preparing myself for what I hoped would not be a long vigil. Yet even as I did this, a horse and rider slowly approached in shadow.

I rose to my feet as the rider stopped in the trees and dismounted. Interposing myself between the glowing tent and darkened trees as the figure came forward, I called out, "Who goes there, please?"

The man stopped. I could not see the visitor's face, but the form in the shadow was taller than me and lean. There was something ominous in the silhouette, an emanating impression of strength. Perhaps it was because of the wide-brimmed hat resting atop the darkened features of his face. Or it could have been because of the way this man, whoever he was, stopped like an Indian when challenged and took several long, unintimidated seconds to reply.

Finally the visitor stepped forward into the glow of the tent's lantern light. I could now make out the gray uniform and a general's insignia on the collar. The face was still hidden by the wide brim of the slouch hat. For a brief moment it occurred to me that General Hardee had returned, but the man before me, while having a similarly short beard, was younger, with a more pronounced step and sturdier frame. I waited.

"I am General Forrest, reporting to General Lee *as requested.*" He took another step forward, and the light from the tent illuminated the thin face with high cheekbones, stern eyes, and an unsmiling mouth. I recognized him instantly.

"Good evening, sir," I saluted.

By way of reply, he laconically raised his right forefinger to the brim of his hat.

"I'll inform General Lee you're here," I said.

Inside the tent, Lee was already buttoning his tunic. "Show the general in, Major," he said calmly. "And then remain. I will have need of your expertise."

I held the tent flap as the cavalry commander entered. This was the first time I had seen him up close. Within the confines of the tent and in the full light of the lantern, the impression of strength and formidability that I had sensed in his shadow was confirmed. The top of Forrest's head, even with his headwear removed, nearly touched the highest part of the large tent. He was thin, but it was the gauntness of a hardy woodsman—no fat, all sinew. Looking at this famous Western Confederate officer made me call to mind a description I had read about him somewhere: "hickory tough."

Yet there was a certain elegance in the way he carried himself. I had noticed it the first time I had seen Forrest in the saddle, straight and commanding. Now I saw it again in the way he stood before Lee, upright in posture, confident, haughty in bearing. Unlike Bragg, he was a handsome man in his severity. Like Bragg, it was impossible to imagine what a smile would look like on his face.

"General Forrest, thank you for coming. I am delighted that you are here." This was General Lee's meeting and he began it with his customary genteelness. Forrest bowed slightly and the two shook hands. I noted that he was taller than Lee by nearly a head.

"Thank you, General Lee. I am here at your request."

I felt the scarcely hidden disdain in this last remark, uttered twice already, and wondered whether Lee had picked up on it.

"I did indeed send for you, General," Lee said. "It was one of the first things I did as soon as I arrived here. Thankfully, you have responded most promptly."

Forrest made no answer to this. He wore a long gray tunic girthed by a wide black sword belt, minus the sword. Tucking his hat under his arm, he proceeded calmly to remove his gauntlets, all the while looking at General Lee with dark, unblinking eyes. Undoubtedly he was taking his measure of the elderly Virginian, and it occurred to me that Forrest was the hard type who took the measure of every man he met so as to define the relationship.

Lee took a seat behind the table, gesturing as he did so to a camp chair on the other side. Forrest sat down slowly, bringing up his heavy-booted right leg to rest upon his knee. He glanced around the tent, his eyes flickering over me with disinterest then back to Lee. As I took in this austere, ascetic Western cavalry offi-cer seated before me, I recalled some of the things I had heard said about Forrest in civilian circles back in Richmond. "Why, the fellow didn't just order charges, he led them! Right up to the whites of the enemy's eyes. And yes, personally killed more of them than most of his own men had. Yes, by God, in person!

Would put the muzzle of his pistol right up against a blue uniform and pull the trigger!"

I decided I believed it all.

"General Forrest," Lee began. "I would like first of all to say that I find it immeasurably gratifying to meet you in person. I have long followed your exploits, as we all have in Virginia, and I would like to add my own commendations to the many you have already received as one of the great soldiers of our cause."

Forrest heard him out, bowed his head slightly in acknowledgment of the compliment, then continued to regard the senior general with what to me was a cold, even supercilious look.

"Thank you for your fine and elegant words, sir," Forrest replied. "And permit me to say that your own glorious deeds and reputation are well known to everyone in this theater. Indeed there are many here who believe that it will be your will and greatness alone that will sustain us and ultimately lead our nation to victory."

That these embellished, insincere words came from a tough, semiliterate warrior made them even more mocking. I groaned to myself. I personally liked Forrest despite his arrogance. I had wanted him to do well with General Lee. But now, right at the start, he had made a big mistake, a great error of assessment.

As honest men, both Lee and Forrest could be expected to detest flattery. But where Lee had been raised in society, Forrest had not. Lee was a Virginia gentleman. Forrest was a rough-hewn, self-made Tennessean. Both were highly intelligent men, yet it was not surprising, given their unfamiliarity with each other, and each other's backgrounds, that a misunderstanding in communication should arise. Not surprising, but unfortunate, and made even more so now by Forrest's arrogance and his unschooled misreading of what the gentleman sitting across from him had meant in a formal greeting.

Anyone who knew Lee in any capacity, or had spent any time around him, was aware of his immense character. It was a personality that embraced truth above everything and eschewed flummery. But it was possible of course, indeed had just happened, that Lee's forthrightness in manner in bestowing a sincere compliment, as well as his highly refined courtesy, could be taken as empty flattery by those who lacked the sophistication to see it for what it really was. Among gentlemen, an honest compliment was just another way of saying, "I respect you." Nothing more. Nothing less. But Forrest missed this completely. I could not help feeling embarrassed for the cavalryman just then, watching a man of his stature underestimate a man of Lee's. Still, I knew Lee would set him right at some point, in his own way.

The general did.

Forrest's words, as well as the way he had uttered them, could not be ignored. Lee's reaction was immediate and without artifice. With a slight grimace he looked down at the table and absently straightened some papers. Then he looked up.

"Thank you for those kind sentiments, General Forrest," he said curtly, "but they are mistaken. The success or failure of our cause is in God's hands, not in the hands of a single man. Those who suggest otherwise would seem to hold in slight regard the sacrifices of thousands of brave hearts. I personally would want no part of that. I serve this cause as a general the same way a private serves it, and both our souls are equal in God's eyes."

My admiration for the old man swelled. This was Lee's aura, his greatness. And I could see that Forrest was sensing this as well.

But he had also heard the reproach, which was something to which he was clearly unaccustomed. A dark look covered his face. Lee stared back calmly. For a tense moment I thought that the cavalryman might storm out. He did not.

Forrest leaned back, his angry eyes narrowed with a new awareness. He had seen his mistake, and now he was drawing back, reevaluating, his gaze still challenged and confronted but the sauciness was gone.

"General Lee, why did you send for me?" he demanded.

Lee's features were steady and his answer deliberate. "I sent for you, General, in the hope that you might be able to answer some questions that I have about certain aspects of this theater of operation. But more important, I requested your presence here to ascertain your willingness to be of continued service to this army."

"You mean *Bragg's* army?" Forrest asked contemptuously.

"Yes," Lee replied.

"And what about service to yourself?" Forrest pressed.

"I am asking for that only in conjunction with my ordered presence here by Richmond, which is to assist that same army."

This brought a snort of impatience from the cavalryman.

"Well it don't appear like this is going to be a long conversation then," he said. He leaned forward. "Let's cut the cards, General, and get this thing over."

"As you wish," said Lee.

"I reckon pretty fairly you're aware of my differences with the great victor of Chickamauga."

"Yes."

"Then I reckon you've got a pretty fair notion of where I stand. The last conversation I had with that officer, I told him flat out that I would serve no more under his incompetence. Flat out, I told him. Right between the eyeballs, so's even a Braxton Bragg could understand. Now I'll tell you, sir, I have no intention of compromising my principles. If you intend me to go back on what I told that man after taking a belly full from him, then I reckon I'll just ride on out of here, and you can go back to your maps!"

Holding the glowering cavalryman in his gaze, Lee replied, "I can assure you, General Forrest, that I did not ask you here to compromise your principles. You do not know me, sir, but I sincerely hope you will believe me. And if you have no desire to hear out my requests, I certainly have no power to keep you here."

Easy, General Lee, I thought with alarm. This is a profane Westerner you're dealing with, not a Virginian. And he's angry.

Once again, to my vast relief, Forrest did not abandon this meeting. He sat where he was with a deep scowl on his face, not at Lee, I felt, but at his memories of Bragg. The fact that he remained seemed to me to be a turning point. Lee, the master of all situations, went on evenly.

"Your dispute with General Bragg is your own affair, General. But I fervently hope you will not be precluded from rendering valuable assistance to this army. Assistance that you and your command are best equipped to carry out." Then he added, "General Forrest, we have dire need of you, sir."

Forrest looked up sharply. For a moment he stared at Lee then demanded bluntly, "General Lee, why are you here? Tell me that, sir. Why? Why are you with this army now instead of with your own in Virginia?"

Lee's eyes flickered momentarily, and the thought crossed my mind that perhaps the old general might have asked himself that same question a time or two since his arrival here and found the answer less than satisfactory. Yet the response he gave to Forrest spoke otherwise.

"I was sent here by order of President Davis," he said. "The president believes that a chance for decisive victory is within our grasp here." He paused then added, "And based on what I have managed to see for myself, General, I find that I concur with Mr. Davis's assessment."

"Keepin' the Yankees from bustin' into Georgia ain't my idea of decisive victory," Forrest snapped, his old impatience returning.

"Nor mine," Lee replied quietly.

"Recapturing that mudhole town down below don't count for much either, if we can't hold it." Forrest declared.

"I agree," Lee said. "I think we can do much better than that."

I wondered if the cavalry commander noticed the fiery glint that had come into Lee's dark eyes just then. Forrest had. He stared at Lee with a new intensity.

"You mean, like destroy that army down there?"

"I do."

For a second the surprise on Forrest's face was unmistakable. He regarded Lee closely. When at last he spoke again, it was to ask a question on a new tack.

"Is it possible, General, that you're fixin' to relieve Bragg at some point?"

"No," Lee answered without hesitation. "I have no such orders. I was sent here by Richmond as a senior officer to look over matters in this theater, thereupon to work with General Bragg to—"

He did not get to finish. Forrest slapped his gauntlets on his boot in displeasure, yet I saw in this act not so much anger as disappointment.

"Well, General, I expect your long trip out here has been for naught then," Forrest said with disgust. His eyes flashed again with anger. "General Lee, with all due respect, sir, 'cause I know you've whupped up on a lot of Yankees back where you came from, there's somethin' needs sayin' right now."

"Please say it then, General Forrest."

Raising his sinewy arm and pointing in the direction of General Bragg's headquarters, Forrest lashed out in heated words. "You hear me now, General, and take warning! Whatever fine ideas you might have a notion to try here ain't gonna amount to a bucket of horse dung so long as that man's left in charge. 'Cause as long as he is, he'll have the power to prevent and countermand all your efforts tomorrow, never mind what he tells you today. I can tell you, sir, 'cause I know him!"

Forrest's resentment was coming into full force, his rage unfettered.

"We lost our best chance to blot them bluebellies after Chickamauga, when they was on the git. Ask your General Longstreet. We could've stayed on 'em then, but that weren't all. We could've jumped 'em after that, as well, when they were all herded up like panicked sheep in Chattanooga. I tell you, sir, we could've come right down off this ridge and shoved the whole lot of them into the Tennessee! Used our bayonets as pitchforks! We didn't though, thanks to what we got sittin' in that farmhouse yonder. You hear me, General Lee, 'cause I'm fixin' to tell you somethin' else that's fact. Them bluebellies down there have run out of mistakes to make. They ain't gonna give us another chance to lick 'em, nor are they commanded by a damn fool right now!"

The cavalryman's countenance was flushed with anger, his eyes snapped. Fascinated, I thought, *This is no West Pointer. This is no Jeb Stuart—nothing against old Jeb. Was it possible there were officers like Forrest, undiscovered, in the Army of Northern Virginia?*

Lowering his voice, Forrest concluded, "I've had my say now, General, and I reckon you know how I feel. So I'll ask the question a final time. Why did you send for me, sir?"

Lee's answer was immediate. "To help bring on the destruction of this invading enemy, General Forrest."

"The same ones that's sittin' behind their fat trenches right now?"

"The very ones."

"And you've a mind to use this army?"

"Yes, as well as elements of my own, which I intend to bring back from East Tennessee."

I stiffened. This was the first inkling I had of this.

"And with Bragg still in his present job?" Forrest went on.

"Yes," said Lee. "And with his cooperation."

Forrest's gloves slapped on his boot again. "Well, General Lee, sounds like all I've tried to tell you was just so much huffin' and puffin'."

"To the contrary, I assure you," Lee said earnestly. "I have not dismissed your words, General Forrest. I happen to believe in the truth of your articulation. And I am still asking for your help, not in disagreement of your views, but with full acceptance of them."

His eyes glittered as he spoke to the cavalryman. And I thought, *It just might be working.* Working in gradual stages.

Working like a spell. Gradually taking hold. Forrest was still holding out, but much less forcefully. And when he spoke again, his tone was not nearly as bellicose.

"Those are fine words, General Lee. But I hope you won't be too disappointed when it hits you on the head that this army and this commanding general ain't like any you've known back East."

Forrest looked at him, waiting for a response. Lee said nothing. Forrest leaned forward; once more his eyes were intently on the senior general. "I must say, sir, you pack a lot of gumption. And now I'll admit, I'm a tad curious. I expect you've got some kind of plan worked out?"

"I have the framework of one," Lee answered tersely. "And the confidence it may succeed if we can bring certain things under our power."

There was strength and authority in Lee's voice now—and a shade of testiness. He's tired of bandying about with this man, I thought. He'll press it home now, hang the consequences.

Lee did just that. "General Forrest, I was ordered here by the president to change the situation in this theater. I therefore plan to act accordingly. Plans to defeat the enemy must be made with all promptness, since time is every bit their ally and our foe. Furthermore, I quite share your view that those people cannot be counted on to revisit old mistakes. Nor in my view, can they be counted on to remain idle for much longer. They are being supplied and reinforced daily. I am certain that this man Grant already has his plan in mind. Success, I believe, will go with whoever acts first here with the wisest course. Therefore, General, I am putting it to you directly. I would like to know now whether I can expect your participation in future endeavors, which I intend to undertake with General Bragg's consent.

"Like goin' for the Yankees?" Forrest asked.

"Of course."

There was a long silence. Forrest's mouth suddenly contorted in what seemed to be a grimace, but then I saw that it was actually the man's way of making a smile.

"And just how would I be a participant in your 'endeavors,' General Lee?"

"Information," Lee answered immediately. "If a sound plan is to be laid, there are certain things we need to know first and foremost. Certain questions of geography. Military dispositions, accurate numbers, particularly of those forces outside of the Chattanooga defenses. More questions on geography. The existence, or not, of serviceable roads into Lookout Valley twenty miles south of here. In short, General Forrest, questions that are within the province of hard-riding, aggressive cavalry to answer."

Forrest had listened intently, studying the old general with a clinical gaze. Lee finished, and the Tennessean raised one of his eyebrows archly and again the mouth contorted.

"Well then, General," he drawled. "If you've a mind to have so many things answered, you'd better write out what you want answers to and show me on a map what points it is what's got you so snake fascinated."

Lee's quick nod was his thank you. "Paper, Major," he said to me. "And bring up the map of Lookout Valley."

I laid out the map and two generals leaned over it. Lee asked many questions, a number of which Forrest answered firsthand. Others he could not. At the end Lee sat down and, taking out some paper, busily wrote out the information he still needed. All the while he did this, Forrest watched him.

Finished, Lee folded the papers into an envelope. Standing up, he handed it to Forrest.

"I am most grateful, General," he said.

Forrest pocketed the envelope silently then said, "You've done right fair work in this war, General. Right fair and right smart. Nobody can say you ain't."

"Thank you," Lee replied.

Forrest continued. "I don't know how it is back where you come from, but my guess is that all you have to do is hum a tune and all kinds of bands will come chimin' in. It won't be so simple out here, as you're likely to find out. And them's not words to gloat, sir, but to put you wise." He paused briefly. "I'll help you in the play you're fixin' to make, General Lee, 'cause tryin's always better than not. Leastwise there'll be some dead Yankees come from it, I reckon, and that's never a bad thing. But hear me, sir. If you manage to pull off what it is I think you've in a mind to, I'll send you my personal respects."

"Thank you, General Forrest," Lee said quietly. "We will succeed, sir. With your help."

Ever so faint, a smile passed on Forrest's face.

"You're a different breed of cat than we've seen out here before, General," he said. "And I hope it won't be to your ill use. But now it seems to me like I wasn't all wrong in what I said at the start of this here meeting, like you made out I was."

"I don't understand, General," Lee said.

Forrest smiled again. "General Lee, you can go on all you want about the 'thousands of brave hearts' and 'not by your will alone' and all that other stuff you said when you was chewin' on my tail. But that don't change the plain truth, sir, which is that you're the one who tells those brave hearts where to go, when to hunker down, and how many of 'em's got to die. Yes sir, you are. But there's somethin' else on top of that, General." Forrest's eyes glittered brightly into Lee's. "You know in your mind you're the only one what's got the ax to bring the tree down. Yes sir, you do. You can't help but know it 'cause you've done it before. And there's other folks knows it as well. And sir, just as other folks knows it, you know you've got to do it."

Lee made no reply. He and Forrest faced each other silently. The cavalryman donned his hat and drew on his gauntlets.

"Good night to you, sir."

"Good night to you, General Forrest."

He was gone. There was a prolonged silence, then I said, "Well, General?"

"It has been a long day," Lee responded. "And tonight we have won for ourselves a great ally. But now I think it is time to put out the lantern."

THE NEXT day, the relocation of Lee's quarters was carried out. His tent was moved in close proximity to the railhead at Chickamauga Station and set up in clearing fronted by a stream. Nearby, but out of sight, was an encampment of Bragg's soldiers who were assigned to guard the station. Lee was pleased with the arrangements, and so was I.

But there was one part of Lee's instructions that I pointedly ignored, even at the risk of incurring the old man's ire. Quite simply, there was no way I was going to leave the general alone while I was busy on my mapmaking. Therefore I went out and found a man who I believed would make the best orderly for Lee in the entire Chattanooga theater.

"The general needs rest badly," I told one-legged Sgt. Goner Wickett of Longstreet's corps. "Whenever he's asleep, try not to let him be disturbed. I'll probably be spending my nights on the ridge, but I'll make a point of stopping by a couple of times during the day to see how things are going. If he wants to send a message, fetch one of the couriers at the camp yonder. If it's a telegraph, take it yourself. Keep an eye on him, Sergeant. It's more important than you know.

More important than any of us might know, I said to myself.

"Marse Robert's gonna be all right, ain't he, Major?" Goner asked.

"Yes, but he needs his rest."

"We gonna have another go at the Yankees?"

"Yes. After he's rested."

As I rode away I looked back in the clearing. There was the tent, inside of which a tired and prematurely aged old man was sleeping off weariness. Outside the tent was the old man's aide, a one-legged soldier hanging on a crutch. Turning away from the scene, I thought, *I hope this war ends pretty soon, because if it doesn't, those of us who aren't killed will end looking like one of them.*

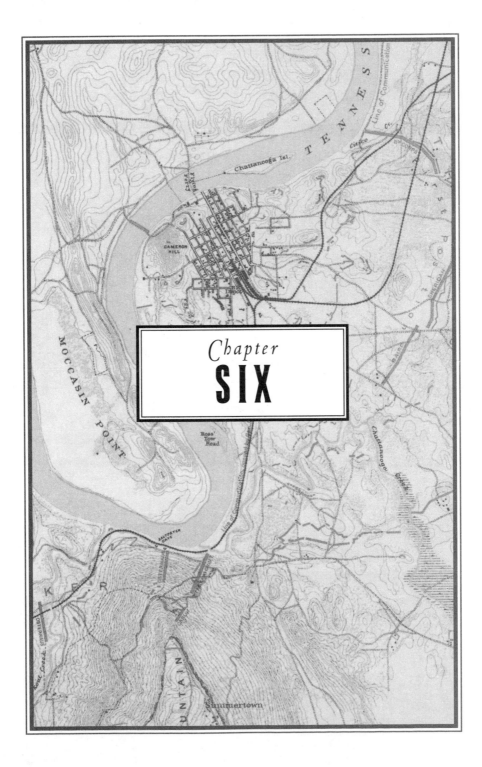

Chapter
SIX

I PAUSED IN MY STORY as the Negro boy came by with another log for the fire. As he tended to the hearth, the innkeeper appeared with the bottle and, without a word, refilled our glasses. To my surprise, Deslauries did not object.

"For three full days I did not see Lee at all," I said, continuing. "For I was, during that time, quite occupied in carrying out the general's 'important clarifications' and 'reexaminations.' In the midst of all this, it was all I could do to visit Chickamauga Station once a day, usually in the afternoon. But the news was comforting. The general was doing well, Sergeant Goner reported—up early in the mornings until late at night, but using the afternoons for long naps. His appetite was good and he looked healthy. Occasionally he received visitors, brigade or regimental officers from the Army of Tennessee, stopping by to pay their respects. Braxton Bragg, however, had not visited, or any of his staff."

THIS ENCOURAGING progress allowed me to go about my business in a much easier frame of mind. My days were busy and I was grateful that there were no distractions. And since Lee was doing so well and apparently needed nothing from me, at night I bivouacked in Cleburne's camp. There was nothing from Forrest during that time. Nor was there any fresh news from Bragg's headquarters about Sherman's whereabouts, something Lee had emphatically ordered me to report to him immediately if it did become known.

During my daily reconnaissances of the Federal line, I was alert to any signs that the Yankees were aware of General Lee's presence above Chattanooga. It was not the kind of thing that could be kept secret for long, and I watched for changes in troop dispositions or any small signs that might signal this knowledge. There were none. If Grant or any of his generals knew anything, they altered nothing. Pickets from the Army of Tennessee and the Army of the Cumberland walked their same posts within plain sight of one another.

Over in Lookout Valley, the daily routine was the norm as well. The Easterners from Hooker's division stayed put and spent their days as all the Yankee soldiers did in camp: drilling in formations, falling in, falling out. Every day smoke from Union supply transports continued to hang over Brown's Ferry. Every day there was a constant flow of wagons back and forth over the pontoon bridge the Yankees had built at Chattanooga.

It was "all quiet along the Tennessee."

But behind all this normalcy I felt the tension. Grant was waiting for Sherman. And I knew Sherman was on Lee's mind as well. The unseen presence of this Western general and his host of Vicksburg veterans was a palpable weight, pressing in on the consciousness.

As I went about my surveys of the enemy defenses around Chattanooga it was impossible for me not to be troubled by the improvements the Federals had made. They had used their time well. Batteries and earthworks were expertly sited so as to allow overlapping fields of fire, and their trenches were indeed, as Forrest had described them, fat ones. The Army of the Cumberland would not be easily pushed into the Tennessee River now.

Yet Lee told Forrest he would attack. Just where he might do so, I could not imagine; every place looked strong. Lee had ordered a particularly detailed survey made of the Union stronghold anchoring the right side of the Chattanooga defenses, Fort Negley; yet upon doing so, I judged it well-nigh impregnable. Still, none of this really mattered. I had no idea of what or where Lee would strike, but it was enough for me to know that he intended to do so. Like everyone who was under the general's spell, so expectant was I of his ability to pull off anything he wanted that I scarcely gave it a second thought. The tragedy at

Gettysburg seriously challenged this notion with some, but that November in Tennessee, I was still a believer.

MAKING MY call to Lee's camp at Chickamauga Station one afternoon, I was informed by Sergeant Goner that the general was, as usual, asleep. As we conversed, a rider came into the clearing, a young cavalryman, small in build but astride a large mount. As he drew nearer, this disparity was made even more apparent, for the horse, quite unlike the rider, was full bodied and muscular, literally a war steed. Crowded and hanging from both sides of the saddle were weapons of war: a saber, a carbine, a Bowie knife, four large horse pistols, and several ammunition pouches. The boyish rider bore the markings of a corporal, and the appearance of so many weapons around one so young might have been comical, especially taking into account his baggy uniform and greatly oversized cavalry boots. But there was a hardness in his face that commanded respect. Not the affected hardness of a boy trying to pose as a man but rather the look of a boy who had seen war and probably would not live to see the end of it.

He halted in front of me and touched his hat in salute. "I was told I could find Gin'ral Lee heah."

His voice was high pitched. He was mud splattered and looked very tired.

"That's right, Corporal," I answered. "And you are . . . ?"

The young cavalryman slid off his animal and took a bulky pouch from one of the saddlebags. Clumping up to me in his heavy boots, he announced, "Corporal Lyle Passengale, suh, and I've got papers in this pouch what's to be delivered personally and only into the hands of Gin'ral Robert E. Lee."

As if to underscore this he held the pouch tightly under his other arm.

"Very well, but what command are you from, sir?" I queried. "You haven't told me that."

The corporal looked surprised. "Why I come from Gin'ral Forrest," he replied.

I had guessed this and received it as welcome news.

Then a voice from behind me said, "I will see the young man, Major."

It was Lee, standing outside the tent, fully dressed.

"And how are you, General?" I exclaimed. It was wonderful to see him again.

Lee smiled. "Very well, thank you, Major. I understand you have been busy."

"I have indeed, sir. And it's very good to see you up and looking well, General," I said and meant it. He did look well. The posture, the clearness of eye. He was the man I recalled from Virginia.

The general addressed the corporal. "You have obviously come far, young man. You may hand me your pouch, if you please." Then abruptly he asked, "Have you brought any news of General Sherman?"

The corporal shook his head. "No suh, I have no such news."

While Lee opened the pouch, the young trooper stared at him intently. Veteran though he was, he was clearly awed in the presence of the legendary personality. Then, as if remembering something he should have said at the very outset, he spoke up shrilly. "Suh, Gin'ral Forrest told me to tell you that the answers to your questions are there enclosed. And if you've a mind to know anything else, you can write them down and send them back with me. Suh!"

Lee regarded him with twinkling eyes. "And where is General Forrest right now?"

The cavalryman nodded to the west. "Just yonder of Lookout Mountain right now, suh, and waitin' on me to come back from here." And he added, "He don't want to set there too long, and my instructions are to come back at the soonest."

"Well done, young man," said Lee. "I will commend you to your general. Meanwhile we will not endeavor to keep you long. Take some rest while the major and I look over what you have brought."

As Lee turned to enter the tent, the youthful corporal suddenly snapped to full attention and raised his hand in crisp salute. "Yes suh! And thank you, Gin'ral Robert E. Lee, suh!"

Again Lee's eyes crinkled. "And thank you, Corporal Lyle Passengale."

RIDING BACK to Missionary Ridge that afternoon, I was in high spirits. Lee was, as Sergeant Goner had put it best, Lee again. And the contents of Forrest's pouch had been priceless. There were several roughly drawn maps that, despite their crudeness, depicted usable roads and good screening terrain west and south of Chattanooga, leading into Lookout Valley. In addition Forrest had provided tallies on the concentrations and numbers of the Federal forces in and around Lookout Valley, including Brown's Ferry. These had pleased Lee the most. Only once did the general express disappointment, and that was on the lack of any information on the whereabouts of Sherman's force.

"I am beginning to see that Tennessee is not like Virginia," he had remarked with unusual causticity. "For here it seems that twenty thousand of those people on the march can manage to make themselves invisible to all eyes."

As for me, this was the day when I would finish my terrain map of Chattanooga and vicinity. I had everything needed by nightfall, and with daylight fading and the raw air of a November night settling in, I set my horse's head toward the welcome hospitality of Cleburne's camp in a very good frame of mind.

After supper I sat with Cleburne and his staff by a warm fire. We smoked and talked, mostly about different generals, and I told them what Forrest had said about Bragg after Chickamauga.

"He would say it that way, old Forrest," Cleburne laughed. "But he's right, though, Jed. We had them beat, top to bottom, and we should've finished it. I still don't know what General Bragg was thinking."

Cleburne puffed silently on his pipe for a few moments then said, "You know, it's not that Braxton Bragg's a fool. It's more complicated than that, I think, although the end result still comes out the same way, I guess. I've been with Bragg for a long time, and more often than not he does all right for himself. Take the invasion of Kentucky last year. That played hell with the Yankees, big time. Don't think it didn't." His officers nodded. "And this last winter at Murfreesboro. That was as nice a bushwhack as ever could have been planned. But there's where the trouble's always been, when things go according to plan. It's like he's got it in his head we can only take it so far. So when we do win, it's almost like he's more surprised than the Yankees. A strange man. Unhappy man. There's parts of his mind where the lanterns aren't lit. Something inside that makes him see darkness in broad daylight. And it's hard to tell him anything. With General Bragg you can never be sure whether you're talking to the soldier or the martinet, the sound mind or the dyspeptic."

"I worked for a dyspeptic once myself," I said.

"General Jackson?"

"The very one."

"So then," Cleburne asked, "what was the difference between him and Bragg?"

"General Jackson was never surprised by a victory. He downright expected it."

"Hmmm," Cleburne said. "Maybe so at that."

Just then one of his officers looked at me. "All this poking and prodding Lee's had you do, Jed. What's his plan?"

"I don't know."

The officer gave me an amused look. "You don't know?"

"That's right," I asserted. "Truly I don't."

"Really, Jed," said another.

I smiled. "You flatter me, gentlemen. I'm just his topographical engineer. General Lee does not take counsel with me when he plots his grand strategy."

"I reckon you could make a good guess, though," the first officer persisted.

"Well now, Captain," I answered. "Asking an engineer for a guess is opening up another deck of cards."

They all laughed.

Cleburne had remained silent. Now he gave me a serious look. "My guess is that he's had a plan in mind for some time, Jed."

"That would be my guess as well."

"Probably for a strong offensive."

"Those are the kinds he tends to favor." I smiled.

"Jed, when you go back tomorrow, you tell General Lee that we're ready. Tell him this division is ready for whatever he's got in mind."

I looked at him, not quite comprehending.

"Are you aware that the day I met General Lee on Missionary Ridge, he spoke to me of using this division in an offensive movement?" Cleburne asked.

"No," I replied truthfully. "Although that doesn't surprise me. What is your assignment to be?"

"He wasn't specific," Cleburne said. "I was hoping you might know, but now it seems we'll all find out together, won't we? But he did say this: He said that he hoped we'd be ready when the time came. So you tell him from me, Jed, we're ready. If whipping the Yankees is what he's got in mind, then he can put us to work."

The fire cracked. Cleburne and his officers stared in my direction.

I nodded slowly. "Rest assured, General Cleburne," I said. "I will relay your message to General Lee."

THE NEXT morning, as I passed through Chickamauga Station on my way to Lee's camp, I heard delightful news. A contingent of officers from Longstreet's corps had arrived by train from East Tennessee during the night. Elated, I galloped the rest of the way. Coming into the clearing I saw horses tethered in the trees. I recognized the first two immediately. One mount was

Longstreet's. The other belonged to Longstreet's chief aide, my
friend and comrade, Moxley Sorrel. And it was Major Sorrel
himself who was coming forward to meet me.

"Sorrel!"

"Howdy, Jed!"

I jumped down from my horse and clasped his hand.
"Dammit, Mox, seeing you here is better than a flapjack breakfast, I declare!"

Sorrel laughed. "We came as soon as we could once we got
word General Lee wanted to see Old Pete. I think he was looking for any excuse to get away from back there. My God, Jed,
what a wild country over there. Remember how when we first
got here we thought *this* was prehistory wilderness? Well, let me
tell you, compared to East Tennessee, this is Society Hill Park."

"And how's Pete?"

"Happy and fit to bust," Sorrel replied. "Jed, when he got
word that Marse Robert was really in Tennessee, really here in
person, why he actually allowed himself a smile. Full blown.
Can't recall the last time I saw that."

I laughed.

"They're both inside chatting," Sorrel said. "Come on, the
general will be glad to see you again."

Sorrel led the way to the open tent flap. Longstreet and
Lee were sitting at a table, both in relaxed poses. Longstreet's
usually dour face was loose and genial.

"Well, Major Hotchkiss," he said to me.

"Hello, General. Very good to see you again, sir."

Longstreet looked at Lee with twinkling eyes. "How's he
been doing for you, General?"

"I couldn't have asked for a more capable assistant," Lee
answered kindly.

Sorrel coughed lightly, and I was aware that this compliment would get back to Lee's aide, Walter Taylor, with relish.

As I took in the scene just then, it seemed to me as though
we were all back in Virginia. Old Pete and Marse Robert, talking

together, conversing lightly, and plotting mischief for the enemy. Just for a moment it could have been one of the old days along the Rapidan. All that was needed was for Stonewall to come riding up.

"What is the news from Missionary Ridge today, Major?" Lee asked. "I suppose there is still no word regarding General Sherman?"

"I'm afraid not, sir."

I placed my now-completed map on the table. Then I told the general what Cleburne had pressed upon me the night before.

Lee gave a satisfied nod and looked at Longstreet, who grunted approvingly.

"That's General Cleburne talking all right," Longstreet commented. "General Bragg's a lucky man to have the likes of that officer in his army. I hope he knows it."

"Whether he does or not, we will need his approval for General Cleburne's use," Lee said. "If we can get that, that young man will be of inestimable service to his army and us."

Lee and Longstreet began scanning my map. After a few questions to me, the two commanders became absorbed and addressed their comments to each other. Sorrel and I quietly abandoned the tent.

"General Lee's ordered the whole corps back here, did you know that?" Sorrel asked.

"I heard him mention something about that recently," I replied. "Can't say I'm surprised to hear it."

"Has he let General Bragg know?"

"I don't think so. Anyway he doesn't have to, except as a courtesy, which I'm sure he'll do. The message from Richmond sending him here specifically set forth that he was to reassume command of First Corps. It'll be nice to see the boys again," I added. "But what about General Burnside's army at Knoxville?"

Sorrel gave a mocking laugh. "Burnside! You know what a sledgehammer that old boy is. Hell, Jed, he's dug in so deep, ten-foot spades couldn't get to him. And he's hoarded up all the food for his bluebellies like a fat squirrel. That adds up to stayin' put, in my book. With the railroad in good order, we can slip away from there, lick the Yankees down here then get up to Knoxville in time to thump General Burnside when he comes out from his trenches."

While Lee and Longstreet consulted, Sorrel and I and the rest of the officers who had come down on the train spent the time catching up on gossip. By every account I heard, life for the First Corps around Knoxville was exceedingly dreary and unproductive. All of Longstreet's officers were glad they were coming back to be a part of whatever Lee had in mind to inflict on the Yankees in Chattanooga.

During the course of the day, both generals would occasionally emerge from the tent and stroll around the clearing. At one point I noticed the indefatigable Sergeant Goner stretched out on a log, face turned to the sun, fast asleep. *You'll be reunited with your friends soon, bless your heart,* I thought. Several times I was called in by the generals to answer their questions and expound on certain features of the terrain and Union dispositions. During one of these summons, Lee questioned me intently on the close-up observations I had sketched and written about Fort Negley, to my mind the Army of the Cumberland's most formidable redoubt.

Late in the afternoon, I was called once more to the tent.

"Major Hotchkiss," Lee began, "I would like for you to ride up to Missionary Ridge and see General Bragg. Tell him, if he is amenable to such a thing, that I would like to meet with him at his headquarters tomorrow morning at the earliest convenience. He can tell you whatever time he desires. Tell him you will be my sole accompaniment."

As I saddled my horse for this errand, Sorrel came up and observed, "Well, it would appear Marse Robert's ready to stir up some trouble."

"Looks like," I agreed. "I guess it's time to see what six weeks of peace and quiet have done to the Yankees."

"The Yankees?" Sorrel snorted. "Hell, Jed, I was talking about General Bragg!"

THE NEXT morning I waited for Lee in the clearing. Longstreet walked with the general to his horse, and I overheard him telling Lee, "There should have been nothing left of that army after Chickamauga but a steady spew of stragglers heading north."

"That could still happen, General," Lee said amiably. "With God's will and the kind cooperation of General Bragg."

Longstreet grunted. "It's General Grant's cooperation that has me worried. He'll stick to his hand, play out his own set of cards regardless of what you're holding, General. That's the way he operates. And some of General Bragg's people have told my officers that General Grant knows you're here, which emphasizes my point. If that's true, he's shown no reaction. Hasn't changed his army's alignment one bit. He's playing his own hand all right."

Lee mounted and took the reins. "Well and good, General Longstreet. Well and good. But the important thing is to not let him find out that *you* are here. And as for that man's army . . . well, perhaps we can change its alignment."

This was classic Lee. I stifled a laugh. Longstreet's bearded face twitched, which was his equivalent of a smile.

"Also General," Lee went on, "as some of your corps arrives, I think it would be prudent to post your own scouts along Missionary Ridge to keep watch on the enemy. That way our intelligence on their movements will always be firsthand."

Longstreet nodded, "We'll make it so."

"Thank you, General," Lee said with a wave of his hand. "Come along, Major Hotchkiss."

As we rode off, I believed there had been a change in the weather. I felt a surge of euphoria that I hadn't experienced since the Army of Northern Virginia broke camp and marched into Maryland four months ago. As we cantered out of the clearing we passed Sergeant Goner, Lee's loyal orderly, sitting under a tree and eating his breakfast.

"Mawnin', Gen'ral!" he called.

Lee touched his hat. I waved. *That's right, you one-legged fire-eater,* I said to myself in kind of giddy elation. *It's just like you said. Lee's here, we're gonna lick the Yankees, and everything's gonna be fine.*

DAYS AGO, when General Lee had removed himself to Chickamauga Station, wild rumors had circulated through the camps on Missionary Ridge that the famous general from Virginia was gravely ill and returning to Richmond. As soon as they saw him this morning, the soldiers came away from their fires and gawked again at this smartly uniformed officer riding through their camps. When we entered the yard of General Bragg's farmhouse headquarters, a sober-faced captain came forward and bade us dismount. Orderlies took our horses, and in a much too formal style of speech, the grim captain said that he would announce our arrival to General Bragg. In the meantime, he added, would we be so kind as to wait in the yard?

Several minutes later we were still waiting, and I fumed as I watched several aides with busy frowns entering and exiting the small house.

I had long ago come to expect this kind of bad theater at Bragg's headquarters, but it had never ceased to irritate me. In the Army of Northern Virginia, when one general wanted to call on another, it was only a matter of going to where that officer was and rapping on the tent pole, without the Napoleonics of self-important staff officers snapping and wheeling about, announcing their arrivals. Yet here, in this unhappy staff organization, where casualness and informality were unknown, grim protocol held sway.

Bragg's chief of staff finally came out of the house. Ignoring me, he saluted the general. "General Bragg will see you now, sir."

"Thank you, Colonel," Lee responded. "I shall be bringing my aide as well. Major, if you please."

The colonel said nothing to this and led the way into the house.

Just as at their first meeting, Bragg was seated at his desk when Lee entered the room. Rising now he bid the general good morning, adding, "I am happy to see you up and around and in good health again."

There was nothing happy about Bragg's face as he spoke these words, but this was nothing new. The tone was sincere and the remark proper. Lee thanked him, and the two generals sat down. Four of Bragg's officers stood along one wall, and I placed myself against the opposite one.

Lee came to his business immediately. He began by informing Bragg of Longstreet's arrival at Chickamauga Station, even though Bragg would have known of this already. As Lee spoke, Bragg's dark face showed neither acceptance nor disapproval. He sat motionless, eyes blinking, listening stolidly. Lee went on to the next subject without pause or waiting for comment, much in the manner, so it seemed to me, of a senior officer briefing a colleague of somewhat junior rank. He relayed to Bragg what Longstreet had informed him of the situation in East Tennessee, emphasizing how Burnside was well dug in and showing not the slightest propensity to move or even to conduct aggressive reconnoitering outside his works.

Bragg heard him out, or at least appeared to do so. I had decided long ago that the man had only two expressions. If he wasn't looking glarish and ill tempered, he was looking nonplused. Now it was the latter, and as he listened to Lee he did not look directly at him, but at some point over my general's left shoulder.

What a strange bird, I thought. Much stranger than Jackson ever was. Darker, too, and quite without that Jackson brilliance that laid so many victories at the Confederacy's feet and made any shortcomings of personality into forgivable eccentricities. I recalled the contrast Cleburne had noted about Bragg, the sound mind versus the dyspeptic, and wondered which man Lee was seeing at present. As yet there was no clue.

Lee still held the floor and moved to another topic. "General Bragg, I have had sufficient time to study and reflect upon the situation here. Having done so, I must tell you honestly that I feel a strong sense of optimism over what I believe to be certain exploitable opportunities."

"Exploitable opportunities? Indeed, General?" Bragg asked with barely concealed skepticism.

"Very much so," Lee answered, his dark eyes glistening. "These opportunities exist here and now. And if we are bold enough in action and ardent in our purpose, I believe we can visit a great catastrophe on those people."

These were powerful words from a commander who never boasted. Along the far wall, Bragg's officers stirred. Bragg himself was clearly on the defensive.

"Well, I am happy to hear you say so," he responded lamely. Trying poorly to affect nonchalance, what emerged instead was uneasiness. "I assume you will tell us what opportunities you have seen to make you feel so sanguine."

Lee's answer was immediate. "General, the enemy force before us is divided. We have the opportunity to strike hard at one or more of the divided segments before they are reinforced further."

"Strike the divided segments," Bragg repeated. "And naturally you have a proposal as well?"

He was stalling.

"I do indeed," Lee said. "A proposal in two parts. The first being that my corps under General Longstreet be brought back to Chickamauga Station immediately. There it will be posted in the rear of your army, out of sight of those people."

Lee seldom used the personal pronoun "my" in referring to his army, preferring the communal "our" instead, but here I understood the reason. He was politely and obliquely telling

Bragg he was taking back the First Corps from the Army of Tennessee. Meanwhile he continued to sketch out the plan.

"I would leave one reinforced brigade on General Burnside's front to keep him in place and maintain the deception that he is still heavily confronted. Meantime, the rest of the corps will be here, hidden, until such time as a surprise blow could be struck at those people below us now."

Bragg was blinking. His staff was looking anxiously back and forth between the two generals. It all sounded so simple. At length, Bragg recovered.

"General Lee, you are proposing to guard my entire right flank in East Tennessee, against fifteen thousand Yankees, with one brigade?" he demanded.

"If I may, I would suggest an alternate perspective on the matter," Lee answered quietly. "Your most important, and your most immediate right flank is right here, General, not in East Tennessee. As long as Burnside is content to sit behind his fortifications and wait for our attack, the threat to your far right flank, as you call it, is only in potential, not actuality. But in bringing an entire corps of ours back to this place, unbeknownst to those people below, it is we ourselves who truly threaten, and not just in potential, sir, but in actuality."

For several seconds there a profound silence echoed in the headquarters. Then Bragg reacted once more.

"Strike a blow?" he demanded testily. "Where along the fortified line of the enemy can you do the things you speak of?"

Lee was ready with a reply. "We cannot know that as yet. That will depend on how those people are situated when the time comes."

This was a very vague answer, but for now Bragg did not press Lee on it. It was obvious he was still thinking about East Tennessee. Bragg's intimidation by Lee was obvious to all, yet so too was his rising level of agitation. *He's being forced to think too much and too fast,* I thought. Easy, General Lee.

When Bragg spoke again his tone was waspish. His eyebrows were knit together. "So let me understand this, General. You propose to bring General Longstreet's entire command, minus only one brigade, back to here—"

"Quickly and unnoticed," Lee interrupted gently. "Especially unnoticed."

Bragg blinked at this, then went on. "—and leave Burnside completely alone. Let him be. Let him keep Knoxville. Have I stated your view correctly, sir?"

"Quite so," said Lee.

Bragg stared at him. "You have great confidence, sir," he said accusingly. "Great confidence that General Burnside will do what you want. Great confidence too, apparently, in the caliber of brigades General Longstreet has in his corps, since one is all you feel is required to hold General Burnside at bay. Will your confidence be the same when he is reinforced by General Sherman's thousands?"

"General Sherman is not marching to join General Burnside, General Bragg," Lee said calmly. "When he shows up, it will be here. At Chattanooga. He is coming to join General Grant, who is waiting for him as we speak. Therefore it is all the more imperative that we act the soonest, before he arrives."

Lee had not said that Sherman "might," he said he "would." I swelled with pride for my general. Meantime Bragg's officers continued to look uncomfortable. Bragg stared at Lee as though he had dropped from the sky. When he spoke again, his voice carried a nasty edge of suspicion. "You have received news of General Sherman's intentions that you have not shared with us, General Lee?"

"None," Lee replied patiently. "It is only my view, but one which I fervently believe will happen."

Bragg said nothing. Suddenly now, Lee became animated. Leaning forward, eyes glistening again, he confronted Bragg. "General Bragg, if left alone, General Burnside will keep himself out of this whole thing. Do you hear, sir? Therefore he must be left alone. General Grant, on the other hand, must not. Whatever he is planning will be in concert with General Sherman, therefore our time to act must be before they unite and before General Grant is aware of the presence of another corps here. We must cause him to shift and weaken his present position around Chattanooga in such a way as to allow your army and my corps to come upon him in full destructive force when he is off balance. That is the only plan, General. That is the only goal. To render that occupying army unfit for any future service against us. We cannot wait any longer. Can you not see that, General? You must surely see that."

Bragg was beginning to wear down, but he was still obdurate. "And how will General Grant be put off balance, sir?" he scoffed. "Or is that the second part of your proposal?"

"It is," Lee said, ignoring the sarcasm.

I listened with renewed interest, for this was going to be news to me as well. Whatever was coming had probably been worked out with Longstreet the day before.

"Once Longstreet's corps is assembled at Chickamauga Station, I would like a force from your army to make a preliminary strike upon the enemy. This being to divert attention away from the defenses around Chattanooga."

"A force from my army," Bragg repeated warily. "What kind of force?"

"Two divisions and artillery," Lee replied. "General Cleburne in command."

Bragg looked indignant. "To strike the enemy where?" he demanded. "Strike where and with what objective? And with what chance of success? Two divisions is no paltry force, sir. And General Cleburne . . ." he began and trailed off, but I finished it to myself, "*is no paltry general.*"

Lee paused before he answered. Then he proceeded, going slowly. In consummate, methodical fashion he unraveled his plan, laying out its design in measured stages, emphasizing tactical objectives and calling for strict adherence to a schedule.

Once he pointedly digressed to discuss terrain and certain aspects of geography that Cleburne's striking force could be expected to encounter. He went on at length, and as he spoke his eyes glittered, his intelligence and aggressive genius fully stoked. Nearing the end he spoke strongly once again on the importance, the absolute imperative, of Cleburne's reaching his objective, which was the key to destabilizing the Army of the Cumberland and disconcerting its generals.

Concluding his presentation, Lee said in a quiet voice, which only served to heighten the dramatic effect of his presentation, "And when General Cleburne achieves this, the rest of us will all go in together against Chattanooga. Our entire force. Strike and press them so that escape across the river is impossible. Indeed, General, they must not be allowed to get across the river."

Finished now, Lee leaned back in his chair. The room was as silent as a tomb. Bragg blinked. His staff gaped. As for me, I had forgotten to breathe ever since hearing what Cleburne's objective was to be. The plan was sheer effrontery. Sheer Robert E. Lee.

Calm and composed, his idea fully divulged, Lee waited, looking at Bragg.

The latter was still speechless, so thoroughly had Lee covered every concern in his explanation that there was not even a vagary that might have allowed Bragg the opportunity to ask a question in order to stall for time. With a nonplused scowl, he turned to his staff. Equally nonplused, they stared back at him. At last he recovered his voice.

"Brown's Ferry, General Lee? Brown's Ferry?"

"Yes, General," Lee replied.

"Why, General Cleburne will have to go through General Hooker and his Easterners to get there!"

"Precisely so," Lee said supinely.

Bragg looked at him with renewed astonishment.

"And what if General Cleburne cannot do it?"

"I'm sure that he can with the force provided, General Bragg. You know the man yourself, sir. I am highly impressed by his qualities." Then Lee added, "At any rate he *must* take his objective. General Grant will undoubtedly gather forces for a quick counterattack once his supply base is taken. Therefore when General Cleburne takes his objective, we here will watch closely, taking careful note of where he weakens his lines. And then we will launch our own assault, General."

Again there was an astonished hush in the room. Bragg blinked, glowered at the map, and stirred in his seat. His astonishment fading, the ill temper was returning.

"Well now, General Lee," he said. "I must say that I find your plan to be very aggressive—and very ambitious."

For once, I found myself in full agreement with Braxton Bragg

"The trouble is, General," Bragg fussed on, "it seems as though there are . . . I rather think there might be some crucial matters that you have overlooked."

"Please tell me what they are," Lee replied, quite unruffled.

Bragg scowled at the map, not meeting Lee's eyes or answering his request. "Yes, quite ambitious . . . and very risky," he grumbled. "But then you are new to our theater."

Suddenly he looked up sharply. "Start again if you would please, General. Let us have your plan again, sir."

Lee showed the first sign of impatience. He was a commander used to acting on his ideas, not justifying them. Nevertheless he did as Bragg asked, going through it all again, much quicker now but covering everything.

Bragg was silent for a time, and when at last he spoke, the recalcitrance was gone. There was no challenge in his voice now but genuine concern.

"You are asking much, General Lee. Perhaps more than you think. General Cleburne is my best divisional commander, I would have you know."

"I know it quite well," Lee said, "but in this thing before us, it is necessary to use this officer's talents to the utmost. Everyone's talents must be used to the utmost, sir."

"Yes of course," answered Bragg, "but you are still asking that I take my best commander, along with two of my best divisions, pull them out of line of my right to make for this round-about objective you would have them take. That leaves only General Hardee on my right. How can he be expected to hold if suddenly pressed along that part of Missionary Ridge? You have seen for yourself that there is much ground to defend. Who will take the place of General Cleburne's division, sir?"

Much as I disliked Bragg, I had to admit that these were legitimate concerns. And I thought, *now we're getting a glimpse of Bragg the soldier.*

"I think it is unlikely that the enemy will press there," Lee responded. "Particularly if the departure of General Cleburne's brigades is done with the necessary circumspection and stealth. At any rate, General Longstreet's corps will be at Chickamauga Station, directly to the rear of your right flank. He can be moved up quickly in the unlikely event that those people decide to suddenly come out of their works and venture an assault there."

Bragg looked at his staff, who shuffled nervously. Then he growled, "Yes . . . yes. General Longstreet. Well, that is your corps after all, and you will do with it as you like."

Lee said nothing.

Bragg was still muttering at the desk, his irritation back in full. "There are many details to be worked out if such a move is to be made," he was saying. "All too often grand designs, elegantly proposed turn into fiascoes for want of proper attention to seemingly trivial details."

"We will attend to the trivial details, General," Lee said quietly.

Bragg fussed on. "And requisite issues of ammunition and supplies are not to be had by a mere snap of the fingers." Suddenly he looked up at Lee with a shrewd glint in his eye. "If

General Cleburne is to start so soon as you demand, General Lee, then his rations from the march must come from General Longstreet's allotment."

This seemed to give him pleasure. His voice rose. "It can only be from General Longstreet, for I have none to spare. If I am to give you part of my army, then I must insist that you feed it, sir. I will not have it any other way, General, and I will not be dissuaded!"

Bragg had found the issue to reassert his authority. He glared at his staff for backup, and they in turn nodded indignantly. Lee at once surmounted the obstacle.

"You shall have it your way, General," he said evenly. "I will not try to dissuade you."

"Very good then," Bragg snorted. "Very good. We are in accord then, sir."

I was jubilant. Bragg had been brought along. At the cost of a few thousand rations, Lee would have Cleburne and his hard force of veterans at his disposal. I stared at him in proud wonder. The stress and turmoil of the last few years had seemingly done nothing to diminish the Old Fox's ability to succeed against his adversaries, those in gray as well as those in blue.

Bragg was on board, but he would remain a troublesome ally.

"Let us hope for everyone's sake your surmises about the enemy's intentions are correct, General Lee," Bragg snapped. He was back into ill-tempered condescension. "I would not have agreed with your plan but for knowing that it is President Davis's utmost desire that I cooperate with you. I fear you have far too much faith in the pliancy of the Yankees in all this, sir.

"My faith, General, is in God and the valor of our soldiers," Lee smiled, standing up.

It made me smile, too. This was a page from the old days, when our army and our cause had everything we needed: God. Our soldiers. Marse Robert.

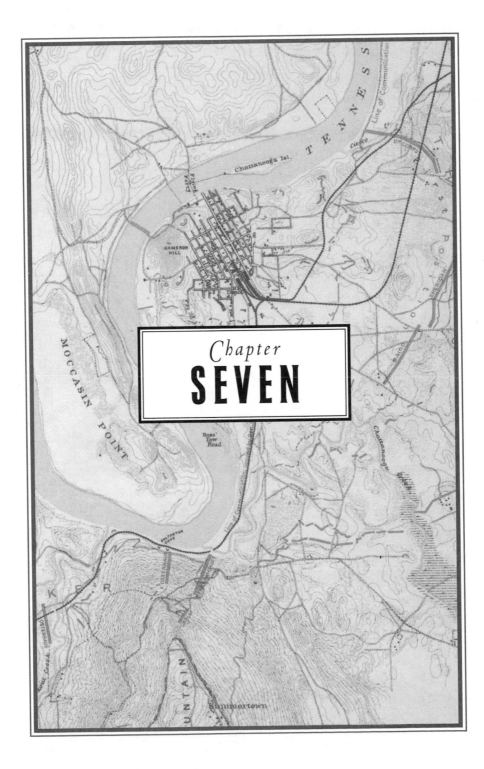

Chapter

SEVEN

THAT SAME DAY THE first trains began arriving at Chickamauga Station with Longstreet's artillery and horses. The unloading took several hours, but by the afternoon the yard was cleared. Just after dark, the long trains of infantry began rolling in.

I was on hand to watch the arrivals. The yard was illuminated by bonfires, and before the hissing locomotives had even come to a squealing stop, lean men were jumping down from boxcars and flatcars. Typically, engineering officers in the army were closest in spirit to the artillery, but there were times, and this was one, when the sight of the lanky butternut infantrymen was an invigorating sight to everyone's eyes. My spirits soared, and I remained for a long time, just watching the trains come in and the troops debark. The bivouacs in the rail yard grew with each arriving locomotive, and soon the air was full of wood smoke, cooking food, and raucous chatter. By midnight, most of John Bell Hood's division, now under command of a young brigadier, Micah Jenkins, had arrived.

EARLY THE next morning Lee rode into Chickamauga Station accompanied by Longstreet and his staff. The first soldiers who spotted the general rushed from their breakfast fires and surrounded his horse.

"It's General Lee, boys! Lee's here!" they shouted. In an instant the entire station and assembly area was alive with frenzied emotion. The volume of the uproar swelled, then shifted to a high pitch as the cheers and cries of "Lee! Lee!" commingled into one vast screeching Rebel yell. Into the tumult rode General Lee, his horse being led by the soldiers. The station area was a resurgent riot of uncontrollable joy, packed with screaming butternuts. They covered the ground and were in the trees as well; they hung from telegraph poles and crowded the tops of sheds and boxcars. Regimental flags were unfurled and passed up to these elevated spots and waved joyfully, the formerly drab station yard now alive with dancing crimson. Above it all rose the ear-splitting Rebel shriek, ceaseless and unslackened.

From where I was riding with the staff, I could see the flush on General Lee's cheeks. Regal as always on horseback, the general looked around with an affectionate smile, nodding and mouthing words of thanks repeatedly, clearly moved by this demonstration. Squarely in the middle of the outpouring, Lee stopped and made as if he wanted to speak. He put up his hand and waited for the fury of sound to subside.

It did not happen. For perhaps the first time, the soldiers disobeyed their commander. Jubilantly they kept up their tribute in full volume. The screaming was incessant. Hats, arms, rifles, and flags waved in the air. He could address them later. Right now they were having their say.

Lee, tears evident in his eyes, looked toward Longstreet. From Longstreet's shaggy black beard I saw a flash of white teeth as he gave a rare laugh.

Seeing that his men were not going to let him speak, General Lee reached up to his hat, and in a sudden, emphatic gesture of salute, he doffed it in the air. As a result of that gesture, the impossible happened. It was inconceivable to me that the din could have grown louder, or the frenzied activity became more so. Yet upon Lee's display of respect to his men, those very things happened. The shrill screeching went another octave and actually seemed to redouble. The crimson battle flags whirled crazily.

I looked over at Moxley Sorrel and saw tears on his cheeks.

Lee began moving through the crowd once more. Only when he reached the outskirts of the rail yard did the noise begin to subside. Parting from his soldiers at last, the general set the pace back toward the headquarters clearing.

"Think the Yankees heard us?" I asked Sorrel when we were clear of the mob.

"Damned if I care!" Sorrel exclaimed, daubing his eyes with his gloves. If it were up to me we'd go down that ridge and light into those blue sons of bitches right now! Damn it all, Jed, wasn't that something? The old man gets it all from his boys, doesn't he? Every last bit. Lawdy, not just in battle, but a salute as well!"

On the hill outside of the station a detachment of soldiers from the Army of Tennessee was standing around a fire by the road. They had watched in amazement all that had transpired, and now when General Lee rode by, they took off their caps, which he acknowledged with a nod.

As Sorrel and I came up, one of these soldiers called out, "That Gin'rel of your'n 'pears like a right tony fellow."

"He is," I answered.

"Wish our'n was," the man said dolefully.

At the clearing, Lee pulled up his horse to let his officers come around him. He had recovered from the tribute, although the flush was still on his cheeks.

"Such splendid, magnificent men, General Longstreet," he said. "How God has blessed our cause."

"They do have a way of expressing themselves from time to time," Longstreet said, and this brought chuckles from the staff. Lee smiled.

"See to them, General. See to them, gentlemen. See that they are fed and rested, and then all of you must do the same. General Cleburne will begin his march this morning. When he strikes the enemy, that will be the call for the utmost exertion from us. If fortunate, and careful as well, the enemy will still be unaware of our presence here when it is our turn to attack."

"It'll be good to get this thing going quickly," Longstreet remarked. "I can't see General Grant staying quiet much longer, General Sherman or no General Sherman. Whatever stew he's cooking up, it'll be best to get ours on the plate first."

"From what I have seen and learned thus far, I share your views on the man, General," Lee said. "Nevertheless, we will see how he stands up to the coming test."

"We might just succeed, even with Bragg on our side," Longstreet said caustically.

"Oh, we must succeed, General," replied Lee. He gestured in the direction of Chickamauga Station. "If only for their sake."

As THE soldiers tramped along, the chatter was incessant. They advanced up the road in loose columns for the march, jabbering and throwing acorns. None of them were similarly attired. Their clothes were motley and crudely patched; all manner of different colors prevailed, although grays, browns, and blacks were predominant. Mostly they wore slouch hats for headgear, but there were a number of forage caps as well, and many of these were blue. There were also top hats, bowlers, derbies, and a smattering of gaudy blue confiscations. They looked not like an organized army but rather like a heavily armed, unruly horde, all moving in the same direction.

It was a frosty, sunny November morning. They had all had their coffee and stepped lively toward their objective.

Off to the side of the road, Moxley Sorrel and I sat on horseback with General Cleburne, watching these men go by. Taking in the noisy files, Sorrel raised his hand in salute and said in a stentorian parade-ground tone, "Army of Tennessee, pass in review!"

The three of us laughed, although Cleburne's was the most wholehearted. "The only time they like to dress-right-dress is when they're getting into battle line," he said affectionately.

"Hey there, Gin'rel!" called one of the soldiers. "This hyar's the road to H'atlanter. We all gawn to H'atlanter?"

Cleburne smiled and shrugged.

"Naw, this ain't no march to Atlanta," drawled another. "This here's a retreat. Bragg's finally gotten smart. We'uns all gonna retreat without a battle this time so's folks won't be put out."

Their high morale was unmistakable. So too was their formidability. Their well-oiled rifles were slung, draped, or carried cross shoulder. Cartridge boxes hung from straps or were secured to belts along with canteens and bayonets. Many of the men carried large, homemade Bowie knives, fearsome-looking things, strapped to boots or tied around waists, which I had come to know were prized weapons with the troops of the western Confederacy.

They passed like rabble, saucy and impudent. They had been with the Army of Tennessee at Perryville, Murfreesboro, and Chickamauga. They were seasoned to a man and knew what they were about. This was veteran Confederate infantry—killers of Yankees.

The last of them passed, and artillery brought up the rear. There were no supply wagons.

"I suppose it's time to get going," Cleburne said. "Tell General Lee to keep his ears cocked. He'll be hearing from us in a couple of days if the roads stay dry."

"When do you link up with Forrest?" I asked.

"I expect he'll find me sometime this evening," Cleburne replied. "One of his riders told me this morning that the general would come in person to lead us up. His cavalry's been busy pokin' at the Yankees over in the valley to keep their scouts from venturing too far from the picket lines. That'll be good for us. Any late word on General Sherman's whereabouts?"

"None," I answered.

"Don't worry about Sherman, General," Moxley Sorrel said carelessly. "We'll all take care of him if he shows up."

Cleburne raised an eyebrow at this and looked at Sorrel with a wan smile. "I *will* be counting on you all to take care of him, Major Sorrel—if he shows up."

Sorrel took a bourbon flask from his saddlebag and held it out to Cleburne. "To success."

"To success, and—" General Cleburne took a drink then passed it to me "—a good cavalry screen."

He shook hands with us, touched his hand to his hat in return to our salute, then galloped up the road after his division.

We watched him go with admiration.

"A fine officer that one," said Sorrel.

"Oh, yes. Let's hope he lives."

BACK AT Lee's encampment, Longstreet gave me my orders for the rest of the day. I was to make my usual rounds on Missionary Ridge in the event some important news arrived concerning Sherman or there was a change in the disposition of the Federals around Chattanooga or over in Lookout Valley.

"If you learn anything at all, it will only be because you were present there in person," Longstreet said dourly. "I would not expect Bragg or any of his staff to make an effort to keep us informed of any tactical developments."

Longstreet made no effort to conceal his dislike of Braxton Bragg from his officers, which was common knowledge already.

"Most important," he continued, "keep your eyes on the signal stations, especially the one on Lookout Mountain. That's the one with the best eye on General Grant and General Hooker, and that'll be the one to spot General Sherman as long as there's daylight."

That day on Missionary Ridge, as I rode about the camps of the Army of Tennessee, I was conscious of a change in the weather there, so to speak. Something in the attitudes and demeanor of the soldiers that had not been there during the weary length of the siege at Chattanooga was present now. It was an air of expectation; something felt more than seen, but a palpable tension nonetheless.

The men knew something was up. A fourth of their army had marched off someplace, and Longstreet's corps, which had been earlier sent off to the wilds of East Tennessee, had returned and settled in their rear back at Chickamauga Station. Camped and waiting just like they were, staying warm around their campfires the same as they, all waiting for whatever it was that was sure to happen. Everywhere on the ridge that day I encountered the belief among the soldiers and their officers that the spirit-killing status quo was about to end.

It was well after dark when I returned to Lee's encampment. I found Longstreet conferring with Lee outside his tent.

"All quiet around Chattanooga," I reported. "Still no sign or word of General Sherman. However, there were reports of some light skirmishing around General Hooker's camps over in the Valley."

"That would be General Forrest," Lee said, smiling faintly. "Tomorrow, Major, you and I will ride to General Bragg's headquarters to see how things are keeping up there."

He looked at Longstreet. "Meanwhile, General, we ourselves must make use of this quiet time for as long as it keeps. We must ensure that we have planned with the utmost thoroughness for any contingency. When this affair begins, we must be completely prepared to move our men quickly and efficiently without becoming entangled with the Army of Tennessee. As soon as you can arrange it, I would like to meet with General McLaws and General Jenkins and have them review the maps again. Perhaps some of the brigade commanders as well, the ones you see fit."

"We can do that tonight," Longstreet said.

"Very good," said Lee. "And speaking of maps, General Longstreet, if you will come inside I will show you an interesting terrain feature near one of the enemy's forts that I think could be used to our advantage."

This was my cue to leave, and I did so with a light heart. My old corps was back. Lee and Longstreet were at work on a plan to beat the enemy, and my day was finished. With a profound sense of well-being, I set my thoughts on finding something to eat.

I SUSPENDED MY story to watch the innkeeper's Negro boy drag a log nearly as large as his own small form to the hearth. With a deft half carry, half roll he placed it on the grate, whereupon the fire blazed up, flooding our table with light and heat.

"You know," I said to Deslauries. "Lee's army never ate well, but in the entire war I was never as hungry, or as cold, as during that campaign in Tennessee."

Deslauries nodded. "That winter after Gettysburg was when all of us in Richmond really began to feel the pinch of the blockade," he said. "And the foodstuffs we were accustomed to getting from the inner regions were becoming much scarcer. But it was on our Sunday nights that we felt it the most." Deslauries gave a distracted sigh, then a wistful laugh. "Pardon my little reverie, Major," he said. "I was referring to my wife and I. Sunday nights were always special to us, because we were married on a Sunday. At any rate that was always our night for a special meal as well, usually a smoked turkey or a fine old ham with a good bottle of French champagne. Afterward I would sit in my chair, and my wife would play the piano. She had a wonderful voice besides, and our favorite song was 'Barbara Allen.'" Deslauries smiled at the memory. "Do you know the song? A most beautiful ballad, and there is a poignant line where fair Barbara Allen tells her hero, 'Young man, I think you're dying,' and each time my wife would sing this part, she would pause and look at me, and we let the angel pass between us." Deslauries gave a sigh. "For a while after the war began, we managed to continue this exquisite formality, meal and all, but eventually it became harder and harder to obtain even the basics, bread and butter, let alone a splendid main course, or a good Bordeaux." Concluding sadly, he said, "You know, at the outset we all knew that war was cruel. Intellectually we accepted that. But—" he shook his head, "Sunday evenings without an old ham or a stuffed turkey seemed so . . . uncivilized."

By luck and constant effort, I had managed to keep a straight face during Deslauries's tale of his and his wife's wartime Sunday evenings. Now I agreed with him in a sympathetic tone. "Yes. Quite uncivilized," I said.

The innkeeper appeared at our table. After a quick inspection of the fire, he refilled our glasses. Once again, I expected Deslauries to object, but as before he did not.

"Would the gentlemen care for anything to eat?" he asked primly.

"No thanks," I answered, then with a wink at Deslauries I quipped, "unless perhaps you have a smoked turkey."

The innkeeper was all business. "No sir, I have no turkeys. But I do have hams. My wife is bringing one in from the smokehouse just now for our supper. It would be no trouble to fetch another."

"That's all right," I said. "We have to be going out shortly."

"As you wish, sir," said the innkeeper, and raising his eyes at the rain pelting on the roof he observed, "Bad night for it, though."

He left and just then the front door opened and a woman entered, dressed against the torrent in a large rubber poncho and cradling a bulky ham wrapped in burlap. The poncho glistened with wetness in the firelight, and streams of rainwater ran down the folds, making a puddle by the door. Placing the ham on a table near the door, she slowly pulled off the dripping outerwear, whereupon was revealed to us in measured, dramatic stages a breathtaking specimen of a woman with long raven hair, full body, and striking beauty. As we gaped at this heretofore unseen member of the innkeeper's household, she hung up the poncho, an act that caused her uncorseted waist and proportioned shoulders to strain against her dress. Thereupon she shook out her mane of luxuriant hair, picked up the burlapped ham, and made for the kitchen, a radiant goddess come to earth in the rude confines of Lexington, Virginia.

"Good afternoon, gentlemen," she greeted us in official tone as she passed by, cruelly refusing to smile, and paying us no more interest than a couple of week-old bird droppings.

Speechless, I looked at Deslauries, but he too was incapable of addressing the vision.

"Pray, proceed with your story, Major," he said glumly.

"On the next day, it was late morning before General Lee was ready to set out for Missionary Ridge," I went on. "At the onset of our ride, the general was in a casual conversational mood, talking of the weather and the terrain of Tennessee."

"You have been here as long as anyone, Major," Lee said. "How have you found this portion of our Confederacy?"

"Rugged and beautiful," I answered. "Sometimes I think it goes on forever, especially taking in the view on Lookout Mountain. But I've got to confess, General, I'll be glad to see Virginia again."

"Yes," Lee agreed. "I was thinking of Virginia this morning. When we conclude this matter at hand, I will take great comfort in planning our return there."

As we came up the ridge we were met by a hard-riding sergeant, one of Longstreet's men posted to watch the Yankees. The man reined up and saluted.

"General Lee, it's good to see you, sir. I was just riding back to the corps to report. Somebody better come up and take a look at what the Yankees are doing right now."

"Is it General Sherman?" Lee asked sharply.

"No, General. It's General Grant, sir, or rather the Army of the Cumberland. They've come out of their works, and they're to-in' and fro-in' right smart like on the plain now. Looks like a parade, it does."

"Are they forming for an attack?" Lee demanded.

The sergeant looked uncomfortable. "I can't say for sure, General. Right now they're just traipsin' around. But there's a whole lot of them, so you gotta figure they have something in mind."

"If we ride up a short way there's a spot we can get a look, General," I said.

"Go report to Longstreet," Lee commanded the sergeant as we rode off.

I led the way at a gallop along the road until we came to a stand of trees where we tethered the horses. Beyond was a vantage point that afforded a full view of Chattanooga and a partial view of the plain, but the partial view was enough to confirm the sergeant's summation. Large columns of blue infantry were on the march out from the town. They were already on the plain, and we could see large formations, probably brigades, in the midst of forming a long line abreast.

Lee was looking intently through my field glasses.

"A frontal assault?" I asked aloud, unbelieving. Rapidly I conjured up the defenses of the Army of Tennessee on Missionary Ridge, flawed but terribly formidable. And many guns.

"General Grant doesn't have the men to take the ridge," I said. "He's got to know that, General. Not without General Hooker at least. He's got to know that."

Lee didn't answer, but I could see he was weighing that same evidence. I went over in my mind Bragg's order of battle on Missionary Ridge, calculating numbers and unit strengths. The Army of Tennessee's defensive advantage was preponderant. Was Grant a fool?

"General Grant did order a frontal assault when he got to Vicksburg," I said, seized with a hopeful idea.

"Yes," Lee agreed thoughtfully.

"And it was repulsed decidedly," I said, finishing the thought for both of us. "Maybe this general is going to provide Bragg with his own Fredericksburg after all."

Lee was frowning as he handed back my glasses. "No Major, I think not. No Fredericksburg here." Then he ordered. "Let us proceed at once to General Bragg's headquarters!"

We regained the road and cantered along the ridge. Along the breastworks and gun positions we passed, the soldiers were in a holiday mood, standing atop their trenches, watching the pageant on the plain and calling their comrades to join them.

"Them bluebellies is havin' themselves a review!" a private shouted to his friends.

Lee said nothing as we hurried along, acknowledging neither greetings nor questions. Coming into the yard of Bragg's headquarters, I saw a group of staff officers standing on a nearby knoll, absorbed with the movement below. As orderlies took our

Missionary Ridge (on the far right) in relation to Chattanooga.
The ridge extends to the north and far to the south.

horses, Lee was already dismounted and calling once more for my field glasses. I joined him on the knoll, noticing to my fury that Bragg's officers had sidestepped away to increase their distance from Lee; no one from the group offered to brief him. Yet as I looked down on the plain, it was clear what was happening.

It was a parade-ground procession; the gawking Rebels had not been wrong. Union columns wheeled smartly and went into line. Regimental flags snapped in the wind. Mounted officers on horseback waved swords and gesticulated. Very faintly, carried by the wind, came the stutter sounds of bugles.

Lee watched without a word, his jaw clenched, grimly silent.

Again the formations on the plain shifted. Swords flashed, flags billowed, and the blue columns wheeled and counter-marched. Nearby, a jovial group of Rebel soldiers applauded.

It was indeed a thrilling sight, and I wished I had brought an extra set of field glasses. I squinted, counting flags and groups as accurately as I could.

"I make it at two divisions, General," I said. "They'll never do it. They'll be destroyed if they try to take this place."

"The enemy is not after this place today, Major," Lee responded tersely. "Orchard Knob is what he's after. And unless reinforcements are sent there now, this very minute, he shall have it."

Lee shot an angry look in the direction of Bragg's officers and beckoned impatiently. A major detached himself from the group and came forward warily.

"Where is your general, sir?" Lee demanded.

"He's gone off along the line, sir," the major answered.

"The enemy is about to test your center, sir. He is coming for Orchard Knob. Are you prepared to receive him there?"

Lee's eyes fixed on the man. The major flushed then stammered, "I— the position is fortified, sir—we—I am certain that General Bragg is looking into matters and does not expect the Yankees to attack."

"You have only to use your eyes, sir!" Lee stormed. He was interrupted by a loud *Pop!*

Above Orchard Knob a thick bloom of sooty white smoke blossomed then hung lazily in the clear, sunny sky. A faint low boom reached our ears, then several booms together, and I saw the distant puffs of smoke where a Yankee battery had unlimbered. Over Orchard Knob there was another pop, louder than the first, and a second smoke blossom hung next to the dissipating first. Two more shells exploded in the trees in front of the knob. Lines of sparks appeared in the sky, whereupon two more airbursts were followed by two solid, direct-hit explosions on one of Orchard Knob's rifle pits. This last drew a moan from the nearby soldiers, whose spectator amusement had now turned to dire consternation.

We watched, transfixed.

The short barrage stopped. Then, once more coming on the air, was the faint stutter of bugles, not a few but many. As we watched, a long, dark wave of Yankee infantry surged forward in splendid alignment, bright flags in the lead, dark masses following, moving fast, sunlight glistening on the wall of bayonets in motion. A successive wave of Union infantry moved out immediately behind them, following the first.

Despite the threat this posed to our side, I could not help but marvel at the sight. It was a picture-book charge, like ones I had seen depicted in accounts of the great European battles. During this time, the major from Bragg's staff took the opportunity to hurry away, unnoticed by Lee, whose attention was riveted on the attack in progress.

The precipitate Yankee charge had ended the holiday celebration on Missionary Ridge. In an instant, the handsome Yankee parade lines had been turned into grim, attacking battle waves. The lone Rebel battery posted on Orchard Knob opened fire. Soldiers in the trenches there loosed a heavy volley, sending a small cloud of smoke up through the trees.

The Federals advanced relentlessly. Their first wave was beginning to be obscured by the smoke, but clearly the Rebel gunners were not slowing them down. Nearby to where we were standing, a battery opened in support of their hard-pressed comrades, but Orchard Knob was at the maximum range for most of the guns on the ridge.

Lee spoke, and his voice was quiet with agitation and suppressed anger. "They will have their objective and quickly, unless the position is supported immediately. Indeed, it might already be too late."

That was my view as well, that it was already too late. The elevated knoll that was Orchard Knob, and the surrounding woods, were all filled with the smoke and roar of battle. The first Union attack wave had completely disappeared into this cauldron, and the second line of bayonets was bearing down swiftly. Scanning out from the base of Missionary Ridge, I saw no reinforcements coming forward, but witnessed instead trickles of gray stragglers leaking back from the smoke-filled terrain of Orchard Knob, making quickly for the safety of the trenches at the bottom of the ridge. As I watched, these trickles soon became steady streams of retreating Confederates scurrying rearward. Through the drifting smoke on Orchard Knob I caught my first glimpse of a Union battle flag on the crest of the hill. Others appeared beside it, and in the woods and slopes on either side of the knob, there were more.

The Federals succeeded in occupying the position. Their sudden attack had caved in the foremost point of the Army of Tennessee, and it had been accomplished in only minutes.

More guns on Missionary Ridge took up the dispute, and for a time shot and shell exploded over and near what had formerly been Rebel property. Yet the shelling was poorly concentrated, and most of the shots were falling short. Lee now had his glasses trained watchfully on the rifle pits at the bottom of Missionary Ridge, in obvious anticipation of an explosive counterattack that he would have ordered immediately. Nothing happened, and I felt the old man's ire mounting.

Yet I still held out hope, the hope that the Federals, buoyed by their easy success, would continue the attack against Missionary Ridge, where it could be broken to pieces. If Yankee pluck could take a forward position, Yankee folly could lose everything just as easily. I had seen it happen before in the East, and it could happen here as well.

So I reasoned, and so I came to see my error as the reality spoke otherwise. The smoke cleared from Orchard Knob, and there, as well as in the surrounding woods and thickets, the Federals could clearly be seen to be consolidating their ranks, not for attack, but for defense. Grant, it seemed, was no fool.

A few more angry shots from Missionary Ridge were sent sputtering toward the newest position of the Army of the Cumberland, but then these too stopped. The thing was over.

Without a word Lee handed back my field glasses. His dark eyes glittered with anger.

At that moment, General Bragg himself came into the yard. Waiting for him to dismount, Lee approached formally.

"General Lee," Bragg said upon seeing him.

"General Bragg," Lee replied coolly. His tone was even, his demeanor calm. Only the fire-lit eyes showed what he was truly feeling. "General, what has happened here?" he asked.

"As you have certainly seen for yourself, General, the Yankees have driven in one of my outposts." Bragg sounded calm, almost nonchalant.

"Orchard Knob, an outpost? If you permit me, General, I must say that I always considered it more than that." Lee's protest was polite, but the heat behind it was substantial. "That was the forward position of your army, sir. That was the place where our final assault on the enemy was to be made. We agreed on that, if I recall correctly. Now it is in the hands of those people, General, and will have to be retaken in order for us to get at Chattanooga and prior to any decisive thrust to destroy the enemy on this side of the city."

Bragg was blinking again. And as was his wont when dealing with Lee, he would not, or could not, look him in the eye, so his response was directed to a point over Lee's shoulder.

"The enemy has inflicted no damage to me, General," Bragg replied irritably. "He has merely seized an outpost of no consequence to the defense of this army."

"I must register my strong disagreement of your assessment of Orchard Knob, General Bragg," Lee said tersely. "That 'outpost,' as you call it, sir, is of enormous consequence to the enemy's defense of *his* army. It is now in the way of our attack on Chattanooga, whereas before there was nothing between us and the enemy.

Bragg said nothing but frowned into the air, blinking darkly.

"They are fortifying as we speak, General Bragg," Lee persisted. He had softened his voice, and there was a persuasive tone in it. "The position will have to be retaken sooner or later in order to carry out our own plans. The longer the delay, sir, the more troops the enemy can bring up there."

Suddenly, Bragg responded. "Then let them do it!" he snapped, looking now directly at Lee. "I say let them do it! Let them all come out of their thick earthworks around Chattanooga and settle themselves at our feet, for that brings them closer to our reach! Had you thought of that, sir? For if our goal is to attack the enemy as you have insisted on the matter, then they have only made it easier for us. We'll only have to go a short distance to get at them, instead of walking across an open plain."

Lee made to argue, but Bragg was not finished. His staff had come up, and he went on volubly. "Yes sir, let them come! Indeed, I hope they do. In fact, sir, I hope they continue the attack! Yes, attack right now!" He waved his arms to left and right, indicating the extensive entrenchments of his army. "Let the enemy try to storm these positions, take this high ground. He'll find it considerably more daunting than the seizure of a mere picket post! We have lost nothing, General. Nothing! The enemy has taken nothing from us. This skirmish has done nothing to further threaten my army, sir, nor has it further threatened yours."

He was finished, his face twitching with animation and anger, and he glowered now at Lee. Behind him, his staff gave frowning nods of approval. I stared at the ground and tried to hide my overwhelming disgust, but I must not have succeeded, for I noticed Bragg make a quick glance in my direction.

There was a brief silence. Then Lee spoke. "Very well, General Bragg," he said quietly. "It is your army of course. I defer to your judgment on this."

Bragg looked startled. Whatever he had expected and feared in reply from Lee, it was clearly not this, Lee's capitulation in the face of his histrionics. Yet I knew this was no capitulation. The truth was that Lee had to continue to work with this officer, and that the really big event was yet to come, the moment where Bragg's cooperation counted for everything. It was for this that Lee was keeping his powder dry.

Nevertheless, what had just happened at Orchard Knob had been a galling setback as far as Lee was concerned. Nor was he entirely capable of forcing good humor when he felt just the opposite. His face was expressionless and his voice was flat. Anybody but General Bragg would have found this formality uncomfortable.

"I actually came by to speak with you on another matter, General, before all this," Lee said.

Bragg, now recovered from his strenuous arguments, nodded stiffly. "Yes, I received word this morning that you would be calling, to discuss terrain and enemy positions I was told. I rather thought we had exhausted those topics previously, but if you wish, we can go inside and talk." Casting a cold, contemptuous eye in my direction, he added, "I suppose you will want your mapmaker along as well."

IT HAD been a terrible day. That night I tried to sleep. I was very tired and had not managed to find anything to eat. I wanted desperately to drop off, but sleep would not come. And it was cold, as usual.

The apprehension I had felt since that afternoon at Bragg's headquarters had not gone away. My old euphoria was gone. Bragg had killed it. Here in Tennessee, it was as though we were all in the throes of some evil malediction, caused by the region itself. A region where nothing worked like it was supposed to. Where nothing worked like it did in the East, for this was certainly not Virginia. Not the place nor the people. Here, the powers of God, the cause, and General Lee seemed to have little sway. Hostile and malignant forces held forth in this wild land, and aside from the industrial cities of Atlanta and Mobile, maybe it was best to let the Yankees have the western Confederacy. Let them have it all.

I stirred uneasily in my blankets. A terrible thought. A bitter observation. Like something I would expect from Bragg.

Through tightly closed eyes I saw again the frowning, obdurate face, with no trace of victory in it, and his sneer as he said, "Bring along your mapmaker as well." This and the other disheartening events of the day rolled endlessly through my sleep-starved brain. The wheeling, tramping blue columns. The slow puff of an artillery shot spreading like a small flower over Orchard Knob. The magnificent, determined charge. Banners of victorious Stars and Stripes dancing through the smoke. Bragg blinking. The gloomy ride back to Chickamauga Station, Lee not uttering a word. Longstreet had uttered words however, a bitter denunciation; "Bragg's a damn fool, General Lee. Now you know it for yourself." And Lee's rejoinder had been, "Please, General, no more such recriminations, for we are all arrayed here by God's will to defeat a common foe."

God's will. Common foe. Grant. Ulysses S. Grant. A distant rider on a black horse on the plain in front of Chattanooga.

I felt a hand on my shoulder and heard my name spoken. Quickly I whirled out of my blankets and sat up. Had I been asleep? A sentry was standing over me.

"What is it?" I asked breathlessly.

"Got a courier with an urgent message for General Lee," the sentry replied.

"Very good. Send him forward."

I stood up and shivered. The air was extremely damp. Striking a match, I looked at my watch. An hour until dawn. The hour when men's hearts were lowest, I quoted to myself and tried to recall the work and the author.

In the chilly darkness before me, a figure approached carefully, leading a horse. I recognized him as a lieutenant from one of the scouting patrols that Longstreet had ordered out earlier in the evening.

"Major Hotchkiss?" he asked quietly.

"Yes."

The lieutenant came forward and gave me his message. I heard it and shivered violently, feeling sick to my stomach and feeling as well the full and somewhat literal meaning of the phrase "despair before dawn."

"Are you absolutely sure?" I asked.

"Yes, Major."

I went forward to Lee's tent. It was dark and still inside, and I tried to make out the shape of the cot.

"General Lee?"

"What is it, Major?" The voice was alert and awake.

"Sir, General Sherman is crossing the Tennessee in force north of Chattanooga."

"Where?"

"At Chickamauga Creek, sir."

There was neither hesitation nor excitement in Lee's words. "Inform General Longstreet at once. Tell him to move General McLaws's division forward immediately to support General Hardee. Let there be no delay."

"Yes sir."

"Inform General Longstreet that I will be with him shortly. What is the time please, Major?"

I told him. He only said, "We will use the darkness."

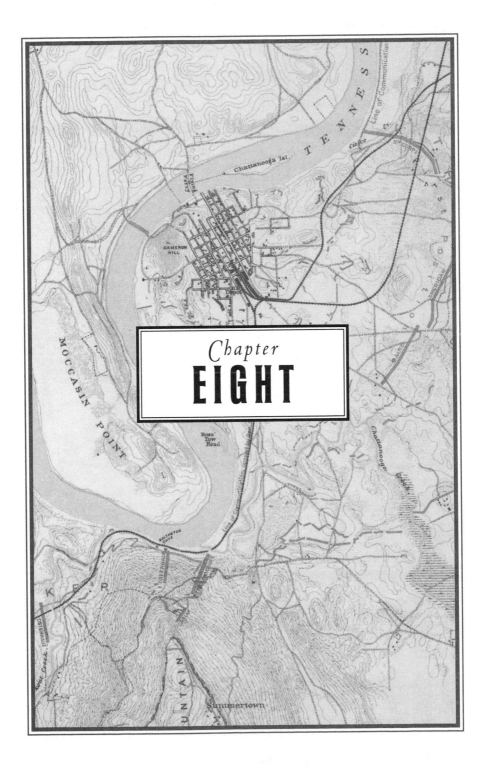

Chapter
EIGHT

*T*HE FOG AND MIST were heaviest toward the river, from whence came the skirmish fire. The shots were sharp and crystalline in the cold morning air—and ominous.

Before long the firing began sounding closer to the hill we were on, a sign that the Yankees were moving steadily in from the river, their skirmishers probing through the fog. Toward the direction of the river there was nothing to see but low-hanging fog and the shadowy tops of the trees, but I fancied I could feel their location in strength down in the river valley. Two divisions were already across, it was reported, and more coming. General Sherman and his Western Yankees had arrived.

Standing with his back to the river, the skirmish fire, and the entire fog-shrouded Federal advance was Lee. With him were Longstreet and Lafayette McLaws. Also participating in this gathering was the Army of Tennessee's William J. Hardee, who looked quite the Southern aristocrat in the cold, sunless dawn. He wore a wide-brimmed hat of quality and was wrapped in a cloak.

With his back to the approaching enemy, Lee was looking up the slope of hills where he intended to stop them. Up from the river and low valleys there was no fog, but there were thin patches of mist. On the tops of the highest hills a drizzling rain was falling. Lee was talking quietly to his generals, pointing to a line of wooded ridges where could be seen soldiers of McLaws's division rolling logs to support the breastworks.

Out of sight in the trees and mist, Lee had ordered artillery positioned. Hardee's corps had been greatly diminished with Cleburne's departure, but those who remained were battle-hardened veterans. So too were the men of McLaws's division who had come up in support and were now fortifying on the right of their Western comrades in arms. As for the terrain, even a superficial glance was sufficient to reveal the natural defensive features.

Yet as far as I was concerned, none of this helped. Even after seeing the preparations for myself, as well as having Lee on the scene right now, I could not shake the depression and despondency that had come over me in the predawn, when the courier had delivered his dispiriting message. I had not slept, and I felt drawn and tired, totally incapable of optimism.

Our position here was strong, to be sure, but the hard core of Hardee's men and his best general, Cleburne, was off and gone on a cross-country hike. Only God knew where they were this morning. And as for McLaws, though his men were doughty fighters, his was the smallest division in Longstreet's corps. And the ten thousand or more men in Sherman's army coming up from the fog below were known to be doughty fighters as well.

Yesterday was when it had all started to come apart, I decided. Grant, not Lee or Bragg, had made the first move and taken Orchard Knob. And now Sherman was here. Not only on hand but also across the Tennessee. I wondered if Lee still thought his plan could succeed. Was it wise to even try it now? I didn't know. And I wasn't a general.

Profoundly depressed, I adjusted my scarf, flicked the reins back and forth in my hands, and tried to think about nothing.

A small fire had been kindled, and an orderly summoned the generals to coffee. Lee looked thoughtful but untroubled. Hardee looked the same. Longstreet was taciturn as usual, but he would be so even if the whole world was collapsing. So too would McLaws, who like his corps commander was a man of few words. Except that McLaws was much shorter than the big-bodied Longstreet, the two men actually resembled each other very much, having identical long, shaggy beards and wide shoulders, a likeness always remarked upon with amusement by staff and strangers alike.

But this morning there was nothing amusing about anything.

The generals stood around the fire and drank their coffee. It was a strangely passive scene. Staff officers dismounted and with their horses formed a semicircle around the generals. We stood quietly, little conversation among ourselves, listening to the skirmish fire and watching our respective commanders.

Moxley Sorrel came riding up from the direction of the river. The fog was thinning, he said, and he went on to corroborate earlier reports regarding enemy unit strength and numbers, but his last statement contained new information. Sherman himself was present on this side of the river.

Lee received this calmly then looked at each of his generals in turn. "He intends to pass this way and take Missionary Ridge in flank. Yet I am very confident that we can deny him the ground he wants. Our own ground is very good, the best we could wish for, I think."

Longstreet nodded. "It is. We can hold him here until spring if we have to. He won't be able to maneuver and will have to come at us on a narrow front. The only place he'll be able to go is back."

"We must only ensure that he does not go forward," Lee smiled grimly. Then he added emphatically. "He must not be allowed to go beyond those hills. It is in keeping General Sherman here that we render his force irrelevant to carrying our own designs."

He looked to Hardee. "When it starts, he will think he is up against your people, General Hardee. As much as possible I would like to keep him from discovering the falsehood of this. To my knowledge, there is nothing that would cause him to believe that General Longstreet's corps is here, as opposed to still confronting General Burnside at Knoxville."

Longstreet turned to McLaws. "General, you are forbidden to have any of your men taken prisoner today."

Lee and Hardee nodded in amusement.

There was a spatter of musketry, sounding close to the hill. The generals ignored it, standing quiet for a time, looking into the campfire. Then Lee said to McLaws. "I would have preferred using your men in an attack role for the coming assault against

Chattanooga, General. But this coming of General Sherman forces us to shift our weight somewhat."

"Sometimes one is forced to cut the cards with the devil, General," McLaws said blandly.

Lee smiled. "Yes. And if your brave soldiers, along with General Hardee's veterans of Chickamauga, are sufficient enough to contain the enemy in a costly and time-wasting cul-de-sac, then I will consider the cut of the deal well in our favor."

Then he spoke to all of them somberly. "There is nothing hidden from us now, gentlemen. The mystery is gone. Here is General Sherman at last. We now know where each component of the enemy force is. There is no longer any further need for worried conjecture or surmise. Our own plan is in motion and moving toward its climax. We must resist any attempts by the enemy to put us off it." He looked at Hardee and McLaws in turn. Nodding in the direction of the firing he said, "Those people cannot be allowed to interfere."

"They shall not do so, General Lee!" Hardee declared with rare emotion.

"Thank you, General," Lee said quietly.

I stared at Lee in wonder. He was talking like we could still win. Was it possible we could?

From the foggy bottom of our hill came a quick flurry of shots then the crash of a volley.

Longstreet looked at Lee. "We probably should go."

"Yes, I suppose you are right," Lee replied, taking a last sip from his cup.

A courier came pounding up, coming from the direction of Missionary Ridge. I recognized him as a junior officer from Bragg's staff.

"What is it, Lieutenant?" Hardee demanded when he came forward.

The lieutenant saluted. "Sir, General Bragg sent me to inform you and General Lee that he is very concerned over what is happening here, and I am to tell you that he is on his way now to consult with both of you in person, as well as to assure himself of your readiness to meet this attack."

There was no doubt that this message came from Braxton Bragg. Longstreet grimaced. Hardee became coldly rigid. Lee spoke politely. "Thank you, Lieutenant. Please inform General Bragg that we are as ready as God can make us to meet this incursion, and that might prove sufficient. Moreover, General Hardee and I will be pleased to consult with him when he arrives.

"Yes sir," said the courier. "There is also another message General."

"Yes?" Lee inquired.

"The signal station on Lookout Mountain reports heavy firing coming from Lookout Valley."

All heads turned toward the young lieutenant. In an instant the air of the campfire gathering had become fully charged.

"Artillery as well?" questioned Lee.

"Yes sir."

"What can they make out from up there?" Longstreet demanded.

"Just sound," the lieutenant answered, slightly flustered. "Lookout's fogged over real bad, but the station sent word of heavy continuous firing beginning at daylight, but they can't see into the valley to see who's engaged."

"It is General Cleburne," Lee announced. "It is General Cleburne and General Forrest engaged with General Hooker." His eyes were flashing with an aggressive glint. "Now the battle is truly begun."

Everyone mounted, and the generals led the way up the slope toward our lines. Before we had gone far, Bragg himself came galloping out of the trees toward us, reining up in front of Lee and Hardee, both horse and rider wild-eyed.

"General Lee!" Bragg exclaimed, ignoring the other generals and cocking his head angrily to the sudden popping of shots nearby. "Well then, General Lee! Well then, sir! What about this?"

"Good morning, General Bragg."

"Good morning?" Bragg snorted. "Oh, I like that, sir! That firing is coming from none other than General Sherman's army, which has crossed the river to our side. And that is them firing, sir!"

"Some of the firing is ours," Longstreet said in acid sarcasm. "We told our men they could shoot back."

Bragg ignored this and continued to address Lee in strident agitation. "This is a different situation now, General Lee, quite different. We had not discussed this happening when we made our plans, and now we must think on how to change them. I would know your thoughts on this, sir!"

Lee regarded him calmly. "I have been informed of the sounds of firing over in Lookout Valley, General, which is good news. That would be General Cleburne, of course."

Bragg gestured impatiently. "And what if it is, sir! Little use he is to us there, when he should be right here putting his men to full employment in order to hold this ground!"

"We already have enough men to hold this ground, General," Lee said with assurance, and something in his tone caused Bragg to cease his remonstrances and look at him.

"We will hold them from up there." Lee pointed to the misty slopes above us. "And we will hold them with the force we have presently assembled."

Lee glanced in turn from Longstreet to Hardee and then to McLaws. Each of them nodded. Lee was every bit the commander now, in appearance and voice. I had seen it often, but it never failed to embolden me. Bragg stared at him, blinking. Lee looked intently back at him.

"No sir. There must be no changes. The thing is happening now—and it is happening as we wished. We are committed. Today will necessarily be an anxious one for us, but it must be so. This part of our army," he nodded uphill, "will contain General Sherman's incursion."

"And what of the rest of our army?" Bragg demanded almost shrilly. He was blinking, fidgeting, clearly unnerved, clearly not liking what was happening, but just as clearly brought under the spell of Lee's influence.

Lee answered him. "The rest of the army, General Bragg, all those not engaged today, will watch and wait for word from General Cleburne and prepare for tomorrow when we all go in to attack the Army of the Cumberland."

Lee turned his horse's head to resume the ride toward our lines. "Come, General. Let us go up together and inspect the defenses that have been prepared. Also we need to begin formulation of our specific plans for the attack tomorrow. How does Orchard Knob look today? Has there been heavy entrenching by the enemy overnight? I am most concerned that retaking that place does not cost undue time."

Lee moved off, the glowering, nonplused Bragg riding beside him. Awestruck, I looked after them, and I marveled at how Lee moved ahead of things that had not as yet happened. On a day that had scarcely begun, and where serious reverses were a real possibility, the general's mind was already on tomorrow.

Longstreet beckoned to me.

"Get up to Lookout Mountain and find out what's going on," he growled. I don't want to have to rely on any information that comes from Bragg's headquarters."

THE FOG was thick at the base of Lookout Mountain, so that it took me several minutes to find the rutted road that snaked and twisted toward the summit. Finding it at last, I began the ascent, going slowly into the chill, dripping wetness. Thick strands of mist hung everywhere, particularly in the trees and gullies. The air was piercingly damp, and I shivered violently in my coat.

Drawing near to the mountain on my ride along Missionary Ridge, I had begun to hear the clump of guns from over in Lookout Valley. Now as I ascended the trail, it was clearly audible. I allowed myself to think about the possibility of a victory only to keep my mind off the cold. *A good general, this Patrick Cleburne,*

I thought. Not a West Pointer though, which was the kind Lee favored. But Lee had picked him as his Western Stonewall, and the results would hopefully confirm the wisdom of it.

A half-hour later I came to a turn in the road that placed me in the vicinity of the signal station. It was not on the road, however, and the rest of my climb would have to be on foot. Tethering my horse, I started up a slippery footpath through massive rocks. Soon I was guided by the luminous glow of what was obviously a large fire farther on. Reaching the top, I made my way cautiously toward it. There were no sentries. I came up on the signalers of the station clustered comfortably around a heaping bonfire.

The reason for their idleness was readily apparent. Visibility beyond the fire was nonexistent. What on a clear day would have been a panoramic view of uncountable miles was now a solid wall of gray fog. But out beyond, coming up from the invisible Lookout Valley, was the unmistakable thump and racket of battle.

The signal sergeant came forward to greet me.

"And how is the major this morning?" he asked as he saluted. "Perhaps you'd care for a cup of tea?"

"You bet I would."

"And what seems to be happening here, Sergeant Kirk-patrick?" I asked.

"We might be asking you the same," Kirkpatrick replied coyly. "It started at daylight from that direction—" He pointed southwest through the fog. "And it has been creepin' north ever since." There was another rumble of guns. "And there it is, creepin' farther still. Didn't know we had anything down there but cavalry."

"And you've not been able to see anything?" I queried.

The sergeant smiled at the gray wall all around us. "Just this. I've sent two of the lads down the far side to see if they can get a peek under. I told 'em not to come back until they did. I hope they didn't fall off the cliff."

"Sounds like a real donnybrook down there," a soldier by the fire remarked.

"Let's hope it is," I said.

"Who's stirrin' the pot?" asked the sergeant. "Some of your Army of Northern Virginia folks?"

I smiled. "No, Sergeant. It's some of your Army of Tennessee folks. General Cleburne."

"Well then!" the sergeant exclaimed. "Cleburne and his boys, what marched so mysteriously off the ridge two days back. So it was Hooker they were goin' for. Bless his Irish heart!"

I remained at the signal station for well over an hour, listening to the guns and hoping for the fog to clear. It did not, nor did the sergeant's men return. At length I decided to go back and report what I had learned to Longstreet.

"Don't worry, Major," said the signal sergeant. "I'll go down myself and have a look around. If we can get a line of sight to the valley from anyplace on the mountain, we'll get something to you. Tell your generals that. And Cleburne's people know enough to keep their eyes skinned for us. After all, it's not Bragg's staff of chuckleheads we're dealing with."

THE SOUNDS of the guns from the valley had receded behind me. But later, as I galloped back along the crest of Missionary Ridge, I picked up the rolling growl of artillery in the direction I was heading. Sherman and his Vicksburg veterans had run into McLaws and Hardee.

I wondered how the affair was going. The booming was constant, signifying many guns at work. Undoubtedly, the fighting had been going on all morning, while I was on Lookout Mountain. It was noon now, and I pressed on quickly.

As I passed along the camps and entrenchments of Missionary Ridge, I looked at the soldiers. They had been told little, but the sounds of battle reaching them from two opposite directions was all they needed to comprehend the new situation as it pertained to themselves. The lulling inactivity of the past two months was ended. There was no skylarking or wandering about this morning. The men clustered in quiet groups around their fires, cocking their heads to each new roll of the artillery and talking soberly. In some places the arms were not stacked but were being held or inspected by their owners while they smoked and tried to relax.

As I drew near to the far end of the ridge, my anxiety heightened. I knew that if Hardee and McLaws were hard pressed and things got really bad, Longstreet's remaining division, Hood's, comprised mostly of Texans, could be ordered up from Chickamauga Station. But that would be a costly thing, for with McLaws on the defensive, Hood's division was the only part of Lee's command left to go on the attack tomorrow, a crucial role.

In the near distance I could see smoke rising above the hilltops and concluded optimistically that this was right about the spot where the Confederate trenches ought to be. At least the line hadn't been broken. I spurred my horse toward the sound of battle.

A short way on I encountered a hard-riding courier from the Army of Tennessee heading in the opposite direction. He had wonderful news. Yes, he told me breathlessly, Sherman's Yankees had been coming on all morning and right into a brick wall. Yes, by thunder, every single time, and yes, it was wonderful news. But no, Longstreet was not there anymore; neither was Lee. Both had returned to Chickamauga Station and left the matter to Hardee and McLaws.

This in itself was a good omen, for if disaster was imminent, or the issue was in any way in doubt, either Lee or Longstreet or both senior officers would have remained on the scene. Yet I was disappointed, wanting greatly to see the battlefront myself. But now, angling off from the smoke and roar of battle two hilltops away, I headed for Chickamauga Station.

The men of Hood's division were disposed comfortably around the rail yard, listening to the close sounds of battle in high spirits. They were aware that their own show would be coming soon, having been informed by their officers that after dark they would be marching to Missionary Ridge, and from there to an undisclosed jump-off spot for an early dawn attack on an important objective identified by their own Marse Robert.

I found Longstreet with Lee and made the report of my ride to Lookout Mountain. Longstreet listened attentively.

"No one has actually seen anything?" he inquired.

"No sir."

Longstreet looked at Lee. "Do we dare proceed with our plans based solely on battle sounds?"

"Yes," Lee replied. "I believe we must. I base this on my confidence in General Cleburne. And as the major has pointed out, the sounds are favorable."

I was about to take my leave when Lee said, "Major, come to the map, if you please. I would have you describe the terrain features near a particular spot." He pointed to the map. "Please be precise. This appears to be a gully, and the distance from there to here is perhaps half a mile. Am I mistaken?"

I drew in my breath. There was indeed a wooded gully where the general pointed, half a mile of open ground was about right, and the "here" to which Lee referred was none other than the formidable Fort Negley. I confirmed the general's surmises, then added hesitantly, "That's unquestionably their strongest redoubt, General Lee, as I assume you know."

"Thank you for pointing that out, Major," Longstreet said dryly, and I lapsed into embarrassed silence.

Lee smiled and laid a reassuring hand on my shoulder. "It is indeed their best-built fort, Major, and in appearance very formidable. It is also the only place along the entire enemy line around Chattanooga where we can get our people the closest without being observed, as you just confirmed for me." He put his finger on the map again. "After dark we will bring Hood's division down Missionary Ridge and take them along this creek bed to the low area of the gully, where they will stay until morning. With your acute knowledge of the terrain, Major, do you see any problems with this?"

"None at all," I answered.

Lee looked at Longstreet and tapped the diagram I had made of Fort Negley. "Yes, I feel quite strongly that this should be the spot. It will also be the best place for our men to resist the strong counterattacks that will inevitably follow. Do you concur, General?"

Longstreet nodded his approval. "If we're going to attack, that's the best place of any, especially with all the advantages you cited. Don't like that open ground, though; they'll have to move quick, but as you pointed out, it's the shortest distance we could find."

"We are in accord then," Lee replied. "We will put General Jenkins down there tonight, under cover of darkness. The Texans will spearhead the assault at first light. The remaining brigades will follow them in." And he added, "We should have sufficient strength to carry this out, provided no extra help is needed in holding General Sherman."

"Yes sir," said Longstreet.

Lee looked at me curiously. "You are troubled, Major Hotchkiss," he said.

I was more than troubled. I was horrified. It was Fort Negley that had done it. Feeling my cheeks redden and making sure not to look at Longstreet, I ventured into the breech. I pointed to the bold black lines I had drawn on the diagram.

"General, these represent artillery batteries." As a former officer of engineers, Lee of course knew what the lines meant, which made me feel even more foolish, but it was his and Longstreet's failure to even acknowledge their murderous presence that gave me the courage to point out something that both generals, for some appalling and inexplicable reason, had chosen to overlook.

"The enfilading fire from those guns will break up the attack long before it gets close to the earthworks." I concluded nervously, "I have seen those guns, sir. Our assault won't have a chance."

I waited for the explosion. To my surprise, Longstreet gave a grunt of amusement. Lee was looking at me with an expression of surprise. "Why, Major Hotchkiss, there are no guns there, sir!" he said. He looked at Longstreet with twinkling eyes. "Be so kind, General," he said.

"The guns have been removed from Fort Negley, Major Hotchkiss," Longstreet said in a weary, very senior to very junior tone. "They were pulled out this morning and put into battery around Orchard Knob, probably because that's where General Grant first expects to use them. Fort Negley is only held by infantry now."

"Of course, going about your duties today as you were, there would have been no way for you to know that," Lee said soothingly.

"Please accept my apologies, sir!" I exclaimed and vowed never to utter another word for the rest of my life.

"That's all right, Major," Longstreet quipped. "We both feel better when you can check our work."

The generals fell silent studying the map again. At length, it was Longstreet who spoke, and his tone was serious.

"I believe we can do it, General," he said with deliberation. "I think we can pull it off if we hit them early and fast. We can be in their works, sitting on their flank if we do our job properly. But that won't be enough, General Lee—if others don't do theirs."

"Meaning the Army of Tennessee, General?" Lee asked.

"Orchard Knob should not be in enemy hands right now, sir," Longstreet said tersely. "You don't allow mistakes like that to happen when you've got a man like General Grant down there. It means my men will be attacking tomorrow with a sizable Yankee force on their right rear. I will hold him personally accountable for the safety of my men in that direction."

"He will be accountable, General Longstreet," Lee said. "As soon as your attack opens, he will open his to surprise and overwhelm Orchard Knob. That is the plan we all agreed upon, as you will recall."

Under Lee's reassuring stare, Longstreet's own eyes wavered. "Yes, I know the plan," he said quietly. "And I heard Bragg. But I don't trust him. I don't like relying on him."

Lee smiled. "It was the noble Wellington who said, 'We must rely on each other.'"

Longstreet shrugged and took his gloves from the table. "I'd better ride over and see how General McLaws is doing."

"Good," said Lee. "I myself will ride up to General Bragg's headquarters. I will ask him to schedule a meeting for tonight. His commanders and ours. And we should have more good news from Cleburne's theater by then."

Lee looked at me. "Major, I will ask you to personally guide General Jenkins and General Hood's division down to their attack point tonight. We cannot take the chance of having them get lost."

"Of course, General," I responded.

"Also, if you would be so kind, inform the staff that we will all be riding to Missionary Ridge shortly." Turning to Longstreet, he said, "It might be a good idea for us to move our own head-quarters up there as well, General." And he added, "I think we should all be together now."

BEYOND THE hills to the north, where our men were engaged with Sherman, came the bump and growl of artillery and the higher, ripping sounds of volleyed muskets. All of us kept turn-ing in our saddles to look toward the sounds and speculate anew on what might be happening. Only General Lee, riding alone in the lead, failed to show any interest.

Just then Moxley Sorrel came galloping up from the scene of the engagement and gave Lee a handwritten note from McLaws. Lee read it calmly, thanked the major, and continued on. I had not seen Sorrel since early morning, so I pulled off and accosted my friend eagerly.

"Blazes, Sorrel, what's going on back there! Are we holding on? Everyone's so damn calm!"

"I'm not calm," Sorrel laughed. "I'm excited. Hell, Jed, I just watched old Sherman's boys getting rolled back for the umpteenth time, just as easy as you please. I'll bet he's fit to be tied. Probably thought he was going to walk right on in here, like a Sunday suitor at a spinsters house. He's learning this ain't no Vicksburg!"

"Wonderful news!" I said exultantly. "How many Yankees are there?"

"Lots, I figure," Sorrel replied. "Hard to say for sure because they're all backed up in the trees. It doesn't matter though, Jed. Sherman can't get at us except by straight ahead. The ground is perfect to defend, not like it could be otherwise with Marse Robert and Old Pete doin' the pickin', and our own casualties have been pretty light, just like Fred'ricksburg." Here Sorrel laughed again. "Jed, them Yankee boys are mad as hornets. They don't stop firing, just keep it up, mad like, even when they're not attacking. Our boys just lay low until they come on again. You can tell these bluebellies of Sherman's have been used to getting their own way out here. It riles them big time when someone says 'Git!'"

"So they'll keep on trying," I said.

"And they'll keep on dying," Sorrel replied, laughing at the rhyme. "I've got to get back, Jed. Old Pete's there now. Anyway I don't want to miss anything. What news of Cleburne?"

"He's attacking and appears like he's doing all right. That's all anyone knows right now. Our observation posts are fogged in."

"He'll do the job," Sorrel said as he wheeled his horse about. "This is our day, Jed, just you wait and see!"

With a wave of his arm he was off.

Catching up with Lee's entourage, I found myself caught up by Sorrel's irrepressible faith. I didn't fight it, for I had been gloomy much too long. I began to see how it really might be if

I dared to think it. If Sherman could be held and if Cleburne succeeded, both of which seemed well on the way to being accomplished, then the opportunity would be there to inflict a very real catastrophe on the Yankees tomorrow.

When our group arrived at Bragg's headquarters, we found his staff officers in a state of uncommon optimism, which as we were to learn, had been caused by the earlier arrival of a mud-splattered courier from Cleburne. The man had been sent off by the general early in the attack, and his message to Bragg had been, "We are driving General Hooker before us." This was indeed excellent news, the only drawback being that it was now several hours old.

For the remainder of the afternoon, while Lee joined Bragg inside the house, the rest of us from the Army of Northern Virginia settled ourselves in the vicinity and waited, listening to the distant roar of guns from Lookout Valley, and the louder booming in the opposite direction, over by Hardee and McLaws. Occasionally Lee and Bragg would come out of the house for a look down the ridge at Orchard Knob and the other Union positions, but the day was overcast and the air gray, and little that was in the distance could be seen with clarity.

Lee was calm. Bragg was nervous, his movements jerky. Still, he was much calmer now than when I had seen him that morning, acting like a rattled second lieutenant.

Throughout the afternoon, riders came and went at headquarters, bringing constant updates on what was happening on the Army of Tennessee's right. Hardee and McLaws were holding firm. All attacks had been repulsed. Our casualties were low. Meanwhile, the guns from there growled nonstop.

Then, late in the afternoon came a rider from Lookout Mountain. It was none other than Sergeant Kirkpatrick from the signal station, and he came into the yard on a shaggy mule, hallooing loudly. Everyone was on his feet. He was waving a piece of paper, which he handed to Bragg's staff colonel who had gone forward, frowning severely, to meet him.

"By thunder, yes!" the colonel exclaimed upon reading the note. He in turn handed it to Bragg who, along with Lee, had been drawn outside by the commotion. Bragg read the note, and his mouth and face twitched simultaneously, his version of a smile. Lee read it, smiled in turn, then placed his hand on Bragg's shoulder. The note was passed around among the staffs of the two generals, followed by more exclamations and handclasps.

Of course, long before the note reached my hands I knew what was in it. The gallant Cleburne had taken his objective. But what I did not expect was the extra measure of private gratification and triumph I felt on behalf of my revered commander, Lee, when I actually read the message:

> To Generals Bragg and Lee from Cleburne (3 P.M.): Have taken Brown's Ferry and am digging in. Enemy is before us but disorganized. Have captured two transports. Our casualties manageable. P.S. Forrest is here. Sends respects to General Lee.

LEE'S FINGER touched the map. "We will begin here at daylight. General Longstreet's division, under the command of General Jenkins, will attack and occupy Fort Negley, on the enemy's extreme right. Our Texas brigade will go in the lead. By taking this objective, our left will be anchored on the Tennessee River. By holding these fortifications against any attempts to retake it, we will have driven a wedge deep in the enemy's flank and rear."

The general moved his finger to another portion of the map, Orchard Knob. "As soon as General Longstreet's attack is opened, we request that General Breckinridge and his divisions from the Army of Tennessee oblige us with an immediate assault to recapture Orchard Knob. With that back in our hands, and the wedge securely driven on our left, we will then be in a position to launch the final assault in concert on the Army of the Cumberland in Chattanooga."

He looked up. The room was crowded with generals. None of them spoke; all were listening. The lantern light flickered on sober faces and intent eyes.

Lee was sitting at the table in Bragg's headquarters. Seated on his left was Bragg, leaning back, looking at no one, staring toward the door. He wore his usual taciturn expression, but it was lacking in some of the old hardness. If it had been anybody but Bragg, it might have been described as agreeable. Standing in the back of the room, I had noticed this and recalled that Bragg had looked this way ever since news had arrived of Cleburne's capture of Brown's Ferry.

Nothing serves to soften hard features on a general's face more than a successfully executed flank attack, I thought in amusement. That had always been the case with Stonewall. And now Bragg. And most important, he could take justifiable pride in the fact that the victory today had been won by a superbly handled striking arm of his own Army of Tennessee. That would suit him well. The fact that it had been Lee's plan in the first place would not matter to Bragg, who cared as little for personal glory as he cared for being liked. It was this selflessness that was one of his few assets.

Sitting near Lee on one side of the room was Longstreet. Standing behind him was the commander of his force who would assault the Union right, young Micah Jenkins, a South Carolinian who had inherited John Bell Hood's division after Hood had been wounded at Chickamauga. On the other side of the room sat Hardee and Breckinridge along with several of their generals. Crowded in as well were some of Bragg's senior staff. The room was full of drifting tobacco smoke. The silence was unbroken. It was Bragg's headquarters, but it was Lee presiding.

"I do not think it possible to overstate the importance of speed and celerity in our first efforts tomorrow morning," Lee declared solemnly. "These are all important first objectives which, when taken and exploited, should undeniably lead us to the fulfillment of the final one."

He paused slightly before continuing. "As of this afternoon, thanks to the superlative leadership of General Cleburne and the heroic endeavors of his men, the enemy's supply line is broken. This will be viewed as a disheartening calamity by many in that camp, I think, particularly the officers. Let us ensure then, by our ardor and singleness of purpose tomorrow, that calamity visits them again. And is visited so totally and in such a way that their countrymen in the future might consider this land cursed to enter."

Calmly he spoke, yet his dark eyes gleamed with a frightening light. His eyes could do that sometimes when his blood was up. I always found it an intimidating sight. There was an absolute hush in the small room. Back against the wall, I listened breathlessly.

Lee looked to Hardee. "There are reports, General Hardee, that enemy artillery from various batteries have been taken across the river and recrossed at General Sherman's location. By this it would appear he intends to put you and General McLaws to another test tomorrow. It is crucial that he not be allowed to interfere in any way with our work in front of Chattanooga."

"General Lee," Hardee answered, "you may visit your calamity on the Army of the Cumberland. I can tell you, sir, that he will not break our line. We eagerly await his test tomorrow."

Hardee sat erect in his chair, head held high as he spoke, eyes aflame—a dramatic, commanding figure of a general just then. I was fascinated and thought that it was Lee who could do that. Lee who could make a man act more than he is.

Breckinridge spoke next. He looked worried. "That is a very strong position your men will be attacking tomorrow, General Lee. That is the enemy's strongest redoubt, as I know you are aware. And over our time here we watched as they made it progressively more so." His eyes lingered for a moment, accusingly, on Bragg, who did not notice.

"You are quite right about that position, General Breckinridge," Lee answered. "But it has been stronger. Not only has most of its artillery been removed, but as we have learned today, a large portion of the troops who once occupied it have been moved closer to Missionary Ridge, which General Grant obviously intends to attack if General Sherman breaks through."

He stopped then continued with a twinkle in his eyes. "By doing this, General Grant is showing us a predisposition to concentrate on offensive details to the subordination of defensive ones. In short, the man is allocating all his energy to the thought of his own attack with no thought at all to the possibility of ours. This suits us, gentlemen, for as I recall, this same imbalance of priorities in the face of a strong enemy was committed by this very same officer once before, and on the banks of this very same river. And if I am not mistaken, there are individuals in this room who made him pay a severe price for it at the time."

At this eloquent reference to the battle of Shiloh, Breckinridge and the other Army of Tennessee officers laughed with pleasure. Stoic Hardee allowed a faint smile to lighten his features. Bragg did not smile but gave an abstract nod of agreement.

"We are all of one mind then," Lee announced. "We all know what must be done. May God bless our cause and all of you. And may he protect our gallant soldiers!"

He stood up. The meeting was over, but just then, as the shuffling started and the assembled officers began to depart, Bragg shot up from his seat.

"Commanders and officers!" he called, and his voice filled the room. "The Army of Tennessee has already achieved a great victory today. Another awaits us tomorrow! Let us have it!"

There was a stunned silence as everyone stared in amazement at the aroused martial figure of Braxton Bragg. Astounded like the rest, I felt an inclination to laugh out loud.

Magic, pure and simple, I thought. *Truly General Lee wields magic.*

OUTSIDE BRAGG'S headquarters I stood by while Longstreet and Lee talked.

"If there is anything to fear, I suppose, it would be that General Grant and General Sherman recross the river tonight and move immediately against General Cleburne," Lee was saying. "They would eventually be assured of opening their supply line while at the same time denying us the chance to strike a mortal blow upon them."

Longstreet shrugged. "Of course that's possible. But I don't think General Grant will do it in actuality."

"Nor do I, in actuality," Lee agreed. "I believe he is intent on seeing his own plans through."

"That's General Grant's way," replied Longstreet. "He'll send some reinforcements to help General Hooker deal with General Cleburne, but he won't leave Chattanooga. That would be admitting defeat, and nothing could be further from his mind right now. He'll look on events today as mere setbacks. General Sherman's getting hung up will vex him, but as you pointed out, he'll try us again tomorrow with more guns. His most serious problem is losing Brown's Ferry and his supply line. That would panic most of the Northern generals you and I have seen, but this one doesn't flush so easily."

"That is good for us then," Lee remarked. "So what do you think he will do tonight?"

"Prepare to continue with what he was doing today," Longstreet answered. "Push General Sherman through and get on Bragg's flank. Send help to General Hooker in the hope he's not as much of a dunderhead as he appears and might be able to whip General Cleburne, which of course as we know, he is and he won't. And let's not forget General Cleburne's got General Forrest down there with him. In addition—" Here Longstreet grew thoughtful. "In addition, General Grant will try to feel us out a little more, I'm sure. He'll look at the size of General Cleburne's force as well as what is against General Sherman, then he'll rethink the numbers and try to figure out how many of us he might really be up against here."

"If we are truly fortunate, he still might not suspect the presence of our corps," said Lee.

Longstreet gave another shrug. "Well, whether or not he suspects it tonight, he'll know it for sure before breakfast tomorrow."

He nodded for me to come forward. "Major Hotchkiss, go fetch the Texans. Bring them first. The rest of the brigades are to follow. Take General Jenkins to the assault position."

"Yes sir."

"They'll sleep on their arms tonight. It'll be a long, cold one for sure, but it can't be helped."

"Yes sir."

I started to move off, but then Lee inquired pleasantly, "And how are you tonight, Major Hotchkiss?"

"Quite well, thank you, General," I replied.

"Be careful on your ride. It's a very dark night tonight. An eclipse I'm told."

"Thank you, General, I shall be careful."

I started again, but Lee wasn't finished. "I suppose you'll be very glad to get back to Virginia when this is all over."

I had not been thinking of Virginia for some time that day, but nevertheless I answered, "I will be glad to get back there as soon as possible, sir."

Lee smiled. "Well, it may not be too much longer. Once we complete our task here we can be on our way in good conscience. You may feel free to tell that to the men, any who inquire."

"I will do that, General," I said.

As I walked away I smiled to myself. *The Old Man's keyed up tonight,* I thought. And maybe a trifle homesick. But then again, so were we all.

SEVERAL HOURS later I was standing by a low-burning fire, watching the soldiers file silently down the slope of Missionary Ridge. A light rain was falling, cold and chilling. Both Lee and Longstreet had been right in what they told me. It was indeed a dark night, and it was going to be a long and sodden one for Hood's division, who would spend it in wet gullies. There was no talking. The only sounds were of the rain, muffled footsteps, and an occasional cough.

Then as I watched, I gave a start. Looking up the dark trail I saw an awkward form picking its way slowly down the slippery path. I watched as it came closer, then I put my hand on the man's shoulder.

"Sergeant Goner!" I exclaimed.

"Howdy, Major," the one-legged butternut smiled cheerily. "Kind of a raw night, ain't it?"

"My God, man! What are you about?"

The sergeant affected surprise. "Why, I reckon it ain't much more than a soldier goin' up to the line with his boys. I sorta figured my time as a headquarters aide was passed. How's Uncle Robert?"

"Sergeant," I said to him sternly. "You're a brave man. Everybody who's ever come in contact with you knows that. General Lee knows that as well. Now I'm going to order you back."

The smile remained on the sergeant's face, but his eyes looked resolutely into mine.

"I'd take it kindly if you wouldn't do that, Major," he said. "This here slope's kinda tricky on a crutch. But right now, if I go on my arse, I've got my boys to pick me up and help me along if I need it. Now if I had to come back here later all by myself, it'd be a lot more difficult, not to mention all the time wasted when I could be getting' such rest as I could for tomorrow. I'd be much obliged if you'd spare me all that, Major."

I understood his meaning, but my own conscience prevented me from relenting.

"For God's sake, Goner," I pleaded. "How can I let you go forward in your condition?"

The sergeant smiled again, this one warm and reassuring. "We're all Rebs, Major," he said softly. "And once you pin that name on yourself there ain't nothin' for it but to go ahead on and see things through, just like we'all been doin' since this thing took up."

I could formulate no reply, and I felt the depressing weight of truth of his words.

"Dammit all, Goner!" I swore violently.

"It's all right, Major."

I looked at him. The rain was dripping off his slouch hat. His face was in shadow.

"God bless you then, Sergeant. And may He protect you," I said helplessly.

He adjusted the crutch under his shoulder. "You're a decent man, Major. I always said so," the one-legged butternut smiled. Then he flashed a huge grin, bright and full of spunk. "Take care of yourself tomorrow, sir. And I'll see you and Marse Robert in Chattanooga!"

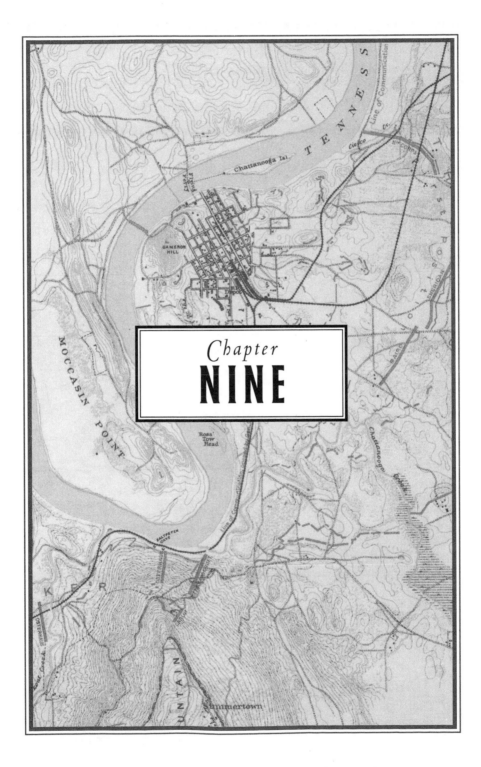

Chapter
NINE

I WAITED FOR THE DAWN, which was not far off, pacing briskly back and forth in a damp, bone-chilling fog. *Like being in a cloud,* I decided grimly. A cloud over a vast frigid tundra. The fog had dropped like a curtain over everything an hour ago, wet and cold and still. I had done everything I could to keep warm: hat drawn over my face, collar up, scarf tight, every button buttoned. Still I could not stop shivering.

I needed to put my mind on something else, so I thought about the attack that would come very soon. Everything was in place. Everyone was in place. The fog was impenetrable then, but in my mind's eye I could see the open ground in front of the gully where Jenkins's division was sequestered, and beyond the open ground and the Yankee fort. It was a daunting plan Lee had proposed. An unwelcome comparison to the charge of George Pickett's division at Gettysburg had been pressing on my mind persistently for the last couple of hours. Yet, as I told myself in rebuttal, this would be no midafternoon charge across a vast mile-long field to where the enemy was waiting, fully braced for the attack. Here the only warning would be the three signal shots from Missionary Ridge, and then the assault would roll immediately, fast and sudden. And, I thought, *if* things were in our favor, *if* the enemy hadn't discovered the whereabouts of a hidden division, *if* the men moved quick, like hell and thunder across the half-mile of plain, and finally and most critically, *if* Marse Robert and Old Pete knew what they were talking about in saying the guns of the fort had been removed, then just maybe . . .

It was growing lighter. On the hilltop where I waited the fog was thinning somewhat. In the gray light I could see the dark loom of Lookout Mountain behind me. A breeze blew up, and the fog began to drift off. Suddenly I could see the terrain around me and in front. The open ground was visible. So was the Yankee fort beyond. But in the hollows and low area the fog still hung thick. The gully and adjacent ravines where Jenkins's men waited and shivered was covered by a dense mist. I looked at my watch. Up in the clear where I was, it was daylight plus.

Then from back on the ridge came a sonorous *Boom!* Its echo was still reverberating when another followed. Then came the third. The quiet that followed, already intense, grew profound.

Anxiously I trained my field glasses on the thick bank of fog hanging between the two hillocks. Nothing happened. The echo of the third and final shot had faded, and the landscape returned to its frosty morning stillness. Still there was nothing, and peering through the thick fog bank was impossible.

Suddenly the lead gray regiments broke out of the mist, crimson battle flags leading the way, the lines arcing behind. Then the second line emerged from the fog, battle flags snapping and followed hard on the heels of the first. These were Hood's Texas brigades, the Army of Northern Virginia's hard hitters. They swept forward, moving fast across the open ground, and from the hill where I was watching I heard, faint yet persistent, the high quaver of the Rebel yell. I was aware of goosebumps.

On a small knoll well forward of the Union fort that was the ultimate objective was an advance Federal signal station, defended by two guns and a couple of companies of infantry. Suddenly assailed now, in the midst of lighting their breakfast fires, the unlucky defenders barely had time to fire off a rattled volley before the gray juggernaut was upon and over them. There was a brief, lively melee among the guns and the rifle pits, then it was over and the Union position ceased to exist, its defenders either dead, wounded, or shoved to the rear as prisoners. I lowered my glasses and took a long, satisfied breath.

The Texans paused only for the time it took to realign their ranks, then they were off at a run. This time they would not stop unless they were either shot down or upon the breastworks of the Union redoubt. I looked at my watch. The brief fight at the signal station and ensuing delay had been less than five minutes, but already Yankee artillery was coming alive, albeit slowly. Two poorly fused airbursts broke harmlessly high above the attacking Texans.

The faint wail of the Rebel battle cry came to my ears again. Swinging my glasses back to the gully, I saw the battle lines of the second attack wave rolling forward out of the mist. The horseback figure of Jenkins was visible in the lead, swinging his sword round and round over his head. These were the remaining brigades of the division, nothing held in reserve. They had watched and waited while the spearhead Texans made their whirlwind pounce on the unfortunate Union outpost. Now it was their turn, and they were up and off, shrieking across the plain.

Just before I had left headquarters in the predawn, there had been glum discussions between Longstreet and some of his officers about reinforcements being sent forward in the event that the attack ran into calamity. If such were to happen, I would take these reinforcements forward and put them in the best spot to support the assault waves, or as in the case of a real calamity like Pickett's attack at Gettysburg, to cover the survivors and break up a Yankee counterblow.

But just what troops these would be I had no idea. Every man of Hood's division was going forward in the initial assault on the Union fort; not a single regiment was held back. This only left McLaws's division, and any force he would be able to send would have to come from the other end of Missionary Ridge.

Therefore there must not be a calamity.

I trained my glasses back on the Texans. They were attacking with their characteristic verve, closing on the enemy fort. Heart pounding, mouth dry, I watched and waited. If Lee and Longstreet's scouts were wrong about the artillery being removed from the redoubt, right about now was when the mistake would be known and hideous carnage would ensue. I watched with rising anxiety. The attack waves rolled closer, and still there were no blasts of canister. Apparently the generals were right, but before I could feel any measure of relief, an eruption of musketry from the Union breastworks exploded in the faces of the Texans. I twitched. Smoke boiled up, and I could see that the crimson battle flags had halted their advance. Another sheet of flame erupted, more smoke billowed. Through it I could see the scarlet flags of the Texans on the move again, tossing forward through the haze. In very brief glimpses I spotted Rebel soldiers swarming up and over the breastworks in frantic rushes. There was the constant flashing of rifles, and the smoke thickened. Finally I lost sight of everything. Attackers, defenders, the entire fort; all were lost to view inside a thick, dirty cloud.

Closer to hand, another tense drama was beginning to unfold. What punishment the Union artillery batteries down the line around Chattanooga missed inflicting on the first wave of fast-moving Texans was now being attempted on General Jenkins's second wave.

It was not unsuccessful. By the time the lead regiments were halfway across the open ground they had come obligingly into range of the Federal batteries in the outer works of Chattanooga. Explosions rocked the attacking columns. Men fell and parts of the long battle lines became disarrayed.

"No! No!" I cried aloud and felt sickened. To my mind, there was no worse sight in warfare than to watch open, unprotected ranks of infantry being raked by artillery. Yet I could not look away.

The attack had been staggered—not stopped. The forward momentum resumed. Through the drifting smoke I recognized Jenkins's horse, with the general still astride, and saw other mounted officers as well darting along the lines. Despite the punishment, the infantry forged ahead, moving fast and covering much ground. Yet as this took place, as the leaden seconds ticked away, it seemed to me that the Yankee shellfire not only dwindled but lacked its customary brutal concentration for which Northern artillery was so adept. There was plenty of open ground left for the attackers to cover, a bountiful killing zone for the Federal guns, but the slackening of fire caused me both relief and bewilderment.

I could only guess that the reason for this had something to do with what was happening out of my line of vision, to the right. From the approximate location of Orchard Knob, the combined rattle and thunder of cannon and musketry reached my ears. Swinging my field glasses in that direction, I saw vast columns of gray smoke spew skyward. Clearly the main assault on the knob had opened, and whatever was happening there was on a large scale. Just then, however, my sole interest lay in what was occurring to my own front.

Jenkins's battle lines maintained a steady advance toward their objective, leaking dead and wounded along the way, but now, as the lines drew near the fort where the Texans were still embroiled with its defenders, the shelling from other parts of the Union line ceased entirely. Through gaps in the battle haze I made out the flashes of rifle volleys but was unable to determine which side was firing. Part of the first line of Jenkins's men to reach the Federal ramparts appeared to recoil from the enemy's fire, but in another spot I saw two crimson Rebel flags going over the works then everything was lost to view.

The fort was once more obscured by smoke, and I could only imagine what kind of confused melee might be taking place in and among the inner works. Impatiently I lowered my field glasses and waited. Several minutes later the smoke was as thick as ever, and I resolved to ride down to the plain myself and go forward until I could make out something tangible on the progress of the battle. I had just begun to do so when the hallooing of a rider coming down the slope behind me attracted my attention. It was one of Longstreet's staff, and he bore a message from the general.

"Pete says to say well done and come on back up, Jed," the captain relayed as soon as he drew rein beside me.

"I need to go forward to find out what's going on down there," I protested.

The captain shook his head. "Pete wants you back on the ridge. We can see the fort from there just as well as you can when the smoke clears. Anyway you don't see any of our boys coming back out, so that's got to be good news."

With this I had to agree. As we made our way back up to the ridge, I saw that the smoke plumes rising above Orchard Knob had doubled, and the air reverberated with the crash and boom of a hot fight.

"What's going on over there?" I asked.

The captain smiled. "Hell, fire, and brimstone for the Yankees," he said. "Bragg's boys pitched into 'em like wildcats. The bluebellies held on for a time, but just before I came down here, their whole line started to give. By the time we get up to the top, we ought to be seeing a first-class rout."

We continued on, and the captain's words proved true. At the top of the ridge I could see in full panorama the extent of the Southern victory in progress. It was a wild scene. Through the drifting gray battle smoke around Orchard Knob appeared countless crimson battle flags. On the plain beyond the knob, amid bursting shells, the Yankees could be seen streaming back toward Chattanooga. The retreat, although disordered, was far from panicked. The Federals were trudging, not running, but the direction of the flow was the same.

The air thundered violently with the sounds of battle. Above the chaotic plain the sky was fiery with airbursts and criss-crossing ordnance as Union artillery in front of Chattanooga dueled fiercely at long range with the captured guns now in Rebel hands on Orchard Knob. Scanning to the north, I could see a heavy pall of smoke rising above the hills, marking the spot where McLaws and Hardee were holding off Sherman. So far, everything was magnificent.

Longstreet had set up his and Lee's headquarters on the far left end of Missionary Ridge, literally in the shadow of Lookout

Mountain. Arriving, I saw the general standing among a group of couriers as he dictated orders. He was as self-possessed as ever, even with his corps divided on two fronts and fighting at opposite ends of our line. When I joined him, a soldier from a nearby signal station was just finishing his report.

"Jenkins is holding on in the fort, General. They just rolled back a Yankee counterattack, but it looks like there's another one massing."

Longstreet nodded, and the soldier departed. "Well, that sounds like good news, General," I said to announce my arrival.

"It'll do for now," Longstreet answered curtly. Then he turned toward me. "Well done down there, Major.

"Thank you, sir."

"This is a busy day and it's far from over. Stay close in case I need you."

I withdrew to a bonfire around which some of Longstreet's officers were standing. There I learned that Lee had gone to visit Bragg at the latter's headquarters, and that the final, all-out assault against Chattanooga would be coming soon. This was more good news.

Suddenly I was aware of a great thirst. I had lost my canteen, so I borrowed a drink from one of the others. There was a tightness in my eyes, and I felt uncontrollably sleepy. Unneeded for now, and feeling grateful, I took myself away a short distance and sat down against a tree. A quick nap before the big assault would not be unwelcome, I told myself, and closing my eyes I heard only briefly the crumping of the guns before falling into a deep unconsciousness.

MY EYES opened and I bolted upright. Quickly I looked around at the surrounding scene. Whatever it was that had startled me awake, there was no clue of it in the camp around me. Other men still stood around a few fires; no one appeared to be in a hurry. Obviously the final attack had not begun. In the distance, the guns maintained their fire, unchanged from when I had dozed off.

I looked at my watch. I had slept one hour. The attack couldn't be long now.

I walked to the crest of the ridge and gazed down on the battlefield. The artillery duel between the guns in Chattanooga and the batteries on Orchard Knob had stopped. The plain between these two positions was speckled with the dark forms of dead and wounded Yankee soldiers. Around and behind the knob, sheltered in the trees and gullies, were large masses of our infantry. Farther back, a train of artillery was coming up, while moving in the opposite direction were large groups of prisoners being herded to Missionary Ridge.

General Longstreet was standing atop a nearby breastwork with several aides. He was peering intently down on the battlefield with his field glasses, swinging back and forth between the assembled brigades of the Army of Tennessee around Orchard Knob then off toward Chattanooga, to the captured Union fort where his own brigades were hanging on, unconnected to any other part of the Confederate line. As the general peered in this direction, a courier from that position rode up to deliver his report. It was good news. The Texans and Jenkins's men were holding. They had just beaten off a determined counterattack with few losses. Jenkins further reported that after Bragg's attack on Orchard Knob, the Yankees knocked loose from there had streamed back into Chattanooga, causing much congestion and confusion. But there was no discernible panic, and since then the enemy had been regrouping and reforming.

The courier concluded excitedly that Jenkins's major concern was not from any counterattack by the enemy upon his position but that the Yankees would have time to pull back across the river to safety, taking up their pontoon bridge after them. Bragg's army must proceed immediately with a full assault or Jenkins's force must in some way interfere.

All our eyes were upon Longstreet. A thick cloud of smoke bellowed from his cigar. To the courier, he responded, "Give General Jenkins my compliments and tell him well done." Then he added, with a touch of asperity, "And tell him he's to stay where he is and wait, just like the rest of us."

The courier rode off, and those aides standing about gave each other sidelong glances and covered up smiles. Yet it was clear that Longstreet himself was chafing at the delay as his field glasses lingered long on the butternut infantry gathered around Orchard Knob, formed in lines of battle but inert, the soldiers disposed for comfort, sitting or kneeling, and the regimental battle flags furled.

As we waited for something to happen, Moxley Sorrel came pounding up with a report from McLaws. On the far side of the line, Sherman's men were coming on fiercely, but he and Hardee were holding on. Losses were light.

Longstreet nodded and without a word resumed glowering at Orchard Knob through his field glasses.

Before Sorrel rode off, I found him. "Methinks thou bringest fair tidings," I said.

He laughed. "Dammit, Jed, how are you? Those Texans really did it this morning, didn't they? Old Hood would have been pleased. Are they still holding on?"

I nodded. "I remember your saying yesterday that it was our day. Today looks like more of the same."

Sorrel laughed. "It'd better be. The left and the right elements have done their share; now it's up to the center." He nodded toward Chattanooga. "That's where we need to finish them off. If Bragg's army goes soon, we'll finish Grant while Sherman sits and watches. Then we'll get him next." With a frowning glance in the direction of Orchard Knob, he asked, "Are they going soon?"

"We're all hoping so," I said.

With a wave, Sorrel galloped off.

It was now noon, and the wait continued. Longstreet, his face dark with anger, beckoned a courier and sent the man galloping down the ridge toward Orchard Knob. None of us needed to guess what the message might be.

"Now that's an impatient, wasted effort, I'll wager," announced a captain next to me. "I'll bet he'll no sooner get there than the attack will open."

"I hope you're right," I said.

He was wrong. The minutes ticked by. The sounds of artillery on the right slackened. To the east, in Lookout Valley, there was also stillness. A pyre of black smoke rose up languidly on the horizon, marking the spot of Brown's Ferry, where Cleburne and Forrest still held. But in the center, nothing was happening. This wait was becoming unendurable.

Nearly another hour passed before Longstreet's courier returned, picking his way up the ridge carefully. The man looked hapless; undoubtedly he was bringing word of further delay, so as he approached he unwittingly became to all of us spectators a harbinger of maddening news.

Longstreet too watched with obvious disapproval. When the man reached the crest at last and reined up his mount in front of the general, he was greeted by a terrible scowl from the large bearded commander.

Clearly rattled, he announced shrilly, "Sir, General Breckinridge says to tell you he can't go till General Bragg says and General Bragg ain't said. He says to tell you they've been ready and are ready and soon's General Bragg says go, they'll go, but General Bragg ain't said and he has to wait till he does. General Breckinridge says to tell you sorry but there it is!"

Longstreet spat in disgust. Whirling about, he glared in my general direction.

"Hotchkiss!" he bellowed. "Mount your horse and come with me!"

I FOLLOWED THE general. He said not a word, and I could not recall a time I had ever seen him in so deep a paroxysm.

Yet in contrast to the general's black mood, the soldiers we passed along Missionary Ridge were in high spirits. Passing near a battery, I heard one officer remark to another as they looked down on the plain, "Still can't believe we licked them blue-bellies so easy. And with Bragg in charge yet."

"We licked 'em in spite of Bragg bein' in charge," his companion noted, and a gale of laughter followed.

For the first time since leaving his headquarters, Longstreet spoke. Turning to look at me, he jerked his thumb in their direction. "Did you hear that, Major?" he said bitterly. "Did you hear that? They take back a position that never should have been lost in the first place, then they act like they won Waterloo!"

We arrived at Bragg's headquarters and dismounted. Several of Bragg's staff were standing about nervously. Longstreet's heavy body stormed toward the headquarters, and then he spotted Lee and Bragg standing together on a nearby knoll. Abruptly he changed direction, making one of the staff officers scurry out of his way. Apprehensively, I followed.

Lee was remonstrating with Bragg. He was talking emphatically, watching Bragg as he spoke. Bragg was somewhat turned away, not looking at Lee, but keeping his field glasses in front of his face. It was a bad omen.

As we came within earshot, I heard Lee say, "General Bragg, I feel your concern on that matter is quite unfounded. The important thing is here and now, sir."

Sorrowfully, I concluded that this was what the Old Man must have been doing for the last two hours. Cajoling, coaxing, deflecting. Anything within the limits of patience and etiquette to get the thing moving again. To pry the thick, stubborn boulder loose and send it rolling down on the enemy. Seeing Longstreet now, Lee greeted him with an enthusiasm that was not forced. Neither Longstreet nor Bragg spoke to the other.

"And tell us, General, how are things on the left?" Lee asked Longstreet.

"Jenkins is holding on," Longstreet said huskily. "But he is well forward of our army. The Yankees are far from being in disarray, and each minute of delay will cost the lives of our soldiers. The attack from the center must be made at once."

Longstreet's words triggered an immediate and angry response from Bragg, who replied, as usual, without making eye contact and in a jerky, irascible voice.

"The optimum position of a single division does not dictate the tactics of an entire army in the midst of a major battle, sir! Much is at stake, and there is much to lose. Carefully planned assaults have carried the day for us so far. Rash ones could well lose it. We have already won too great a success to hazard it all to impulsiveness, sir!"

Longstreet was like a projectile ready to explode. Without a word he pivoted on his heel and began pacing back and forth behind Lee and Bragg, glowering at the ground.

"General Bragg, we are now at an extremely crucial time." Lee said in a persuasive tone. "I beg of you, sir, to order the attack on the enemy. His line is bent and he is unable to summon help. The great success to which you allude is only a beginning. He is hoping for darkness and will meanwhile use all the time given him to strengthen his defenses against us. It is getting late, General, and we are now forced to hurry with the daylight remaining. If those people are not attacked before night, they will escape, and we will not be able to get at them. With the river between us, they will be able to consolidate. Brown's Ferry will be for naught, and we will have lost the offensive."

Bragg turned to face Lee. "But we will have Chattanooga, sir!"

At this, Lee displayed his first flare of temper. "The town itself means nothing, sir!"

"Clearly not to the Army of Northern Virginia," Bragg shot back, and there was an unpleasant tone in his voice. "But it means much to the Army of Tennessee!"

Behind the two generals, Longstreet spat in disgust.

Lee, aware now of the sudden and dangerous turn the conversation had taken, attempted to defuse it.

"General Bragg, if you please." His tone was firm but soft. "If we do not take the opportunity to strike those people while they are divided before us, we will lose it for good. They will retreat and leave you in possession of the field, it is true, but for them it will only be a temporary setback. Undamaged, this very same enemy army will regroup and come on again. They will be free to revisit this theater whenever they choose. All that was gained by your brave army at Chickamauga will be obviated."

Lee paused. A flush appeared on his cheeks. "General Bragg," he asked calmly, "will you order the attack?"

Bragg did not answer. Nearby stood a group of his staff, watching and looking troubled. From a distance others witnessed this scene, soldiers and officers alike, all waiting to see what would happen, all sensing that so much was hanging in the balance.

All while Lee spoke, Bragg fidgeted. His nervousness was such that when Lee at last concluded, finishing with the all-important question, Bragg unconsciously gave a spasmodic shake of his shoulders, as though clearing himself from some great encumbrance. Still silent, he walked slowly away from Lee, his eyes blinking, his mouth in a tight scowl, and a look of self-absorbed agitation on his face. He put up his field glasses, focused on Orchard Knob then at Chattanooga, lowered them, then brought them up again for another look. Putting the glasses down once more, he paced a little farther off and his scowl deepened.

Lee waited where he was, his dark eyes following every move of the general. Longstreet stood beside Lee, refusing to look at Bragg, his back squarely to him.

Just say yes, Bragg, you damned fool! I wanted to shout. Caught up as I was by the frustration of the moment, I was feeling something else for Bragg that I never would have imagined possible, much as I disliked the man.

There before us stood the wretched general, distancing himself from everyone. Apart from Lee and Longstreet, apart from his staff, apart, saddest of all, from the officers and soldiers of his army. Apart with no hope of it ever being otherwise. Apart forever. To me there was only one word to describe Bragg just then, and that word was "pitiable."

I had always suspected that if one dug deep enough into this strange and disagreeable officer, there would be found the same bedrock of soldierly principle that was in Lee himself and Longstreet and all the other good ones. A code of ethics where duty and selflessness would always take ascendancy over everything. But this high devotion to duty, this simplicity of purpose had not been sufficient to make Bragg a successful military captain. In all three of his brilliant triumphs—the invasion of Kentucky and the battles of Murfreesboro and Chickamauga—his adeptness in confrontation had been followed by an appalling breakdown in the follow-up. Action bereft of totality. Lack of totality in victory, lack of totality in visiting destruction on a rival army. This was the summation of Bragg's inability as a fighting commander—a zealous, committed starter but a poor and distracted finisher. Cleburne had put his finger on it. Bragg was all twisted up somehow, with a deep uncertainty about himself running loose inside. Bad for Bragg. Bad for the Army of Tennessee. Worst for the cause. And now he stood here alone, looking alternately dazed and combative, a pathetic-looking figure just then and about to be made more so in front of many witnesses.

Nearby was a wagon trail leading down from the crest of Missionary Ridge to its base. Last night it had been full of soldiers going down to their jump-off positions for the attack on Orchard Knob. This afternoon it was the route by which groups of Yankee prisoners were being ushered to the rear. A large group was being brought up now, trudging along and catching their breath from the climb. A few were wounded, most were not. Bragg stared at them absently. They looked back curiously, at Bragg and Lee and Longstreet and the rest of the collected Confederate officers. One of the Federal prisoners, a tall bearded man, called out defiantly to Bragg as he jerked his thumb over his shoulder. "There's your town, General, down yonder. Go ahead and take her. If you can, that is!"

Everyone heard this, Bragg especially. The prisoners slogged off, but Bragg kept staring after the man, his words obviously having had some kind of effect. My dismay began to rise. Twitching, fidgeting, intimidated by Lee, and now clearly daunted by the words of a Yankee prisoner, it was almost too much to watch.

Suddenly Bragg wheeled about and walked back to Lee.

"I am riding over to the right to see how Hardee is doing," he announced tartly. "I will make my decision upon my return."

No one moved in the slightest. Longstreet grimaced. Lee's eyes were aflame.

"General Bragg," he intoned, "you know that if you ride over there now, by the time you return there will not be sufficient daylight left to carry out an assault. Therefore you must give the order now, sir! Now in the name of our cause!"

Bragg looked in the direction of his staff. "Get my horse!" he snapped savagely, and an aide went running. Turning back to Lee, he said frostily, "I am going to the right, sir, to inspect that flank of my army. I believe I am within my authority to do so. We will continue this discussion upon my return, sir, if you still wish to do so!" And with that he stalked off.

If you still wish to do so, I thought with despair.

Lee looked after him, hands clenched at his side, controlling his fury. Longstreet spat again.

"Could have told you about that man," Longstreet said with venomous disgust. "Could have told you. Should have known he would do this. What now?"

For a time Lee did not speak. Then he answered quietly. "Nothing," he said. "Nothing at all."

THE NIGHT air was icy brittle. It was not only the bitterest night of our stay in Tennessee, it was quite possibly the coldest night I could ever remember. Fortunately for those of us out in it, there was no wind, only profound, frozen stillness. The air was painful to breathe. Frosty plumes of vapor ballooned and whirled about the mouths and nostrils of men and horses. In the saddle, I pulled my blanket closer. Beside me was Sorrel, similarly bundled but with a scarf around his face so that only his eyes were visible.

The generals were up in front, their dark forms in silhouette. General Lee was to our left, and at his right side stood the tall, wide bulk of Longstreet. Beside the latter was the shorter shape of McLaws. Hardee was at Lee's left. All of them were draped in blankets, even Lee.

Looking back over my shoulder, I could see the crescent of Missionary Ridge ablaze with bonfires. So too was Orchard Knob. The invigorated Army of Tennessee was keeping close to their fires. On the plain between Orchard Knob and Chattanooga was only empty blackness. It was black as well in the area where Chattanooga lay. Complete darkness. The Yankees were lighting no fires. Not even by the river, where they had their bridge, was the glow of a single torch visible. Evidently they would retreat in darkness and give their enemy no satisfaction in watching.

To our front was more unlit darkness, the black mass of hills looming before us. All the generals were silent, listening. When no one stirred, the faint and distant tramp of a large force on the move was audible, sounding like a running river. Occasionally there was a rumble or the piercing whinny of a horse carrying crystal clear through the frigid air.

Sherman was pulling out.

Lee finally looked toward McLaws. "When did they begin to recross?"

"Just after dark," McLaws answered. "And it's been steady ever since. They're doing it blindlike, just a couple of fires at the bridge. But one of my scouts swore he saw General Sherman go across with the first bunch."

"Do you believe him?"

"Yes."

"Keep a close watch on them," Lee ordered. "Keep me informed of any changes and send me word when their entire force is across."

"Yes sir."

Lee turned to Hardee. "My sincere compliments on your performance these past two days, General, and on the valor of your soldiers. And most of all, my heartfelt thanks. We are indebted to you."

Hardee bowed his head in response. "You honor me, General Lee. For my part I would like to say how much I regret the turn of events that has caused your plan to go astray. You begin to see now what we all—" He went no further. There was no need to elaborate.

"Thank you, General," Lee replied.

Taking leave of Hardee and McLaws, Lee and Longstreet returned to their headquarters on Missionary Ridge. They went slowly, and to me, what with the disappointment of the day and the chill of the night, the ride seemed interminable. All along the ridge, we passed on the periphery of noisy bonfires where soldiers celebrated the day's success.

"Behold the Army of Tennessee," Sorrel sneered. "Triumphant victors of the battle of Orchard Knob!"

Reaching the headquarters, Lee addressed a group of Longstreet's officers. "It appears the enemy will escape us tonight gentlemen," he said. "For this I am sorry. Very sorry. Nevertheless, you all performed your individual duties in every way expected, and for that I thank you."

There was a prolonged silence. Lee stared into the crackling fire before going on.

"Several days ago, I believed that if we were properly alert, were persistent and assiduous in our preparations, we could expect as a reward that fortune would favor us with just the opening needed to strike a fatal blow. With ample time we would have been able to press it home. As a result of our plans we were so rewarded. One day only to achieve our purpose. As all of you know, in the past that always sufficed. Today was that day, gentlemen. Today is when it should have been done. But we all know that it was not, and now the day is gone."

There followed a dismal silence.

"We can expect that our foe is now aware of the presence of your corps," Lee went on. "He will know the numbers before him now and can be expected to look to the safety of his army. By a mere recrossing of the river, the Army of the Cumberland will be augmented with General Sherman. Thus united, the formerly separate portions of their army will outnumber us. Moreover, it is to be expected that General Grant has already notified General Burnside that the corps which he believed was in front of him at Knoxville is actually here. General Burnside, therefore, can be expected to advance immediately on Chattanooga. It is therefore a new situation confronting us, gentlemen. New and very dangerous."

The Old Man's voice was flat. He looked tired, even haggard. Turning to Longstreet he said, "I desire that you should send a courier to General Cleburne. Inform him that the attack on Chattanooga was not made and that General Sherman is now recrossing the Tennessee. Undoubtedly General Grant will do likewise, whereupon both will probably move in his direction in strong force. My prayers are with him. I can offer no more assistance than that."

"Don't you think General Bragg will inform him of that?" asked Longstreet.

"I cannot count on that, General," Lee answered.

"I'll see to it," Longstreet assured him, then added, "General Lee, I want to bring General Jenkins back to Missionary Ridge right away, under cover of darkness. They're no good anymore where they are, and there's nothing to stop the Yankees from massing batteries right across the river and pounding the place into rubble."

"Yes," Lee nodded. "Quite so. Quite so." He frowned, and the light from the fire showed the anger in his eyes. "And such a splendid effort. Such a marvelous—" He broke off. "By all means bring them out, General Longstreet."

Then one of the other officers spoke up.

"General Lee, will we stay here or go back to Virginia?"

There was a long silence. All eyes were on Lee as he brooded into the campfire. Finally he said, "We will not stay here simply to serve as a garrison to a line of fortified works. You were all sent here, you have all been here, to serve as instruments of victory, instruments to be wielded so as to bring about the destruction of the enemy down there, and so render his invasion a defeat. Only for that reason did I agree to your being sent here!"

Lee was angry. Everyone waited, "I have sent President Davis a request that sufficient rail transportation be hurried to Chickamauga Station without delay. Tomorrow, if the enemy is quiescent on our front, I intend to evacuate the corps to Atlanta."

"I will be in my tent, General Longstreet," he concluded abruptly. " I wish to know of every report that comes in and to be kept informed on the progress of General Jenkins's withdrawal."

With that he left the fire-lit circle and disappeared into his tent.

I assumed that I would be the one to take the withdrawal order to Jenkins, but Longstreet had another assignment in mind for me.

"Go see Bragg's medical officer," he said. "Tell him we'll have quite a few wounded coming in later, and we'd appreciate any arrangements he could make. With General Bragg's permission, of course."

There was no humor behind Longstreet's sarcasm.

I carried out my orders, speaking to the medical officer at the Army of Tennessee's field hospital, a genial man by the name of Durwood. "Tell General Longstreet we'll do all we can," he promised, then added morbidly, "and the ones we can't help won't have long to suffer on a cold night like this."

As I was leaving the hospital I was approached by an orderly. "Major, there's a Yank prisoner bein' questioned over yonder. One of Sherman's boys. Says they all know General Lee's here. The captain figured you'd be interested in seeing him."

The Federal was being interrogated by one of Hardee's captains. He wore the rank of sergeant and had been wounded in the leg; he was sitting up and smoking a cigar. I crouched down beside the captain.

"So tell me, Sergeant, at what point do you think Sherman decided to order you fellows to retreat?" the captain was asking.

The Union man puffed calmly on his cigar. "Naw, you got it all wrong. Warn't no retreat. We all just went back across to fetch up some more ammunition."

"I might just believe you. You sure used enough of it on the trees and rocks these last two days," the captain laughed.

The Yankee's eyes flickered at this, but he made no reply.

Pointing to me, the captain said amiably, "This here's one of Lee's officers. Anything you'd like to say?"

The man gave me a long, clinical look. "Is that true?" he asked.

I nodded.

The captured bluecoat took the cigar from his mouth. "You tell that old man we're coming to get him," he said. "If he knew what was good for him he'd take his granny white locks and skedaddle quick back to Virginia!"

I shot up instantly, glaring down on the prisoner. "You are impudent, sir!" I exclaimed furiously.

The Federal gave me an icy smile as he replaced the cigar in his mouth. "Well now, Major," he said, "I reckon you could say I was raised wrong."

BACK AT headquarters, there was nothing for me to do but try to stay warm. This proved to be no easy thing. The wind had begun to pick up, and those officers and orderlies not off on errands for the generals crowded en masses around whatever campfires stayed lit.

Near midnight, a courier from McLaws brought the word that the last of Sherman's men had crossed the Tennessee, taking up their pontoon bridge after them. Soon after, two more officers arrived, Moxley Sorrel and Micah Jenkins. Longstreet went forward and shook the latter's hand warmly.

"Glad to see you back after this day's fiasco," the general growled. "Did you have to put up a rear-guard action?"

Jenkins shook his head. "They let us go clean. Don't know if they missed us or just didn't care. Couldn't see a thing, but we heard an awful lot. Lots of commotion coming from the bridge. I expect they were pulling out just like we were." A pained look came over his face, and he said wearily, "The boys really did it today, General. The way they took that fort— Hood would be proud. If only we had— if only we could have—"

"I know," Longstreet interrupted tersely. "Let's go see General Lee."

There was nothing else to do that evening. I would have given anything for some warm food, but tea and captured Yankee hardtack was all there was. Dreadfully tired, I spread my blankets by a fire on the frozen ground. Closing my eyes tightly, I tried to shut out the cold, the dark night, and Missionary Ridge.

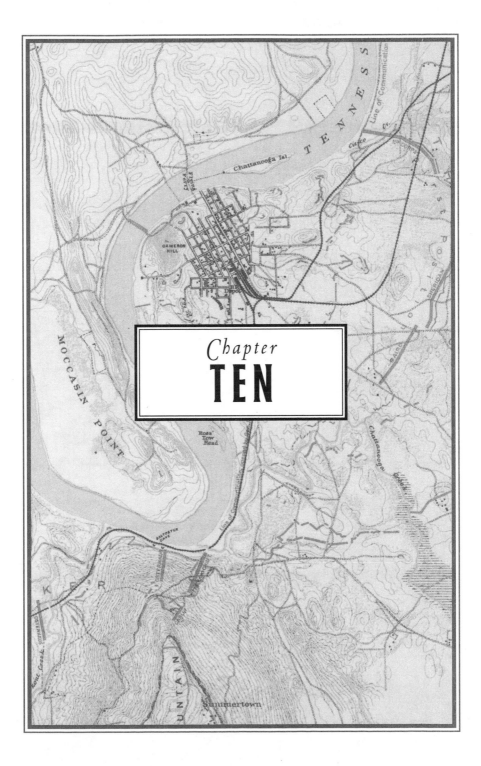

Chapter
TEN

I AWOKE COVERED IN ASHES. My clothes and my blankets were caked in it. Soot was in my hair and eyes and nostrils, and I stood up, coughing and spitting.

I had rolled in the stuff while I was sleeping, a not uncommon occurrence on a cold night when the body instinctively chases the remaining warmth of a fading campfire. As I slapped and beat at my clothing, Moxley Sorrel came up. Ordinarily my predicament would have been cause for laughter and ribbing, but not this particular morning on the ridge.

"The Yankees ain't gone, Jed," said Sorrel, and his voice was flat. "You'd better come and have a look."

We walked to the crest of the ridge, and when I looked down I caught my breath.

The Yankees had not gone. Thick ranks of blue infantry covered the plain in front of Chattanooga, hard at work digging earthworks out of the frozen earth and piling abatis in front of their lines. Batteries frowned from new positions. Already the enemy army seemed to be settled into a nearly unassailable defensive posture if an attack was what the Confederates were planning, which it was not.

I looked at Sorrel. "My God," I said forlornly, "yesterday was all for nothing."

Sorrel pointed glumly to the west, to the open ground that had been crossed the day before by Jenkins's and Hood's brigades. Now the same ground was occupied by Federal troops, digging and fortifying.

"Those are Sherman's boys," Sorrel said. "Jenkins thought he heard Grant pulling out across the bridges last night. What he was really hearing was Sherman coming back into Chattanooga to join Grant. You got to hand it to that bluebelly; he's got sass. Gets thrown out the window and comes right in the back door."

My heart was sick. "They probably outnumber us two to one down there," I estimated.

"It won't matter," Sorrel replied. "Bragg himself won't be able to stay here more than a couple of days. We got word last night that Burnside's on the march from Knoxville as we speak. Grant probably told him to get his arse moving after Longstreet's corps was identified here."

"The Yankees won't have to attack Missionary Ridge now," I noted. "All they need to do is wait for Burnside to come in on the flank."

Sorrel pointed in the direction of Orchard Knob. "Bragg's troops evacuated there last night to strengthen the line at the ridge. Probably not a bad idea. Orchard Knob's no use to him anymore. Nor to us."

I shivered in the cold and said nothing. There was nothing to say. Coming off duty as the night staff officer, Sorrel went to get some sleep. As the day staff officer, I reported to Longstreet's camp and learned that he and Lee had gone off for an inspection ride along the line. There was little breakfast to be found at the camp, and no one was in the mood for conversation.

As soon as the generals returned, Longstreet sent for me straightaway.

"Ride to Chickamauga Station," he said. "General Lee is expecting a message from Richmond. Also find out anything you can about the trains we requested. We're pulling out tonight, and I want to get the artillery loaded and off as quick as possible."

As I traversed the ridge I passed numerous vantage points providing disheartening views of the Union host in front of Chattanooga. After a while I gave up looking in that direction.

At Chickamauga Station there was a confidential telegram waiting from Richmond to Lee. Another telegram was for Longstreet from his rear-guard commander in East Tennessee. The message, sent from a station twenty miles west of Knoxville, reported that Burnside's army was advancing rapidly on

Chattanooga. The commander added that he was putting his brigade on flatcars and would be in Chickamauga Station that night. From the stationmaster I learned that every available train was being routed up from Atlanta; the first one from Resaca would be arriving in less than an hour.

I returned to Missionary Ridge with the dispatches and the news. Lee and Longstreet, heavily cloaked, were standing before a fire and talking quietly. After Lee read the Richmond telegram, he handed it to Longstreet, who nodded gravely.

"Wait here, if you would, Major Hotchkiss," Lee told me and went inside his tent. After a time he emerged and handed me an envelope.

"Major, I desire you to ride to General Bragg's headquarters and deliver this into his hands. I am informing him that General Longstreet's corps has received the approval of President Davis to rejoin the Army of Northern Virginia. We will begin our trek after dark for Chickamauga Station. I am asking permission for the right of way on the main roads to move our artillery."

I arrived at Bragg's headquarters and reported my business. I was shown into the farmhouse room where the general and his chief of staff were sitting at the desk and poring over maps. When I entered, Bragg looked up and scowled. The colonel did likewise.

Saluting, I announced my errand and placed the letter before Bragg. Then I stepped back and stood at attention.

With the impatient air of a man involved in weighty matters who was now forced to attend to some triviality, Bragg took the envelope disdainfully. He read it through, then to my surprise and disgust, he laughed. It was a harsh, unpleasant sound. He handed it to the colonel and fixed me with a steely look.

"And just what, pray tell, was General Lee's purpose in writing this letter?" he demanded. "Does he think we don't receive telegrams from Richmond just the same as he?"

What Bragg meant by his hostile words and tone I had no idea, but it was nothing new to deal with.

"The letter was to keep you informed of his intentions," I answered. "He wanted no misunderstandings."

"Your General Lee is too kind," Bragg said unctuously. "What is there to misunderstand? President Davis has made it quite clear that he does not want his number-one general twisting one more day in the chilly winds of Tennessee." His eyes glittered darkly. "Tell General Lee he may evacuate Missionary Ridge whenever he chooses. We will not stand in his way."

And the colonel added, with a malevolent smile, "And please tell General Longstreet that this army will cover his retreat."

Turning about crisply, I departed.

THAT NIGHT, Chickamauga Station was a busy, noisy place. Bonfires blazed, warming the troops of Longstreet's corps as they made their bivouacs in the station yard and along the tracks. Lee and Longstreet had moved their headquarters to the same railroad car that had brought Lee to Tennessee. It seemed like a long, long time ago.

In contrast to the somber attitude around the head-quarters, the soldiers were robust and cheerful in contemplation of returning to their homeland, where campaigns and battles usually worked out according to plan. Trains arrived all night, interrupting sleep, but there was no complaining.

Just before dawn the first long train pulling Longstreet's artillery rolled out of the yard. Shortly afterward, the low roll and rumble of cannon reached our ears from away to the north-west. The sound persisted and intensified.

"Are those Bragg's batteries or the Yankees?" Sorrel asked.

I continued to listen. "I don't know," I confessed.

As was expected, the distant firing drew the attention of Lee. He came out onto the platform of the railroad car, looking off in the direction of the sound.

"What guns are those, gentlemen?" he asked.

"We can't make them out for certain, General," I answered.

He considered for a moment. "Major Hotchkiss, be so kind as to ride up to the ridge and find out what you can. I fear those guns might belong to our enemies, and if that is so I would be most anxious to learn what is happening."

On the way out of the rail yard I met Longstreet astride his horse. When I told him where I was going and what Lee had said, he nodded. "I was just going up to have a look for myself," he said. "I don't like the sound of them either."

We went hurriedly up to the ridge, and I led Longstreet to the spot where I had first taken Lee on the day the Yankees came out of Chattanooga and attacked Orchard Knob. From here we could ascertain that the firing was coming from Federal batteries drawn up around Orchard Knob, with the target evidently being the rifle pits at the base of Missionary Ridge. Yet our view of the plain from this vantage point was only a partial one, and Longstreet was not satisfied.

"Find me a better spot," he commanded. "I need to see what they're up to down there."

"There's a good place farther along the ridge, close to Bragg's headquarters," I told him, both as an acknowledgment and a warning.

Longstreet was unconcerned. "Let's go, then," he said.

When we arrived at this new spot we found two of Bragg's staff officers there. As we dismounted, they saluted Longstreet then wordlessly mounted their own horses and cantered away.

From this vantage point it was evident that the rifle pits at the base of the ridge, opposite Orchard Knob, were the object of all the Federal activity, undoubtedly an incursion in the making to give them more room in front of their key position. The Union cannons blazed away as marching lines of infantry left their own works and advanced to the attack. This was a sizable force coming out, an entire beefed-up division, I calculated, with probably another division drawn up in reserve behind the blur of Yankee powder smoke.

Almost immediately as the blue battle lines had stepped out from the shelter of the trees and brush in front of Orchard Knob they were taken under fire by the batteries atop the ridge. Damage was inflicted on the advancing blue columns, but it was much less than it should have been. Shooting as they were from their separate and insular spots along the ridge line, each battery operated independently, so the fire, instead of being concentrated and steady, was disjointed. Moreover, I noted with exasperation, many of Bragg's gunners were overshooting the dense Union formations. I was about to say something to Longstreet regarding this, but the dark look on his face as he glowered through his field glasses made no comment necessary. The Yankees were taking their worst hurt from the rifle fire of the Rebel infantry, although this was not sufficient to slow the attack. As the Federal advance bore down on them, the defenders of the rifle pits cracked in a final volley, then, under cover of the drifting smoke, began an orderly withdrawal up the slope to the next line of trenches.

With loud hurrahs, which were clearly audible from where Longstreet and I stood watching, the Yankees rolled up, over, and into the abandoned works. But their shouts of triumph were short-lived, for now our men began causing serious damage to the attackers. Artillery shot and musket fire rained down from the slopes above, and in the crowded rifle pits below the Yankees cowered for any cover they could find and took heavy losses.

"That's better," I said out loud, and Longstreet grunted approvingly.

I looked at my watch. Only five minutes had passed since the Federals had swarmed into the evacuated rifle pits, but under the punishment they had taken I surmised that for them, this time must have seemed like hours. Nor had the Rebel fire slackened, and I sensed that very soon, something had to give.

"They're in a real box down there, General," I proclaimed. "Sooner or later they've got to break for it."

Even as I spoke these words, several units of blue infantry began doing just that, although not in the direction I expected.

Singly and in small groups, blue soldiers began to dash out into the open from the deadly rifle pits where they had been trying to find shelter—and they began clambering up the slope. In some instances these rash soldiers were immediately shot down, but as scores of other Federals came out of the shot-ravaged trenches to follow their lead, many more of them survived. And so, fully armed and on the loose once more, these men were allowed to begin the ascent.

Longstreet frowned.

I felt my own tension begin to build and waited anxiously for some titanic blast of cannon or heavy volley of well-aimed rifle fire that would send these bluecoats rolling back down the ridge, but instead, the Confederate fire continued as before, accurate and heavy on certain spots, ragged or poorly aimed on others. Meanwhile the exodus of Yankees from their pent-up positions became widespread. The thin trickles of reckless Union soldiers who had begun toiling up the steep slope toward the next line of Rebel trenches were now joined by more of their comrades. There were officers among them now, I could see, not waving their swords to bring their men back but to encourage them on. And the trickles turned into streams, and then entire regiments were out and clambering upward in V-shaped wedges. On the leading point of each was a flag.

Longstreet's face was a dark cloud. He neither moved nor made a sound but continued to watch in portentous silence.

The Federals came on doggedly. In several places where the incline was very steep, they crawled on their hands and knees. And as the panting, sliding, hurrahing wedges of blue infantry came up to the second line of Rebel trenches, the butternut defenders began slowly to abandon them, once more fading back up the slope, many of them stopping to fire as they did so. Yet, had they been aware, this display of casual, over-the-shoulder-and-kneel-to-shoot defiance toward the attacker served only the attacker, for as the Rebel defenders made their way up to the next line of trenches, the Yankees followed after them and so were protected from serious harm. What would have been a murderous fire that should have opened on the advancing enemy was held in abeyance to spare friends.

I watched with growing alarm, and all at once other things began to happen.

From the moment the Federal charge out from Orchard Knob tumbled into the abandoned rifle pits at the base of the ridge, Yankee batteries from all other parts of the line facing Missionary Ridge opened a slow and steady bombardment on whatever Rebel positions were in front of them and within range. But this was a thing to be expected from artillery while a major attack was in progress, and neither Longstreet nor I paid it any mind as we grimly transfixed our attention on the infantry engagement closest to us.

Now the sounds of the distant Union batteries increased to a constant, thunderous roar, the reverberations of which rolled and echoed off the hills, even above the small-arms racket of the battle below us. There was true malice in the sound of the Federal guns now, and both the general and I swung our glasses to the distance. It was difficult to see much through the haze of powder smoke, but on the portion of the plain that was held by Sherman's divisions, I could see long lines of blue infantry advancing in a general movement straight toward Missionary Ridge. Whether this was to be a real attack or merely a spirited diversion to draw off some of our troops from resisting the first Yankee attack that was already halfway up the ridge was too soon to tell, but in light of the disaster that appeared to be slowly unfolding before us, this new menace was not to be dismissed quickly.

All at once, something akin to panic came over me.

"My God!" I exclaimed. "My God, General! Do you think the Yankees will—"

He held up his hand. His face was grave, and he was thinking hard. For a long time he did not speak, and when he finally did, he spoke calmly but with an urgency I had never heard before. That made it all the more alarming to me.

"Ride at once to General McLaws," he ordered. "He is to move every man of his division forward immediately for the defense of Chickamauga Station. Every man up! And without a moment's delay! Where the station road intersects the ridge road, he is to deploy for defense. Keep the road to Chickamauga Station open at all costs. At all costs, do you hear? The rail yard must not be allowed to fall to the enemy! Do you understand?"

I gulped and nodded, my head swimming with the dizzying and sickening turn of events that now had me galloping frantically to one of Longstreet's generals to relay the astonishing order that Chickamauga Station must not fall into enemy hands! I could imagine the reception I would receive from McLaws and his officers. Having only the distant crumping of the guns to go on until now, which might mean anything, and not having seen for themselves this fantastic and impossible thing that the Yankees were about to pull off, and for that matter not even being able to imagine it, they were sure to be thunderstruck.

"General Jenkins is to move in behind General McLaws as reserve," Longstreet commanded. "And if there's any artillery that the trains haven't yet taken, bring them up too. And everybody move quick!"

Again I nodded, and Longstreet fell silent, brooding down the slope. Judging him finished, I started to leave, but he put his hand on my shoulder. When he spoke his voice was quiet. "Jed, after you've reported all this to General Lee, I want you to give him a message from me personally. Tell him we'll do all we can, and that may serve. But tell him that there's nothing more that *he* can do here, so I want him to get on the train now and get away from here—" Longstreet interrupted himself with a quick shake of his head. "No. Don't say get away from here. Say 'Get back to Richmond and Virginia.' Tell him we'll be fine here, but I must insist that he leave immediately and return to his army, for the sake of the cause!"

I stared at the general wide-eyed.

Just then there was a pounding in the earth behind us, and Bragg's chief staff officer came galloping up on a lathered horse. He had come fast and was much keyed up. Without dismounting, he fired off a hasty salute to Longstreet. His excited horse whirled around, and while the colonel got him back under control Longstreet waited, a dark look covering his face.

Facing around again, the colonel shouted, "General, our line is threatened!"

"I'll say it is!" Longstreet snapped.

The colonel gave him a startled look, then continued with his message. "General Bragg says that the enemy attack must be counterattacked at once, and he demands that General Lee and the soldiers under his command come forward in support! He demands that they come forward with all haste!"

I could feel the heat emanating from Longstreet throughout this tiny, shrill diatribe. Now the smoldering projectile exploded at last.

"Demands, does he?" Longstreet roared. "Demands? Yes, that is *just* how Bragg would say it, wouldn't he? And do you know what I say to that, sir? I say damn him! Damn him! Tell him that for a reply to saucy impudence, sir!"

He stepped forward angrily. He was a big man with an equally large black beard, and in his present state he looked totally fearsome. Both officer and horse drew back.

Longstreet thundered again, "Demands, does he? Demands? And after the last two pathetic days and my dead who had to be buried by Yankees? The gall and nerve, sir! The impudence and smug conceit! Ever since we've been here, we've heard of little else from you and your general but about the Army of Tennessee's much vaunted line of defense on Missionary Ridge! Are you aware of the one, sir? The one that you and your general said could be held by a line of skirmishers if the need arose? The great blue slaughter pen, if only 'they' would come on? Do you recall, sir?" He thrust his finger at the shot-torn slope of the hill, where the blue-shaped wedges advanced. "Well, they are indeed coming on, sir. And I would suggest that now might be the time to deploy *your* skirmishers!"

The colonel flushed at the general's goading. "You are refusing a legitimate call for support then?" he shot back angrily.

For answer Longstreet turned sharply. "Major Hotchkiss, do you understand your instructions?"

"Yes sir," I answered breathlessly.

"Then be off at once," commanded the general.

As I twirled into the saddle, Longstreet's booming voice came to me again. "Major Hotchkiss! Make sure General Lee gets my personal message. It is most important."

I nodded emphatically and was gone.

I GALLOPED MY horse full speed along the ridge road, avoiding ammunition wagons and double-timing squads of soldiers. The crash and thunder of battle reverberated behind me, and as I sped along I did so with a deep sense of dismay. The "bill," it seemed, had finally arrived. For all the flaws, the carelessness, and the complacency of the Army of Tennessee, the payment was now due in full, and foreclosure on the last stronghold of the Confederacy in the state of Tennessee was a real prospect.

I had only gone a short way along the crest when I spotted a group of officers coming toward me from the other way. It was Lee himself cantering in the lead, with a kite tail of officers behind him. One of these was Jenkins, two were from McLaws's division, and the last two I recognized as from Bragg's staff.

The general did not stop when I reached him, looking wholly intent on getting to the scene of the engagement. I whirled my horse and fell in beside him, reporting to him of the peril to the Army of Tennessee's main line, as well as Longstreet's orders to his corps. Lee nodded in acknowledgment, although not taking his eyes from the direction of the firing up ahead. But he said to me, "You may save yourself the ride, Major, for I have already given those exact instructions to General McLaws myself. His and

Jenkins's divisions are coming out of Chickamauga Station as we speak." Behind Lee, Jenkins nodded to me in confirmation.

What was left then was for me to give Longstreet's personal message to Lee, but this was clearly not the time to suggest that he return to Chickamauga Station, so I held off. Lee's eyes were dark with concern and, I noticed, extreme anger. He pressed his horse to go faster and ordered me to lead the way to Longstreet. The last half-mile along Missionary Ridge was at a gallop.

Longstreet turned as we came riding up, and when he saw Lee, a spasm of alarm passed over his dark face. Lee, Jenkins, and McLaws's officers dismounted and gazed with outright horror at what they saw was happening down the line of Confederate works atop the ridge. In the center of the crest, near Bragg's headquarters farmhouse and right at the point of a poorly sited battery, Rebel gunners were trying in vain to depress their barrels to take the Yankees under fire even as other bluecoats breached the crest nearby and came swarming along the flank and rear. Past the drifting smoke of this inferno I could see two more places where the summit of the ridge had also been pierced.

Longstreet and Lee conversed, Longstreet talking with animation and pointing to various parts of the ridge and Orchard Knob. Lee nodded, frowning deeply. Then the conversation shifted, and I saw Longstreet pointing back in the direction of Chickamauga Station in an imploring manner. When this apparently had no effect, his gestures became ones of sharp remonstrance. At this last, Lee turned and fixed the general with a look of supreme annoyance. I came close enough to overhear him.

"General Longstreet, such a thing as you suggest is quite out of the question. I would take it most kindly if you would speak of it no more. But in the meantime, sir, do not let me hinder you from checking on the progress of your corps."

Thus rebuffed, Longstreet saluted and turned away in frustration. He made a sharp gesture to his officers, and he mounted his horse and was joined by Jenkins and McLaws's officers.

"Don't let him slip the leash, Major," Longstreet growled as he rode past me. "We've already lost more than we can afford today."

Lee's attention remained riveted for a time on the many wedges of Union infantry that were continuing to ascend the steep upper slope toward the crest.

"We must get closer!" he cried impatiently as he remounted. Looking at Bragg's officers, he declared urgently, "I must find General Bragg at once. Take me to him, gentlemen."

Wholly characteristically, I noted, whether in peace or battle, the first reaction of a couple of Bragg's aides to an imperative order was to give each other nonplused looks.

"I don't think I know where he is, sir," stammered one.

"I think I might, sir," said the other, but he was clearly uneasy about going out on such a limb.

We galloped off along the crest road, past the wounded and the inevitable fugitives and stragglers, until it seemed to me that these fools were going to lead us right into the middle of the melee around the battery. Yet as we got closer, and as I was wracking my brain for some way to get us to stop, Braxton Bragg came riding toward us out of the wisping smoke. He was as flustered as ever I had seen him, and as he approached Lee, he was shouting. "Here you are, sir, but what help did you bring? Where is your corps, sir? I must have support! I must have support!"

"And so you shall, General Bragg!" Lee shouted back, not with anger, but with encouragement and, much to my surprise, what sounded like enthusiasm. "They are coming up to the ridge as we speak, sir!" He was looking past Bragg now at the widening breach at the crest of the ridge and then with frowning disapproval at the vast flow of gray fugitives streaming past. Addressing Bragg once more, he shouted, "General, we must look immediately to this break in our lines before anything else. We must repair this at once!"

"Yes! Yes, at once!" Bragg repeated, his eyes wild.

Lee stood up in his saddle and raised his hand. As he looked all around him, he began to speak to the fugitives in a resonating voice: "No, men, no, no! This is not the way! Soldiers of the Confederacy, this is not the way. Turn around! Turn around!" The flow continued, not a soldier looked Lee in the face, but he continued on. "This is not the way, soldiers. You know this is not the way! Turn around! Turn around! Are you afraid to look at your enemy again? No, no soldiers, you must not be afraid. Stand your ground. Stand your ground, sirs. Your enemy is there!"

One soldier stopped, casting a contemptuous look over his shoulder toward the Yankee breakthrough. Reaching into a leather pouch he drew out a cartridge, which he then bit into and poured the powder into his rifle barrel, all the while with a look of annoyance on his face, as though he had important business elsewhere. But to humor this old grandfather of a general, he would load and fire one more time. Another man joined him. Then another.

"Yes!" cried Lee. "Yes, soldiers! There is your enemy! Who will go with me to retake our position?"

"I will accompany you, General Lee!" Bragg thundered.

"Yes, very good, General Bragg! We will go together. And who else? Who else, men?

Others were stopping, others were slowing their pace and looking back over their shoulders. I saw that things were quickly getting out of hand. The wrought-up Lee was capable of doing anything just then, including drawing his sword and making a dash toward the Federals whether anybody followed him or not. And there were no cries of "Lee to the rear!" with this army. Something had to be done—and at once.

"General Lee!" I called, pushing my horse forward, and he whirled his head at the sound of my voice, looking at me not in pique but as though, suddenly reminded of my presence, he instantly saw in it a fortuitous opportunity for a tasking he had in mind. This turned out to be the case.

"Yes, Major Hotchkiss, very good, sir. Come here please." His voice rose above the increasing din. His white cheeks were flushed pink, and his eyes glittered with battle fever.

"Major, we are going forward now to drive those people off, but we will soon need help. If we are to continue to hold them, we will need our guns. Do you understand, sir? Ride at once and with all haste to Chickamauga Station and inquire after our artillery train. See if there is any way to have it brought back at once. Indeed, do all you can, Major. And tell whoever is in control of such matters that it is imperative that our guns be returned at once!"

My heart sank. This was a hopeless mission, and I knew it. Lee himself surely was aware of the nigh impossibility of getting his artillery train back, already two hours gone down the railroad line, although I understood from his point of view that there was nothing to lose in trying. We were already looking at a deep disaster in the making, and regardless of what Lee was trying to do, I knew from what I had seen with my own eyes that it was past being prevented or unmade; our losses could only be minimized. And I was tormented by my own dreadful responsibility as well, recalling Longstreet's admonition to me and knowing that I was the only one on the spot just then who might somehow, if I stayed close by and waited for my chance, bring this battle-crazed old general back to his senses and to a place of safety, for the sake of the entire Confederacy. Wholly desperate now, I played my final card, and played it very badly.

"In the name of God, General Lee, you must come back to Chickamauga Station with me! This is not the place for you, sir!"

The ensuing explosion caught me fully within its burst and caused me the most terror I experienced in the entire war. Lee's terrible eyes flashed with scalding rage, and worst of all, both his eyes and his rage were fixed entirely upon me and no one else.

"How dare you invoke the name of God for such a thing, sir!" he shouted furiously. "How dare you! Be off at once, sir, and do as you are ordered!"

I recoiled at this rebuke. Even Bragg, the master of violent outbursts, looked at Lee with a stunned expression. So too did the nearby soldiers, although some let out a whoop of pleasure at the sight of the famous Lee breaking his fierce wrath over the head of an aide. Before I was even aware of it, I had turned my horse and was gone, fleeing like a panicked deer away from Lee and toward Chickamauga Station.

THE ENTIRE Confederate line behind which I galloped as I sped along the ridge was now engaged. The rifle pits crashed with volleys, aimed downhill at an enemy I could not see, and the artillery batteries roared, sending clouds of smoke spewing skyward. I guessed that the Yankees were now pressing their attack along the entire length of the ridge to keep Bragg from reinforcing his perforated center. I did not stop anywhere to look or ask questions but pressed on in my hopeless errand for Lee. Turning off the ridge road I came upon the first regiments of McLaws's division, slogging their way up toward the ridge with grim faces. On a slope nearby was McLaws himself, equally grim. I spurred my horse up to him, looking for Longstreet, being most anxious to explain why I had left Lee.

"Is General Longstreet here?" I asked.

"He's somewhere on the ridge," McLaws said then nodded dourly toward the sound of the firing. "Is all that as bad as it sounds?"

"I'm afraid it is, General," I answered. "And if you see General Longstreet, would you kindly tell him that General Lee ordered me to Chickamauga Station to try to get our artillery back here?"

McLaws lowered his head upon hearing this, his opinion of the success of the endeavor obviously coinciding with mine.

"Carry on, Major," he said finally without looking up.

I hurried on to Chickamauga Station and the stationmaster's office. The end result was as I expected. The stationmaster, although totally sympathetic, explained apologetically that the artillery train had already passed through Resaca and was beyond the reach of the telegraph until it came to Adairsville, another twenty miles down the line. Even then, bringing the train back up the track would require rerouting the trains following behind, carrying the corps' sick and wounded. The logistical problems were legion.

By then I had heard enough and was loath to linger another second in the stationmaster's office. Thanking him, I leapt back on my lathered horse and spurred off in the direction of Missionary Ridge, but the poor animal was nearly played out and could only manage a fast walk. So I rode along, fuming at the pace, and the sounds of battle rumbled ahead and the dark clouds around my own thoughts hovered closer.

I soon encountered the stragglers from the battle. Many were walking wounded; others were lost or cut off. I had long ago made it a practice, learned through experience, not to question frazzled or disordered soldiers about what had happened on the battlefield. Yet the odds and ends I heard from this backwash I could not discount.

I looked at them, listened to what they were saying, and all the while tried not to think of what had become of General Lee. All along the ridge, it seemed, the Yankees had come storming up the slope, and the sullen Southern soldiers I was seeing now had been jarred with the shock that the enemy had reached them at all without having been decimated by the artillery. Yet one soldier I encountered was neither jarred nor wounded. He came toward me in fully good health, rifle slung on his shoulder and stepping lively, as though he had just come off picket duty and was making for the campfire.

"What's going on?" I called to him.

"Yankees swarmin' on the ridge," he replied nonchalantly.

"Well, what are you going to do about it?" I demanded with heat.

"I reckon Bragg'll figure things out on his own," he retorted and walked past me.

I hurried now, trying not to think about what might have befallen Lee and wondering where in this chaos I was moving into I might find Longstreet.

All at once I came upon an ambulance. Longstreet and Sorrel were following behind it. I stopped my horse and stared crestfallen. It was all I needed to see to know everything there was left to know about our war of secession.

LEE WAS in the ambulance. Longstreet spoke in somber conversation with Bragg's chief medical officer, Dr. Durwood, who was leaning out of the back of the wagon. Sorrel looked pale and goggle-eyed, gazing distractedly in my direction and not recognizing me at all.

"Dear Lord," I uttered aloud. "Was this necessary? For this man who was always Your faithful servant. Was this Your will for him? Here and in this place?"

I stared numbly. The ambulance drew closer, and Sorrel recognized me at last. General Longstreet came forward to address me.

"Well, Major Hotchkiss," he said.

I touched my hat in salute and in a thickening voice began to ask, "Is he—"

Longstreet cut me short. "The leg's got to come off. They'll do it aboard the railroad car."

He nodded grimly in the direction of the wagon and the surgeons. "As soon as they do what they've got to do, get the train rolling. I told them as well. I'll try to come back to the rail yard later if I can, but if I don't make it back, get the general out of here. He'll get better care in Atlanta anyway."

I saw that Longstreet had wearied in the past few hours, looking very much as fatigued and enervated as he had been on the last day of Gettysburg.

"Do everything you can for the general," he added, quite unnecessarily, and then he was off.

I looked at Sorrel then at the ambulance.

"Go ahead and have a look," Sorrel said, his eyes glistening with tears. "If he's conscious he may recognize you. He spoke to me. Told me he was glad I was safe."

Going up to the ambulance with my heart in my mouth, I leaned to the side of my horse and looked inside. The prostrate form of the general was lying in the well of the vehicle. Bending over his naked and bloody leg was Durwood, and just opposite him was a young Union officer. My astonishment at seeing this was interrupted by a deep moan from the old general. The sound went to the very depth of my psyche, and I quickly turned away. It was not the piteous outcry itself that was so traumatic to me, but he who had made it. So deep was my childlike reverence for the commanding general that I believed only other men, even other generals, even generals like Stonewall Jackson, could be expected to cry out when in deep pain. But not General Lee.

"Who's the Yankee?" I asked Sorrel.

"Dr. Durwood brought him," Sorrel replied, his voice flat and dull. "Joe Hooker's surgeon supposedly. Captured at Brown's Ferry. Pat Cleburne sent him along to be of use to Dr. Durwood." And Sorrel added softly, "Let's pray to God that he is."

As we advanced on the railroad station Sorrel related the inglorious details of how the commanding officer of the Army of Northern Virginia had fallen. Despite the heroic legend that evolved from his wounding after the war—and the many overwrought paintings by artists who were not there, depicting an American version of the charge at Baclava at a place called Missionary Ridge—Lee fell not in a heroic charge but as a working general directing his troops under fire.

Moxley recounted the tragedy. Lee and Bragg led the men forward, the collection of soldiers rallying around Lee having grown to a sizable number. The battle line advanced, giving for a time a good account of itself. But the winded Yankees fought back doggedly, and the fight grew hot. Close-in volleys dropped a lot of men in their tracks. Both General Lee and Bragg rode back and forth behind the firing lines, exhorting the men. Then all at once, General Lee and his horse were down. The horse was killed, the rider severely wounded, and the Confederacy doomed.

We came into Chickamauga Station by way of an old road that the driver knew, which, although not a direct route, had fewer ruts than the other roads. At the railway we covered the general with blankets and secured him tightly to the stretcher, whereby, with the help of the train crew, we managed to transport our burden inside without causing him any undue pain.

As the two doctors removed the bindings and the blankets and tried to make the general more comfortable, Lee's eyes flickered. Despite his weakened condition he scrutinized the blue-uniformed officer attentively.

His lips moved and he asked hoarsely, "And who might you be, young man, and where are you from?"

The Union surgeon gave an abashed smile and nodded his head deferentially. "Dr. Stephen Quist of Stamford, Connecticut, at your service, General Lee," he said, then catching himself, as though he had somehow misspoken, he added hastily, "My parents are Virginians by birth, sir."

Lee's lips quivered slightly, in what at first I took to be a grimace of pain, but it lingered, and I saw to my surprise that it was a faint smile.

"Let us hope, gentlemen," the general said softly, "that at some later time perhaps, we can all recollect and appreciate the irony which God has seen fit to bestow on this situation."

"You must rest quietly now, General," said Durwood. "We've given you a sedative, and you must let it do its work."

Sorrel and I wept silently. Unseen by Lee, the Union doctor began to remove some tools from Durwood's bag and line them up neatly on a nearby table. When he took out the bone saw, I motioned to Sorrel that we should leave.

"We'll be outside if you need anything," I said softly to the surgeons.

Durwood was engrossed in examining the general's leg, preparing to remove the tourniquet. The young Yankee surgeon looked up from his inventory and smiled at me in acknowledgment, a charming, boyish smile full of optimism and confidence.

"Thank you," he said and, as though we were a pair of bereaved sons or nephews, added, "Try not to worry. We'll do the very best we can for him."

Outside the caboose and far enough away so as to be out of earshot of any sounds coming from within the railcar, Sorrel and I stood in heartbroken silence amid the sounds of battle pumping and pulsating from the direction of Missionary Ridge. In addition to the wounded men who had been brought here, the rail yard had become a bedlam of disordered, disheartened, and frazzled Southerners who had been knocked loose from their supposedly impregnable positions on the ridge and were now seeking food and rest or both, leaving the responsibility of their shattered army to the aggressive and plucky rear guard of Longstreet's men. Most of them had held on to their rifles, and it was probably a safe bet that they would be willing to fight another day. But it was plain to see that they were not going to fight any more this day nor take orders from any of their officers. That being the case, the small caboose—with two aides standing nearby and the flag of a full general attached to the roof—was given a wide berth.

No more than ten minutes passed before the door of the railcar opened and Dr. Quist, his white shirt besmirched with blood, emerged and proceeded cautiously down the steps with a heavy bundle in a dark-stained blanket, holding it away from his body.

"Oh, dear God," Sorrel whispered in anguish.

Thoroughly sickened as I was, I followed the young surgeon. He placed the bundle next to a pine sapling near the track and looked at me blankly as I approached then at the soiled bundle on the ground. "I do not know where else to put it," he said distractedly, obviously in haste to get back to his patient.

"I'll take care of it," I said. As he hurried back up the steps of the car, I inquired, "How is he?"

"Alive and breathing, God be praised," the young doctor said then disappeared inside.

I summoned Sorrel, and borrowing a couple of shovels from the train crew, we set about digging a hole. The earth was hard, and our task was no easy thing, but finally we made a suitable indentation in the ground. With our shovels we gingerly laid the ghastly bundle into it and thereupon piled the excavated dirt and stones.

Our task finished, we stood before the small mound in mute silence.

"I expect we ought to say a prayer," Sorrel said at length.

"But he's not dead," I replied.

"Let's say a prayer anyway," he all but demanded.

We prayed aloud the Lord's Prayer. Afterward I turned away, but Sorrel stayed where he stood.

"Wait, Jed, we can't leave it like this."

"Leave it like what?" I asked.

"Like this. Without some kind of marker. We have to mark it somehow."

"Mark it?" I protested, but Sorrel had become exasperatingly fixed in his purpose. "We can't just leave it like this, Jed," he repeated.

"But it's not a grave, Moxley. And it's not a man in there," I argued. "It's a leg!"

"I know, Jed!" Sorrel burst out. "But hang it all, that ain't no ordinary leg. It's Marse Robert's leg!"

Suddenly the matter had become one of ludicrous importance.

"We'll find a good rock and carve something on it," he said, and this we did. As I watched him scraping out the letters, I had an idea of my own. Taking off my kepi, I removed the insignia so that, in the end, on a fresh mound in a bleak region of northern Georgia rested a round stone with the rough-hewn inscription: LEG OF GENERAL ROBERT E. LEE, ARMY OF N. VA., NOV. 27,

1863. Before the stone was a gold letter "E" in Germanic script, symbolizing an officer of engineers.

After a time, as we stood disconsolately by the railroad car, I became aware of a new sound in the tumult coming from the ridge, the sharp tearing crack of volleyed rifles. It was coming from the direction of McLaws's line, and it could only mean that Yankee infantry had already pressed forward that far. I listened darkly, and Sorrel pulled out his watch. Then a short time later General Longstreet came riding toward the siding. A buckboard wagon full of soldiers followed a distance behind. He reined up before Sorrel and me.

"How is he?" he demanded.

I told him. Sorrel pointed to the earthen mound. The general lowered his head and for a long time did not speak. When he looked up again his face had a look of grim acceptance.

"Well, that's that, then," he said softly, and I knew he was speaking not only for his revered general but for our cause as well. "I expect it's all gone up now. But then there isn't no use cryin' about it."

He rose up in his saddle and gave orders to Sorrel and me in a voice easily heard by the train crew.

"Gentlemen, get this train to Atlanta as soon as everyone's aboard," he commanded. As soon as he issued the directive, the buckboard came rolling up. At a nod from Longstreet the soldiers piled out; two sergeants moved forward and joined the train crew in the locomotive cab. The rest of the men swarmed onto the top of the tender.

"It's not much of an escort, but it's the most I can spare," he said. "Anyhow, you ought to be a safe distance away soon enough if you leave now, before the Yankees come bustin' in. They're moving hell and earth to get their artillery up and into line against us. Once that happens, the dam won't hold much longer."

"And our own artillery rolling south and away from us even as we speak," Sorrel lamented bitterly.

Longstreet fixed him with a look of grim amusement. "But that's a good thing, Major, for at least our guns won't be falling into enemy hands like many of us undoubtedly will be before this day is done."

"Then is there . . . is there no possibility of stopping them?" asked Sorrel.

"Well, I'm fresh out of my *own* ideas on how to do that," the general said dark-humoredly. "But if you've got any of your own, Major Sorrel, now's the time to speak up."

Sorrel said nothing.

"Gentlemen, I ask you to attend well to the general's needs," Longstreet directed us.

He wheeled his horse around and rode back toward the sound of the guns. Suddenly moved, I called after him, "Attend to yourself as well, General Longstreet!" but I don't think he heard me for he made no acknowledgment as he galloped back toward the ridge. It was the last I was to see of him until long after the war. Beside me, Sorrel stood silently, watching him go, his eyes blurred with tears.

"Let's get aboard," I said.

Inside the car Durwood and his young colleague had moved Lee into his private compartment space. Great blots of blood streaked the floor and the wall where the operation had taken place. The air was foul with the smell of medicine and human rot.

The young Union doctor came up to me and placed a piece of paper in my hand.

"It was in his trousers pocket," he said with a formal, dignified expression. "Please be assured that I did not read it."

Looking at it, I saw that it was a personal telegram to Lee from President Jefferson himself, two days old. It was a very short dispatch, and I unabashedly read the contents.

"My dear General Lee," it began. "Words are inadequate to express my thanks to you, General Longstreet, and all your brave officers and soldiers for everything you have done, and all that was attempted in your present theater of operation, so far from your accustomed environs. I concur now with your belief that it is time to bring them all back. Do so now at once—and safely."

As if in afterthought, the president's final sentiment stood alone at the end. "My prayers are with you, General. It appears that you were right all along. How sad. How sad."

"SO THERE it is," I said.

Deslauries was silent for a long time. Then he said softly, "I was not present when Mr. Davis drafted that message. But that would be just like his style of heartfelt utterance." And he repeated dolefully, "How sad. How sad.

"It was the one we had to win," he repeated mournfully. "Chattanooga could have been our new hope."

As before, I said nothing to dissuade him. After all, he was a civilian and had spent the war among politicians. But my experiences in the field had given me a much sterner insight. The reason Chattanooga had to be won in the first place was because Vicksburg and Gettysburg had been lost. In a beleaguered nation such as our Confederacy had become, assailed on all fronts by numerous foes, every battle was related to survival. The hard truth was, they all had to be won.

Neither of us spoke for a long time. Eventually I said, "You know, I'm very hungry."

It was an abrupt and discordant change of subject from the topic of the last two hours. Deslauries looked up from his mournful reverie.

"Well, aren't you?" I persisted. "Goodness, Deslauries, do you smell that wonderful ham? Why it smells positively succulent." It did. I had noticed the aroma steadily growing over the past hour. Thus I confessed to him again, "I find myself to be quite famished."

At first Deslauries looked at me as though I had taken leave of common sense. Frowning and with dignified ceremony, he removed his gold watch from his vest pocket and studied it attentively.

"I think perhaps we have been sitting here too long," he declared. "I believe we are overdue at the Lee residence. His family is surely expecting us."

"Are they?" I asked.

Deslauries looked positively shocked. Recovering, his gaze became censorious. "I might also remind you of our duty to General Lee," he said. "Mine as well as yours. Have you considered that, or has your appetite made you forgetful?"

I ignored his reproach, looking squarely back at him. "I don't believe I care to trouble the Lees' hospitality any further."

Deslauries's expression changed. "Major Hotchkiss," he demanded. "What on earth are you trying to say?"

I looked at him. I was going to do exactly as I wished, with or without his approval, but the fact was, I liked the man. Despite his academic provinciality, I knew that the heart of the man was an honest one, and around an army campfire he would have been an amiable comrade. I did not want a quarrel if it could be avoided, and I felt sure that it could.

He was regarding me sternly, with his offended dignity, waiting for my response.

I frowned. "I don't think I have ever failed before in considering my duty to General Lee," I said, and Deslauries dropped his eyes. "And as of this moment, I consider that duty fully discharged. I would not presume to speak for you, of course, Mr. Deslauries, but I am surrendered, sir. My war was over and lost a long time ago." Then I smiled at him. "I have also considered that my overcoat must still be very wet, while right now I am warm and dry. And, as I told you before, famished. Especially that. So much so that I intend to have a meal, Mr. Deslauries, and probably another drink, a good smoke, and then to sit in front of this fire until I grow drowsy, whereupon I shall go up to bed."

Deslauries said nothing, but he seemed to understand. He looked ponderously at his satchel full of notes and papers; the draft of a book on what the infant Confederacy would have said about the great topics of the world had the infant, already sickened and deformed with the disease of slavery, lived. I hoped he would stay and eat, not to talk about those things, but about the war years, for there were many events and people from those fiery times still to reminisce about, not to mention two good cigars left to smoke. Yet Deslauries had not spoken to me, and I was sadly beginning to conclude that he would presently take up his satchel and go over to the Lee house. But still he stayed where he was, staring thoughtfully at the table.

I looked toward the kitchen to catch the innkeeper's eye. He was gone, but to my visual pleasure his wife was present.

What a lissome creature, I said to myself as she approached, bringing all her tortuous beauty with her, which was enhanced all the more by her staid, unsmiling demeanor. She looked at me expectantly, and I asked how long it would take to prepare another ham.

"Why the one you've got in your nostrils right now is ready if it's a meal you want," she replied.

"But I understood that the one in the oven was to be the meal for you and your husband and the serving staff," I said.

"It's for the guests of this inn first and foremost," the woman declared. "It's a cardinal rule of innkeeping, and neither my husband nor I would dream of having it otherwise." She gave a dismissive shake of her head, a gesture that encompassed a couple of things at once: formal refusal of my chivalrous concern, misplaced as it was as well as being unsolicited, and adjudication of the matter from any more superfluous discussion in an expectation that now we could get down to business.

"It's two for supper then," she announced.

Meanwhile, I was studying the engineering techniques she had used in trussing up her bountiful raven hair and speculating as to its texture, weight, and total mass when she let it all down.

"*I* will be having supper," I corrected her, coming reluctantly out of my languorous contemplation. "And I am hopeful that my companion will join me unless he has to venture out again."

The innkeeper's wife looked somewhat incredulously at Deslauries with a "why would the gentleman want to go out in weather like this unless he is some kind of a dotty old schoolmaster" expression. "And *will* you be staying, sir?" she inquired.

"Most assuredly, hostess!" Deslauries replied with a gusto and lightness of spirit that I found quite astonishing.

The insurrection against common sense having been quelled, the woman was free to turn her efficiency elsewhere.

"It's half a ham," she said. "I'll bring several slices."

"Bring the whole thing," I told her. "We'll pay for it all. What we don't eat we can take with us."

Deslauries looked at me in protest, but to the innkeeper's wife this was eminently sound reasoning. "Very good," she said approvingly. "Cheaper as well to buy it whole than by the slice."

"I suppose it wouldn't hurt to have something to eat, after all. Especially after the last couple of days," said Deslauries after she had gone, with an equanimity that was in stark contrast to his very recent reproachfulness. I was glad he was staying and glad for his company now that he was back in an agreeable mood, although still in bemusement over what had caused it.

A few minutes later the innkeeper's wife returned with a large, steaming tray.

"I'm sorry I can't offer you any vegetables due to the fact that our cellar is flooded," she said. "But I've brought extra plates of hot bread and gravy, and here's butter."

She set the plates and dishes before us, and lastly the prodigious ham. For once I wasn't paying attention to her but to what she was placing on the table, which was the heaping plate of pork, where the moist glaze of the cure glistened and the sweet scent of hickory wood smoke exuded from the thick, steaming slices.

"Now then, can I get you gentlemen anything else just now?" she asked.

Neither of us spoke but shook our heads mutely as we stared at the food, whereupon she returned to the kitchen.

We ate ravenously.